PRAISE FOR FICTION RIVER

"A sugary Christmas treat for those who love romance."
—*Publishers Weekly* on *Fiction River: Christmas Ghosts*

"The stories in this anthology are reflections on the inner conflicts of the human heart. Superhero stories should be human stories after all, and that is always worth your time."
—*Tangent Online* on *Superpowers*

"What I particularly like with the *Fiction River* series is the way it simply gives a writer a title as a central premise and allows them to run with it. Try it sometime... it's harder than you'd think to do on the spot. And yet these fertile imaginations take these ideas to wild and wonderful directions."
—*Astro Guyz*

"[*Fiction River*] is one of the best and most exciting publications in the field today."
—Keith West, *Adventures Fantastic*

FICTION RIVER SPECIAL EDITION: SUMMER SIZZLES

An Original Anthology Magazine

EDITED BY KRISTINE GRAYSON

Series Editors
KRISTINE KATHRYN RUSCH & DEAN WESLEY SMITH

Fiction River Special Edition: Summer Sizzles
Copyright © 2019 by WMG Publishing
Published by WMG Publishing
Cover and layout copyright © 2019 by WMG Publishing
Editing and other written material copyright © 2019 by WMG Publishing
Cover design by Allyson Longueira/WMG Publishing
Cover art copyright © Razihusin/Depositphotos
ISBN-13: 978-1-56146-088-5
ISBN-10: 1-56146-088-5

"Foreword" © 2019 by Dean Wesley Smith
"Introduction: The Toughest Subgenre of All" © 2018 Kristine Kathryn Rusch
"Night Moves" © 2019 by Katie Pressa
"Safe Like Cedar" © 2019 by Lisa Silverthorne
"Flying Above the Hindu Kush" © 2018 by M. L. Buchman
"Love on the Run" © 2019 by Kelly Washington
"Need to Know" © 2019 by Sabrina Chase
"Bribing Ghosts" © 2019 by Leah Cutter
"Come Summer, Come Winter, I'll Come for You" © 2019 by Rei Rosenquist
"Totality" © 2019 by Kristine Kathryn Rusch
"That Summer on Blue Heron Island" © 2019 by Dayle A. Dermatis

CONTENTS

FOREWORD

Dean Wesley Smith

I have to admit, I got very excited when Kristine Grayson proposed the idea of *Summer Sizzles* as a special volume of *Fiction River*. I flat love reading romantic suspense stories and seldom find many that are done well. And the idea of a special edition of romantic suspense stories focused on the summer made it sound even better.

There is just something about the heat of a summer day to add to both the romance side and the crime side of these kinds of stories. Heat, in all of its different incarnations, can make all of us do some very strange things at times. And doing strange things makes for great stories.

Just to be clear, I mean heat of the day on a hot, muggy afternoon, and the heat between two characters madly in lust with each other.

And all the other types of heat imagined between.

Combine that romantic heat with suspense of some sort and great characters to attempt to deal with the suspense and you have romantic suspense, one of the best subgenres in mystery fiction.

And in romance fiction.

I had no doubt that acclaimed romance writer Kristine

Grayson could put together some of the top writers she could find to contribute a story. And wow, did she.

Newer writer Katie Pressa takes us into the world of her novels with a stunning story to start off the volume and Dayle A. Dermatis wraps up the volume with a novella you won't soon forget.

And between those two amazing stories, Kristine has stories from acclaimed military romance writer M.L. Buchman and award-winning mystery writer Kristine Kathryn Rusch. Plus others. Nine great romantic suspense stories in total.

Fiction River is known as an anthology series that stretches genres, combines genres, and explores the edges of genres in every issue. Even though this issue has a focus on the sub-genre of romantic suspense, I think you will discover just how wide that focus can be.

And how powerful stories in romantic suspense can be when told by a great writer.

In this volume there are nine great writers telling nine great stories. I would suggest you read it from the first story to the last to also get the real power of Kristine Grayson's editing.

An amazing volume in the *Fiction River* tradition. I hope you enjoy it as much as I did.

—Dean Wesley Smith
Las Vegas, Nevada

THE TOUGHEST SUBGENRE OF ALL

Kristine Grayson

I love romantic suspense when it's done right. When it's done wrong, it's seriously mind-numbing. I read a novel years ago where the Big Bad Serial Killer is chasing Our Heroine and The Love Interest whom she had just met. They're attracted, of course—Our Heroine and The Love Interest, not all three of them (although... well, never mind). And as the Big Bad Serial Killer crashes through the woods, clutching an ax (I kid you not), Our Heroine and The Love Interest hide in a closet in a cabin in the woods.

And have wild bunny sex.

I mean, c'mon! They can hear the Big Bad Serial Killer outside, and they worry—not that he's going to open the door and chop them to death with his sharp ax (or shoot them with the pistol he's carrying)—but that they might not be able to finish before he enters the cabin.

Um. No. That's not good writing *at all*.

You won't find any stories like that one here. When the protagonists make choices, they make smart choices. And yes, the protagonists might meet the love of their life in these stories, but if they're being chased by a Big Bad something or other, they take care of the Big Bad (usually together) before getting a room (or a closet).

In all seriousness, romantic suspense is a very hard (okay, the puns write themselves. I'm sorry for that. I'll be good now) genre to write well. The romance and the suspense are equally important. Both must be present to be in this genre, and the romance part needs a happily ever after or at least a happily for now as the ending.

Writing romance short stories is hard (um, sorry) all by themselves. Within the space of twenty or so pages, the writer has to convince the reader that the happily ever after (or happily for now) at the end is really a true ever after. Usually romance shorts focus on the meeting or they focus on a reunion.

But short romantic suspense needs *suspense*. And it can't be a five-second worry that the guy Our Couple sees down the street is a pickpocket. It has to be a true suspense story as well.

The writer has to balance a suspense story, with all that entails, with a love story, and a happy ending.

Tough task. And because it's so tough, I didn't think I'd ever be able to put a full volume of romantic suspense together.

Then I ran some writing workshops and got some great romantic suspense stories. Once I saw Dayle A. Dermatis's "That Summer on Blue Heron Island," I knew I had to edit this volume just to give that novella a home. It became my anchor story.

Then I got Katie Pressa's novelette "Night Moves," and knew that I had enough to work with. I took the risk of putting out a call for stories for *Summer Sizzles* at WMG's annual anthology workshop.

I got some surprising stories. The kind of romantic suspense that takes the edges of the genre and pushes at them. Kelly Washington's "Love on the Run" pushes those boundaries hard. A few others give the genre edges a gentle shove. I'm not going to say which stories those are for fear of giving you spoilers. But be braced for the unexpected.

I organized the volume for the reader who wants to read from beginning to end. The book starts with three classic romantic suspense stories—the kind you'd think of when you think romantic suspense. The middle veers all over the world as well as the subgenre, mixing dark with humor. The book ends with Dayle's novella, which is (at its heart) a modern gothic.

If you like romantic suspense, these nine stories should thrill you. If you're new to the genre, you're in for a treat.

Here's a sampling from my favorite subgenre. I hope you'll end up loving it as much as I do.

—Kristine Grayson
Las Vegas, Nevada
February 3, 2019

NIGHT MOVES

KATIE PRESSA

Katie Pressa writes novels that hark back to romance novels of the 1980s and early 1990s. Those novels were sometimes called "problem romances" because they focused on difficult issues of the day. As the romance genre grew in size and publishing became more corporate, editors frowned on romance novels that dealt with real life issues, going more for escapist fare.

Pressa's four novels (so far) delve into violence against women's clinics, racism, and #MeToo, while the couples at the center of the novels discover the safe harbor provided by true love. Her most recent novel, Shotgun Wedding, *appeared in November. Find out more about her work at katiepressa.com.*

About "Night Moves," Pressa writes, "I received a challenge to write a classic romance amnesia story. I don't believe in amnesia in the way it appears in most romance novels, which is little more than a plot device to create complications where there are none. Just as I was about to give up on the challenge, I realized that I had already introduced a character in Gentleman of the Old School *who would have the kind of amnesia that actually exists in real life. Once I found my amnesia victim, the story flowed."*

And became a classic romantic suspense story with a twist. Using old tropes to explore the modern world, "Night Moves" is the perfect story to lead off this volume.

CHAPTER ONE

August 10, 2015
2:07 AM

Hands over his mouth, thumb and forefinger pinching his nose closed. Thought he got a brief whiff of garlic and sweat before he woke entirely. Training kicked in immediately. He didn't struggle even though he couldn't breathe.

Later, he would wonder why his attacker didn't just grab a pillow and press it hard against his face. Did the attacker know the walls in this facility were extraordinarily thin? Sometimes he fell asleep at night, listening to the sobs of the elderly woman in the next room. She was like him: no one visited her, either.

If the attacker had pushed a pillow over his face, he would've kicked the wall, hard; kicked outward and upward even harder—but the attacker didn't.

The attacker opted for the way that worked only with the weak, the ones who didn't know what he knew.

He didn't bring his hands up to pull those fingers off his face. Instead, he slid his arms upwards and slammed his forearms hard against the inside of the attacker's elbows—once, twice, three times until the grip on his face loosened.

Good thing, too, because he was seeing dots in front of his eyes —the precursor to blacking out. He kicked upward, ankles together, his bare feet a single weapon, not going for the nuts, which his attacker was probably prepared for, but for the backside. With the hands busy, the elbows compromised, pressure from an unexpected angle should send the unprepared forward or cause an arm to buckle.

Forward the attacker went, head banging on the wall so hard that the entire building must have heard it.

He pushed the hands off his face, then grabbed his attacker by the waist and slammed the attacker into the wall again, then tossed the attacker off the bed. He rolled the other way, landing on his feet, feeling his own knees buckle.

He caught himself on the edge of the bed, startled at how weak he was. That was what six months recuperation would do. He'd only been out of bed a month, maybe less. He hadn't been counting.

He made himself stand, legs wobbling, his own head aching— the concussion, all that remained of the head injury, making him woozy all over again. Mild concussion, he reminded himself. He'd lived through a lot worse, just this year.

Staggered to the end of the bed just as his attacker was trying to stand up. He grabbed the hospital rails at the bottom, and using a strength he didn't know he still had, upended the bed on his attacker, who went down with a grunt.

He reached the wall across from the bed, hit the secondary emergency button, the one that was for staff, not for him, and saw the blue light start blinking over his door. Then he used the wall to help him stay balanced, worked his way around the room, away from his attacker, reached the door, and winced as the dim floures-cents of the hallway stabbed his eyes.

He kept moving, saw one of the night nurses—Florence, ironi-cally enough—running toward him, saying, "John, John, you have to get back to bed," and it took a moment, just like it always did, to realize that when she said *John*, she meant him.

It wasn't his name. They all knew it wasn't his name, but that's what they called him. John Doe. If he couldn't remember who he was by the time they released him, they'd help him with a new name, new identity, but up until this moment, he hadn't minded John.

At this moment, though, it grated, like fingernails on a chalk board. And that was when he realized what his brain had done.

He grabbed the smooth edge of the nurse's station, held himself upright, and glared at the door to his room, expecting his attacker to emerge as he ran over what had leaped to his mind as he woke up.

The training kicked in.

What training?

Good training, that was clear. The kind of training regular citizens usually didn't have, not even those who had gone through self-defense class. He knew how to disable someone trying to suffocate him with sheer force.

And he had an expectation of strength as he moved, as if he had stepped into a completely different body. Not the one he'd been trapped in since February, when he had slowly come to.

"John," Florence said as she reached him, hands supporting him as if she expected him to buckle further. "We need to get you back to bed."

He shook his head and sucked air through his teeth as the movement made him dizzy.

"Call security and 911," he said. "There's a person in my room."

"Now, John," Florence said with the voice she used for the delusional patients. "You know—"

"I flipped the bed on him, but he won't stay down for long," he said.

As if to confirm, something metal banged in his room. He pushed himself off the nurse's station, away from Florence, and took five long difficult strides to his door. He grabbed the solid metal knob, pushed the button above the latch he wasn't supposed to know about, and slammed the door shut.

7

That button activated the door's lock. Only someone with a key could open the door now, and could only do so from the outside.

His window didn't open, not that it mattered. It overlooked a corner of the building—brick and more brick. No one could get in through the window. He'd checked when he first moved in here. They kept telling him he worried too much.

Apparently not.

He put a hand on the wall, felt the room spin. Couldn't pass out. Not now, not if that yahoo in his room somehow got out. Couldn't trust security in a long-term medical care facility to know how to handle a professional killer.

"Did you call 911?" he asked Florence.

"I'm sure Ralph can handle it," she said.

John felt a surge of irritation, even as he understood why she was humoring him. He'd been the guy who didn't talk much in Room 5476, the guy with the serious brain injury, the guy whose memory should return as soon as the swelling went down...no, wait, it's down...then maybe the memory would return slowly over time...only it hadn't, so maybe the brain was more damaged than they thought...maybe, one doc said, all he needed was the brain to rewire itself because neural pathways were extraordinarily resilient...maybe, the nurses whispered, his memory would never come back.

Except...

His training had kicked in. More than once.

Banging from inside the room. Not on the window, not on the door. On the extra-thin wall.

That didn't bode well.

The security guard—Ralph, apparently—sauntered into the round area near the nurse's station. Of course, the only security guard working tonight was the one with too much girth. He frowned at Florence who was starting to look alarmed. At least she had the phone in her hand.

"911!" John said, pointing at her. "Call now!"

The pounding had grown loud, and the elderly lady in the room started to feebly call for help.

Ralph didn't seem to notice, or if he did, he didn't know what to do. John was banking on the fact that Ralph didn't know what to do. John was so dizzy he was nauseous, but he made himself move on his wobbly legs—damn those muscles—and hurried into the room.

It smelled faintly of urine and antiseptic. The bed was pushed against the wall, and the elderly woman was clinging to the metal hospital rail as if it could help her out of the bed.

She was small and frail, maybe one hundred pounds on a good day. He didn't even think about it, just reached over the rail and grabbed her in a fireman's carry, because his body could handle that.

Barely.

She screamed and he didn't care, feeling her small fists pound at his back, and the not-quite-healed ribs from the last surgery. His eyes watered and he nearly stumbled, but as he reached the door, Ralph was there.

"I'll take her," Ralph said, and even though John didn't want to, he handed her to Ralph, who then carried her to a gurney that Florence had brought into the hall.

John turned around and locked the old lady's room too. The dizziness wasn't quite gone, but it was better—maybe because he was taking deep, deep breaths.

Florence was still on the phone.

"911?" he asked.

She nodded.

"Is there more security tonight?" he asked.

"Just me," Ralph said, as he took the phone from Florence. He nodded at the elderly lady. "You gotta tend to her."

"Should we evacuate?" Florence asked John, her voice tremulous. She clearly didn't want to, and he wasn't sure how they could.

Most people on this floor were ambulatory, but not everyone was. Besides, thre was a difference between ambulatory and taking

9

five flights of stairs to the ground floor. Even though there was one nurse per floor at night, that wasn't enough to get the hundred or so patients out of this facility.

He wasn't sure how to answer Florence's question though. Because if he were the guy locked in the room, he would be figuring out a way to escape. A chair through the elderly lady's window with wadded up sheets as a ladder, maybe, because that window overlooked the parking lot, and would provide a quick escape. Or maybe he would start a fire because places like this had the doors set to automatic unlock when there was that kind of emergency.

How he knew that, he wasn't sure, but he did.

And as he had that thought, the sound of breaking glass greeted them all.

He cursed, and pointed at Ralph. "Get downstairs. He's going out the window."

"And do what?" Ralph asked. "I don't got a gun."

"You got a cell, right?" John asked. "Take pictures. Get his license plate. Do something."

Ralph set the landline receiver down and ran to the stairs—thank heavens he didn't try to wait for the world's slowest elevator.

John wanted to follow, but he couldn't. His legs finally gave out and he slid down the wall, his limbs trembling, his eyes watering from the pain in his back and his head.

"John," Florence asked from across the room. "John?"

The old lady was clinging to her, clearly terrified. And oddly enough, no one else in the place seemed to have awakened despite the noise.

Or maybe not oddly. In his five months here, he had learned to sleep through all kinds of commotion.

"I'm okay," he said to Florence. "Really. I'm okay."

Thank God he wasn't hooked up to any monitors, because his heart was pounding, and his blood pressure was probably through the roof. Not because of the exertion (well, maybe a little because of the exertion), but because he had a sense of himself.

Not John. Not the person without i.d. who had been found in the winter woods behind Sanger House Clinic, confused, badly injured, and half dead from exposure.

But the person he had been before, the person he'd never been able to touch, the person who felt like he had been locked behind a wall in Not-John's head, and—like the attacker—was trying desperately to find a way out.

CHAPTER TWO

August 10, 2015
2:54 AM

The parking lot was a sea of blue and red. Police vehicles from all over Kaykakee County had turned up, including a few from the City of Three Fires itself. Detective Lita Montillo wished none of them were here. All she needed was one squad filled with officers from the sheriff's department and she was good to go.

But they'd all been on the other side of the county, dealing with some big to-do caused by the Fighting Patriots of America, a domestic terror group that had infiltrated half the counties in the state. The Fighting Patriots picked 2016 as the year that they were make a stand—for what, she had no idea, but they were spending all of 2015 prepping for that stand.

When she'd been a lowly officer with the Kaykakee County Sheriff's department, she'd had several run-ins with those bozos, and it had always been ugly. They hated her on sight—a woman in uniform. A woman with dark brown skin in uniform. A woman with a Hispanic name in uniform. It just got worse and worse as far as they were concerned.

She was, from their perspective, all that had gone wrong with

America. And from hers, the existence of fringe groups like them was one of the prices America paid for the liberty it claimed it valued.

At least she didn't have to deal with them tonight.

Tonight, she was dealing with the weirdest case she'd had so far. Dispatch seemed confused by it, and the nurse on site even more so. Someone had broken into the Chimay Recovery Center, attacked two of its residents, broken through a wall, then escaped through a window.

Lita wasn't supposed to have any preconceived notions of the crime, but she couldn't help thinking on the way over here that the only way this thing made any sense at all was that someone had been trying to steal drugs from the Recovery Center, got trapped, and went crazy.

She climbed the stairs to the fifth floor where the event had taken place. In addition to calling out every law enforcement officer within miles, the Recovery Center had also called in some extra staff to deal with the distressed patients.

Which was all she needed. Extra people, extra upset, extra cops.

The fifth floor was one of the floors that the center called an Ambulatory Floor. In theory, everyone who stayed on this floor could move under their own power. It was a Level 1 Ambulatory Floor, though, for people who were basically not able to walk very far.

She knew all of that because she'd spent too much time here, first with a cousin who had lost the use of her right leg in a car accident, and then on several cases. The center had been funded by a foundation run by a hidden benefactor who believed that everyone in the county deserved the kind of rehabilitation services usually reserved for people with great insurance or great wealth.

Half the patients here were the working poor, a third were homeless or destitute, and another third were poorly insured middle-class folk who had had the misfortune of some traumatic injury that would cut into their earning potential. When Lita had been on county patrol, she'd ended up here at least once a week to help security deal with an out-of-control patient—usually a recovering meth-head who had managed to escape.

She'd had her boss submit requests to the foundation for additional security here, but so far, no one had hired anyone—or the folks they had hired were like Ralph Constantine, who might've been good at walking the rounds, but couldn't corral an out-of-control patient if his life depended on it.

The fifth floor had the same circle design that the lower floors had. Every room opened onto the nurse's station to monitor patient care. The upper floors resembled a hotel instead of a medical facility, but here, no one was trying to hide the fact that medical care was the top priority of the floor.

Although tonight, it looked like medical care was the last priority. Two uniforms from Three Fires PD guarded the door—maybe in case someone came back?—and a nurse that Lita didn't recognize bent over an elderly woman on a gurney. The elderly woman watched everything with bright, alert eyes, as if she hadn't experienced anything this exciting in decades.

Two doors across from the elevator were closed, with another police officer standing in front of them, this one from the sheriff's department. Simon Luddington was one of the good guys. A little too young, maybe, a little too enthusiastic, but given some time and seasoning, he would be one of the better officers in Kaykakee County.

"What've we got?" Lita asked as she approached him.

"A real mess. Anders is with one of the security guards downstairs getting footage. I'm waiting for the crime scene techs. Everyone wanted to go in and out of these rooms, so I had the nurse—Florence something?—lock them back up again to preserve them for the techs."

"Locked them up again?" Lita asked.

"Yeah, the guy who was attacked first thought fast, and locked the attacker inside. That's why the attacker went out a window."

"These rooms are connected?" Lita hadn't seen that in the Recovery Center, but she hadn't been in every room.

Simon smiled. "They are now. The guy broke through a wall."

"The patient?" Lita asked.

"The attacker," Simon said.

She shook her head a little, trying to understand it. "Where's the fast thinker?"

"Rec room," Simon said.

She let out a small sigh. She had always thought of the recreation room as more of a torture chamber. She'd sat in one of the rooms on a lower floor through Christmas programs and Sunday sing-a-longs, gamely trying to cheer up her cousin. But it had been depressing as hell.

But Lita had to start somewhere, and since Simon had the rooms under wraps until the techs got there, and Anders was getting the security footage, and the other cops—all seventy-five million of them—were ruining her crime scene in the parking lot, she might as well talk to witnesses.

She would wager the elderly woman missed nothing, but that woman would want to talk at any point.

Lita was much more interested in the fast thinker.

She went down the only long corridor on this floor. The rec room ran along the back wall, which overlooked the grounds and the Burnt River beyond. The view from this side of the building was spectacular—in the daylight.

At night, the windows reflected the dreariness of the Recovery Center itself.

The only lights on in the rec room were the fluorescents on the left side, and the standard emergency lighting that prevented any public area on this floor from being too dark. A pool table was set up near the far wall, apparently something the barely ambulatory could enjoy. There were a number of tables with tabletop games on them, just like on the lower floors, chairs near the window, and couches closer to the door.

A man was stretched out on one of the couches, forearm over

his eyes as if he was resting. He was wearing the standard-issue pajamas, blue with a light checked pattern. No one had brought him his own clothes from home, apparently. He was barefoot, and probably chilled, since the AC seemed particularly high in here.

As she got closer, she realized that the arm over his face was covered in bruises.

"I'm saving my statement for the on-site detective," he said. His voice was a low rumble.

Interesting that he knew what the county called their detectives who handed cases like this.

"I'm the on-site detective," she said, grabbing a wooden chair and pulling it toward the couch, then sitting down beside him. The guy was young, if his feet were any indication, and too thin.

He lifted his arm from his face, slowly, as if the movement cost him pain and effort. He had incredibly bright blue eyes, memorable eyes—movie-star eyes, her mother would have said. His brownish-blond hair was in need of a trim, and he had a bit of stubble on his chin.

But that wasn't what caught her attention; what caught her attention were the handprints forming on his cheeks and lower jawline. He already had bright purplish bruises on his nose.

She circled her hand around her face. "That happen tonight?"

"God," he said, more to himself than to her. "I'm bruising."

"Yes, and I'd like to take pictures. If that happened tonight." She had to ask, both for confirmation and because he was in a medical facility. She had no idea what kind of procedures he was subject to. To make things worse, he had that nearly translucent skin some white people had, the kind that seemed to pick up every touch as an affront, the kind that bruised so easily those folks usually had no idea how they got injured.

"Oh, it did," he said, and pushed himself up by his elbows, wincing with each movement.

"It's okay," she said. "You don't need to sit up."

He smiled at her, just a little. The smile promised something—

warmth, great good looks, something that she couldn't quite define.

The smile made him seem stronger, if that were possible.

"I do need to sit up," he said. "I'd like to see you."

She scooted her chair closer to his hips. "There," she said. "Is that better?"

He nodded, then winced again, and she finally understood. He was dizzy.

"Let me get the photos of your face first," she said, "then you can tell me what happened."

She took out her smart phone, pointed it at him, and snapped a series of photographs. He didn't move as she did so, as if he knew exactly what she wanted.

"You were wearing those clothes?" she asked.

"Yeah," he said. "I know, I'll have to change, right? Give these to your crime techs."

"Yes," she said, not surprised by his question. Too many people watched crime shows on TV. Usually she could tell people they didn't have to contribute their clothing, but in this instance, he'd had direct contact with the person who had tried to kill him. "You haven't washed your face yet, have you?"

"Oh, no," he said. "I know the drill."

Then he looked a little surprised at his own words.

"All right," she said. "I'll need to take your statement. You mind if I record it?"

She waved the phone at him. She always took concurrent notes, just in case the recording failed, but she wanted to make sure she had his permission.

"Yes," he said clearly. "You can record my statement."

Most people nodded. He really did know this stuff.

She spoke into the phone, listing date, time, location, and her name. He watched closely, a slight frown marring his forehead.

"All right," she said. "Now state your name for the record."

"Well," he said, a little sadly, "that's the thing. I don't know my name."

She had encountered this before. Patients sometimes got confused. She suppressed a sigh.

"We can get it from the records, and delay the statement until later," she said.

"No," he said. "It won't make any difference."

Now it was her turn to frown. "What do you mean?"

"I had a head injury in February," he said. "I have no idea who I really am."

CHAPTER THREE

August 10, 2015
3:16 AM

Although he was starting to get a clue. Tonight had triggered something, something that was eating at him.

The detective—she had identified herself as Lita Montillo—was watching him a tad too closely for his tastes. She was beautiful, the kind of beautiful he hadn't seen in years. Her eyes were a dark brown that matched her hair, which had been cut short, probably so she wouldn't have to do much to maintain it.

She obviously eschewed maintenance—her lovely dark skin had no makeup on it at all, not even a hint of blush, not that she needed it. Her eyelashes were naturally long, and her eyebrows naturally trim. Her lips were kissable, a thought that almost made him smile.

He would not have thought that he would have been attracted to a detective. Although at the same time, the thought that came right behind that one was that of course he would be attracted to a detective.

Those kinds of contradictory thoughts were the very things that had confused him for months. At one point, he would be certain he thought a particular way, and then the next thought would convince him that he didn't think that way at all.

He told her his story, what he knew of it. Back in February, shortly after Sanger House Clinic in Three Fires had had a bomb scare, the security the clinic had hired found him in the woods. The security team thought he was homeless—and for all he knew, he had been—but they never found any of his stuff. No tent, no grocery cart filled with the things he collected, nothing.

Most of his clothes didn't fit—not unusual for a homeless guy —and he smelled so bad that people backed away from him. Or so they told him, because he didn't really remember any of it. He was ambulatory, kinda, and people who found him believed that he had known about the clinic and had been trying to get there.

The odd thing—though, that wasn't fair, there were a lot of odd things—his T-shirt, underwear, and socks were in good shape. They also fit. Not that he would be able to look at them and jog his memory, since they had to be cut off him.

Because, once they started to examine him in the clinic, they realized he needed to go to the ER immediately. He had been beaten severely, burned in a couple of places, and had a days-old head wound that had frozen closed on his skull. His brain was swelling, and if they hadn't found him, he would have died.

Although he might have died anyway, from the punctured lung or the slow-bleeding nick in a blood vessel near his heart or all the broken ribs. Or from exposure.

They didn't find the knife wounds until they hosed him down in the ER, and then it became all hands on deck. Triage upon triage, which he thankfully could not remember. They induced a coma, he went through more than a dozen different surgeries, and eventually, he ended up here to recover.

The doctors—and he had a bevy of them—believed that he been subject to one of those beatings homeless men suffered, and someone with the edges of a conscience had dropped him near the clinic. But that's all the thought they gave it. Because for weeks, they didn't think he'd make it.

Eventually he did, but he was still recovering. The docs believed he would probably regain his memory, although probably not the memory of the attack or the rescue near Sanger House.

He had been lucky; he knew it, and was trying hard to be grateful each and every day.

He gave the detective a small smile—and the damn thing hurt. Those bruises were deeper than he had realized.

"They call me John Doe," he said. "They want me to pick a name, but I'm not willing to yet."

"You think your memory will come back," she said.

He raised his right hand and crossed his index and middle finger like a six-year-old. "I'm hoping," he said.

"I'm finding this fascinating," she said. "You were attacked and left for dead, and then you get attacked here. Tell me about that."

He did, from waking up to the moment he collapsed in the hall.

She was eyeing him as if she didn't quite believe he could do all of that.

"Who trained you?" she asked.

"Several people," he said, surprising himself.

"Who taught you hand-to-hand combat?" she said.

"Military," he said before he could think. Then he shook his head. "But that can't be true. They've already checked my fingerprints. If I'd been in the military, there'd be a record of me. And there isn't."

"What about IAFIS?" she asked.

"I'm not in there," he said.

Her eyes sparkled just a little, and he realized she had asked with an acronym. No one had done that before. And the acronym she used was the right one, not the one used on TV.

"And NDIS?" she asked.

The National DNA Index System. He felt as if he was taking an oral exam.

"Not there either," he said. "Or CODIS."

The Combined DNA Index System, of which NDIS was a

part. He almost said that as well, feeling like the A-student who still needed to prove himself. But underneath that feeling was a sense of...joy. A small sense. Because he felt as if he had found a piece of himself.

She nodded, that little hint of a smile gone. But there was something in her eyes, something that seemed a bit brighter than before.

"Not many people would have responded like you did," she said. "Almost no one would have known how to break the attacker's hold on your face."

He stared at her.

"I'm not sure I would have known how to do it," she said.

He nodded.

"And then locking the doors, carrying Mrs. Tucker out of the room, even though you're still compromised—"

He liked that she didn't say *injured*. He was beginning to hate that term.

"It all sounds like deep training to me," she said. "Combined with muscle memory."

"Meaning what?" he asked.

She was about to answer when someone said, "Detective. We need you."

One of the sheriff's deputies stood in the door. He was reflected in the windows across from it, the light at his back. John was grateful for that, because he didn't want to turn and look.

She flicked off her phone, put her notebook in her pocket, then stood. "Stay here. Don't wash till the crime scene techs swab you. I'll send them, because you look like you need rest."

Now that she said that, he realized just how tired he was. God, he hated not having enough strength. He hated feeling weak.

He closed his eyes and thought, just as he started drifting off, that only he would consider exhaustion after rescuing himself, an elderly lady, and maybe part of the fifth floor, weak. And, he noted, that thought seemed strong and coherent, and didn't have a second contradictory thought at all.

CHAPTER FOUR

August 10, 2015
3:45 AM

Even though it was nearly four in the morning, the heat was stifling. There was no breeze. Bugs congregated in the light pouring out of the four halogen streetlights that overlooked the parking lot. The place was well-lit if nothing else.

Half the squads still had their lights on, red and blue forming patterns on the cars in the staff parking lot. Lita wiped a hand over her face, feeling tiredness hit her with the heat.

Her exhaustion made her think of the gorgeous guy upstairs, the one who had somehow thwarted an attack, saved an old lady, and could barely lift his head off the couch. Something about him appealed to her, and it wasn't just his half-smile, nor the fact that she was between relationships.

Although it was fair to say she wasn't really between relationships. She had sworn off relationships, because most of them came from work, and the men she met at work—well, none of them could have stopped an attack like that, and they were all healthy.

Anders was the one who had fetched her from the rec room.

He had walked down the steps with her, leading her outside and briefing her along the way.

The security cameras had caught the assailant climbing down the side of the building. The knotted sheets were still attached to the window, their bright clean whiteness reflecting the light.

The assailant had apparently been bright enough to park somewhere else, but not bright enough to realize that the Recovery Center had security cameras.

"Or maybe he didn't care," Anders had said, which caught her attention.

"Why?" she asked.

Anders gave her a steady look. "You'll see."

They had caught the assailant in the thin woods that sloped down to the Burnt River. He had apparently gotten turned around, thinking he was going toward the road when he was going away from the road.

Fortunately for her investigation, sheriff's department officers were the ones who caught him. They had him in a squad parked haphazardly near the Recovery Center's main entrance.

The back doors were still open, probably because of the heat, and four officers stood around it, two with their hands on their weapons, the other two near the open doors. As she reached them, one of them, Jamari Lucaan, came toward her.

"Guess we can't get away from them after all," he said.

She frowned her incomprehension at him.

He pointed at the squad. "Fighting Patriot," he said, and rolled his eyes.

"How'd he get in?" she asked.

"Walked in around four, visited some catatonic person on the third floor, and then apparently hid in the men's room until lights out." That was Anders beside her. "We're going to have to work on improving security here."

Lita nodded. That was clear.

She walked the handful of steps to the squad, and put her hand on the roof. The metal was hot, although not as hot as it would be during the daylight. Still, hotter than she expected at this time of night.

She peered inside, saw shredded jeans and a ripped T-shirt, along with shit-kickers that had to be much too hot in this heat. His hands were cuffed in the back, and his feet were cuffed together as well, which usually wasn't done when they were transporting someone accused of something. He must have kicked at whoever grabbed him.

The tats on his neck looked familiar—the coils of a rattlesnake, and the words *On Me*. He didn't have to turn around for her to realize who she was looking at.

"Russell Wilkins," she said, her tone deliberately snide, "what the hell do you think you were doing?"

He turned, the lower part of his face distorted by the rattlesnake's tongue. The words around his neck read *Don't Tread On Me*. The Fighting Patriots had coopted the old Revolutionary War symbol, like so many other right-wing crazies had.

His eyes met hers, and his narrowed. Then he leaned over and spit on the ground at her feet.

"Get this abomination out of my presence," he said to the nearest deputy.

She rapped on the roof, startling Wilkins. "Russell, we have security footage of you trying to kill a man upstairs. What were you thinking?"

And why hadn't he brought a weapon? That seemed out of character for him.

"I don't talk to creatures like that," Wilkins said to the deputy.

"Will you talk to me?" the deputy asked, his voice low.

"Yeah," Wilkins said. "But I don't recognize your fucking authority. You're a stooge for a fake government, one that lets critters like her into its ranks."

"I missed you too, Russell," Lita said. "And like it or not, I'm the detective in charge of your case. Be nice to me, and maybe we can figure out what this is about."

Wilkins whirled so fast that the deputies around him drew

their weapons. She had remained motionless. She'd seen that movement from Wilkins before. He was a big thug, but he wasn't a smart tactician—clearly, considering a beefy gym-muscle guy like him had been defeated by a man who had spent six months mostly in bed.

"What this is about," Wilkins said, "is that fucking traitor up there. He needs to die."

"What did he do that was so bad?" she asked, keeping a small taunt in her tone. "Did he offend your delicate sensibilities as much as I do?"

"He stole from us," Wilkins said.

"Did you recover what he stole?" she asked.

Anders leaned forward, and whispered in her ear, "I don't think he's been Mirandized."

Not that it mattered. Wilkins wouldn't argue guilt or innocence when he went to court. He would argue improper jurisdiction, like all of these Fighting Patriots did. They didn't recognize the authority of any courts except their own.

Which meant he had been sacrificed. Or he had volunteered to be sacrificed, which was even stranger.

His non-answer of her question told her that he hadn't found whatever it was he was looking for. He would have bragged about finding it otherwise, bragged and taunted her, telling her that she'd never find it.

"We don't have any record that the man you tried to kill was a Patriot, Russell," she said, using the word they used to describe themselves.

"Patriots don't steal from each other," he said.

"It must have been a big betrayal for you to try to kill him," she said, her heart pounding more than she wanted it to. "How did someone you grew up with become so bad?"

"He's not from the first families," Wilkins said, talking about the incestuous inner circle of the Patriots. "He's a hanger-on."

"Did you vet him?" she asked.

"Why do you care?" he snapped.

"Just thought it was odd that you would try to kill John after you got to know him," she said, deliberately using the name the staff had given the man upstairs.

"His name ain't John," Wilkins snapped. "It's Darby."

"Darby Walker," she said as if she knew him.

"Ezekiel Darby, you freaking bitch," Wilkins said. "Don't you know anything?"

She hadn't known that, and Wilkins was too stupid to realize what he had given her.

He was glaring at her, his piggy little eyes filled with hatred. He was clearly near the end of his usefulness in this conversation.

"Why'd you come out here, Russell?" she asked. "You know this was a suicide mission, right? Brody"—one of the leaders of the FPA—"had to know that you'd get caught—either here or back at the ranch. They sacrificed you."

Rather than piss him off further, the idea that they had sacrificed him did not upset him. He seemed calmer when she said that.

"I volunteered," Wilkins said.

She hadn't expected that. She let her surprise show. "I'm impressed, Russell. You knew this was a suicide mission and you volunteered. That's a lot more courage than I would have pegged you for."

His eyes narrowed again, as if he couldn't decide whether or not she was complimenting him. Guys like Wilkins were not the brains of the organization by a long way. They were clichéd dumb muscle, although they usually had someone watching out for them so that they wouldn't get into trouble—legal trouble.

The FPA must have wanted John Doe—or Ezekiel Darby—more than they wanted to keep Wilkins out of jail.

"Still," she said, "you screwed up. Darby's alive, and you're going to jail."

Wilkins spit again, the spittle landing perilously close to her Nikes.

"They going to send someone else after him?" she asked.

Wilkins didn't answer that either, turning his head away from her. Apparently, he was done.

She was too. She'd had enough of the heat anyway. She would rather talk to him in the pretend-cool of the sheriff's office.

She slammed the car door closed. "Get him out of here," she said to the deputies.

Then she walked away from the squad, not certain what had twisted her stomach so. She had dealt with the FPA many times. Their racism used to nettle her, but didn't any longer. She expected the hatred and the ignorance. She had come to appreciate their overconfidence, thinking that their argument that the government didn't matter would sway a jury or a judge. She actually found it amusing that they did not see the contradiction in their worldview: they didn't recognize the court, and yet they continually planned a strategy in which they tried to convince the court that they were right.

A bead of sweat ran down the side of her face. This was the hottest August that she could remember, and she had lived in Michigan her entire life. But it wasn't the heat that was bothering her. Nor was it the crime.

No, it was a not-so-internal worry that the man upstairs, the man who had thwarted the attack on himself, the man who had saved an elderly lady—that man might not just be a racist, but a member of one of the most hateful racist organizations Lita had ever had the misfortune to encounter.

And she had found that man attractive. She had liked his half-smile, the way his blue eyes electrified the room. She had found him intelligent and appealing, even though he claimed he had no idea who he was.

She paused, looked at the parking lot, saw that many of the squads were leaving. Claimed. She had changed her opinion of his veracity because Wilkins knew him.

Ezekiel Darby. Who hadn't grown up in the FPA. Who had stolen from them. Who had angered them so badly they were willing to sacrifice one of their lower-level operatives to kill him.

Ezekiel Darby. Who had nearly been beaten to death once before.

She veered to the left, stopped at her own car, and grabbed the laptop the department gave her. She ran Darby's name, found some cursory arrest records—the kind that would have provided fingerprints. She saw some arrest photos. They were definitely of the man upstairs, with a fuller face and thicker hair, and barbed wire, with little Nazi barbs, tattooed all the way around his neck.

She frowned. The man she had met did not have a tattoo on his neck.

Did the FPA have the wrong man?

Possible, but not likely.

She had an idea, but she wasn't willing to express it yet. Instead, she shut down her laptop, got out, locked her car, and pocketed the key. Then she went back inside.

As she did, she called Simon on the fifth floor.

"See if you can get permission from John Doe to let me see his medical records," she said.

"John...Doe...?" Simon sounded disbelieving.

"They don't know his real name. That's the guy who was attacked tonight. And keep a wary eye out. I'm not sure the FPA is done with him."

"The FPA?" He clearly hadn't been privy to the night's developments.

"Have Anders update you. But make sure everyone knows this isn't over."

"Okay," Simon said. "I'll see what I can do."

She nodded as she hung up. What Simon could do in five minutes was more than most people could do in an entire day.

After she hung up with him, she got on the phone to the sheriff, not even worried about waking him up. She rarely did, so he knew when she called it was important.

She briefed him on everything, then asked him to call the FBI with one simple question:

Did they lose a man named Ezekiel Darby, and did they want him back?

CHAPTER FIVE

August 10, 2015
5:01 AM

The couch in the rec room was uncomfortable. The pillow didn't help. John put the pillow on the floor, then pulled up the thin blanket they had given him. His feet were cold in the air conditioning, but not the rest of him.

There was only one open room on the fifth floor, and he convinced Florence to let Mrs. Tucker have it. Mrs. Tucker looked happier and wider awake than she had all night, but he had a hunch the adrenaline that had gotten that old lady out of her bed had probably dissipated rapidly once she had a new place to sleep.

His adrenaline was long gone as well, leaving him with a thousand aches and pains, worse than the aches and pains he had felt before the attack.

Clearly someone hated him and wanted him dead. Maybe the beating he had taken in February had nothing to do with his homelessness and had something to do with whoever or whatever he was.

He knew the man had come for him, not just because the man

had entered his room. If the man was a random killer, there were a lot of other targets—easier targets—on the lower floors.

No, the man had come for him, and only three days after the fundraising posters got plastered all over Kaykakee County and the Internet. John wasn't a focus of the poster—that was upstairs rec room with its penthouse views. He had been up there, playing chess with another resident, when the photographer had come in. Their chess game had made it onto the poster, John's face small but clear, as he concentrated on his next move.

He had thought nothing of the poster when they first showed it to him. He liked the graphic design, the announcement of the annual fundraiser, the appeals to the good cause.

But when one of the nurses told him that the posters were all over the county, including the small towns and rural post offices, his stomach had clenched. He felt a panic so severe that it almost shut him down. A warning panic—a *danger, danger, danger* kind of panic.

By then, it had been too late.

Maybe that had been the first whisper of memory, the first sense of who he truly was. Or maybe it had been simple self-preservation. He had been beaten within an inch of his life, literally. Anyone would be frightened after that.

Except, maybe, someone with military training. When Detective Montillo had asked him that, and he had responded without thinking that he had learned his survival skills in the military, that felt right. And then something contradicted it. Something insidious.

A sharp pain ran through his lung and down his back. No matter how altruistic he was, he wasn't going to be able to rest here. They had placed Mrs. Tucker on a gurney. Maybe the gurney was still available. It had to be more comfortable than this couch.

He sat up slowly, ran a hand over his face, felt the swelling along his cheeks. Bastard had hurt him or maybe he had simply been that weak.

He had to keep reminding himself that he was better than he

had been. Maybe, when he got even healthier, he would have enough energy to flirt with a woman as beautiful as Detective Montillo.

Her dark eyes had held a lot of sympathy as he told her about his last few months. She hadn't reached out and called him a poor dear, like some folks here, nor had she told him that she understood. He valued that a lot. And had he been himself, he would have flirted with her.

But he wasn't himself, and he had nothing to offer, so he hadn't even tried.

Although, as he sat there, he thought it odd that he had the thought "had he been himself." He couldn't remember having that thought at all in the past few months.

Something moved in front of him, and his heart rate spiked. Then he realized that he was seeing a reflection in the glass. Something had moved behind him, probably Florence, or her replacement.

The sky was lightening just a bit. Dawn was at least an hour away, but the darkness out those windows seemed thinner. Or maybe that was only because the lights from the police vehicles had stopped flashing while he was lying down.

"Mr. Doe, sir?" someone said behind him. He made himself turn slowly. He wasn't going to think everyone was a threat. Besides, that tone was respectful. He had a hunch it was one of the police officers—sheriff's deputies, actually.

He was right. The tall one who was supposed to be guarding the floor.

"Detective Montillo asked me to find out if it would be all right if she viewed your medical records," the deputy said.

What did she think she would find in the records? And why hadn't he ever thought to ask for them? They would have a lot of detailed information that he hadn't gotten from the attending physicians.

Maybe he hadn't asked because he had been so deeply ill that figuring out what, exactly, was going on hadn't been a priority.

"Mr. Doe?"

"Um, yes," he said. "It would be fine. I suppose you need me to sign something?"

"I don't have an official form, sir, but if you'd write that it's okay on this paper, sign it, and date it, that'll work for now. We'll get the right paperwork later." The deputy handed him a clipboard with some computer paper in it.

John felt a small thread of amusement and that odd joy again. The question about signing something, that had come from his past as well. Because right now, he didn't even know his name, so he didn't have a legal name at all. He probably didn't really exist.

He didn't point that out to the deputy, just scrawled the fact that he gave permission on the paper, and then signed *John Doe* and felt vaguely ridiculous as he did so.

"Did she tell you what she hoped to find in my records?" he asked as he handed the clipboard back to the deputy.

"No, sir," the deputy said. "Thank you, sir."

And then he headed out of the rec room before John could ask him to send Florence in.

That was probably all right. He needed to move around anyway. His muscles—the ones he had strained with all of that unusual activity—were stiffening up.

He stood like an old man. His eyes were grainy, his body ached, and he walked hunched over. But he felt better than he had in months.

He felt as if he was on the cusp of something, as if his brain was finally going to cooperate. As if he might finally get a clue as to who he really was.

CHAPTER SIX

The Recovery Center had paper and online medical files. Apparently, the paper was a back-up for the online files. Or something like that.

The nurse on the first floor near the paper records room was a bit vague. She was more interested in what had happened upstairs. She had also tried to hold off Lita from examining the records until the actual business staff showed up. They had been called after the crisis to come in early to make sure nothing had been tampered with.

Lita soothed the nurse, told her that she would be respectful, and then pointed to the security cameras scattered throughout the room.

"If I screw up," she said, "someone will notice."

She hoped. The security team, which was still Ralph, probably wasn't paying a lot of attention to the cameras.

The nurse nodded, though, pulled John Doe's file, placed it on the metal table in the center of the room, and left.

Lita did not sit on the nearby chair. She felt an odd sense of urgency, maybe the leftover adrenaline from the chaos around the Recovery Center. She was also chilled. This was one of the few rooms where the air conditioning worked—that and the fact that she had been sweating like crazy when she was outside.

The file was thick, stuffed with extra sheets of paper, and had a hand-scrawled note on the manila surface. The note read:

John Doe #65, admitted March 13, 2015.

She felt a slight chill that had nothing to do with the overactive AC as she realized that the man upstairs was the sixty-fifth John Doe to have a file in this facility since the place opened five years before.

So much happened in this county that she never saw, and she had seen more than her fair share.

She opened the file, and flipped over the recent papers. She wanted to see the hospital admittance forms from February, the doctor's write-ups, and photographs if there were any.

The photographs were easy to find. Blurry printouts from the online files, but clear enough. He looked even thinner, his face ruddy from exposure. Other photos, clearly taken for a possible legal case, should he want to bring charges, showed his torso and lower body.

They were painful to look at. Essentially, there was not a part of him that did not have a bruise, a wound, or an obvious broken bone.

How he had made his way to Sanger House was beyond her.

She was convinced the FPA had done this. She looked at the intake information, saw that his outer garments were burned because they were so filthy—after the staff checked the pockets and found nothing, which would have bothered her if she didn't already have a working theory.

He hadn't been homeless at all. Homeless people filled their clothing with their most important small items, in case they couldn't return to their stash or they got rousted away from their usual stuff.

She had had a hunch he wasn't homeless before she looked here, but she wanted confirmation.

Then she stared at the only real photograph of him, printed on actual photography paper, probably from the hospital file itself.

He had a tattoo on his neck. It circled his entire neck, like Wilkins' tattoo did. Instead of the rattlesnake, though, John Doe's tattoo was row after row of barbed wire, that went from his clavicle to his jawline. And, instead of actual barbs, the drawing had tiny swastikas.

The entire tattoo made her cold.

Then she closed her eyes, remembered looking at him in those pajamas, open at the collar, showing his entire neck.

She had noted the handprints on his face, but not a tattoo—and this tattoo wasn't something that got missed.

He stole from us.

Initially, he had been beaten within an inch of his life because he had crossed them. The FPA did that with the members it expelled. They usually died, after a horrendous few days of lingering, often in the woods near whatever place the FPA was using as its headquarters.

He hadn't died. He hadn't served as a warning, so they had come back—probably not to beat him. Probably to recover whatever he had taken from them.

The reason that Wilkins hadn't stabbed him or shot him was because killing John Doe hadn't been the plan. Killing John Doe had been a spur of the moment thing.

Because his tattoo was gone. Wilkins couldn't have missed that. When he looked down at the sleeping John Doe, Wilkins knew he had the right man, but that the man had fooled them. Betrayed them.

Deeply betrayed them.

Rage made Wilkins forget his mission and try to kill John Doe with his bare hands.

Because John Doe had been undercover with the FPA.

John Doe was some kind of Fed—which was why he wasn't in

the database. Organizations like the FPA might check arrest records, if they could, but they never checked official records like CODIS or IAFIS.

They had believed John Doe was one of them. They had shared secrets.

And Wilkins had been furious enough about it to try to kill John Doe.

Then Wilkins had lingered in the woods—not because he was lost, but because he had been contacting the FPA. Wilkins had probably seen the name on John Doe's door, on his wrist, in his room. Wilkins wasn't the brightest bulb in the chandelier, but he was smart enough to realize that John Doe hadn't reported on them yet. Wilkins might've thought that John Doe wasn't even conscious yet.

She hauled out her phone and called the sheriff. Before she could get out a word, he said, "The Detroit office of the FBI is sending someone to you."

"Screw that," she said. "Get those cops back here. Get us backup now."

And then she explained why.

CHAPTER SEVEN

August 10, 2015
5:15 AM

The gurney was infinitely more comfortable than the couch, even if it was in the dimly lit hallway near one of the public restrooms on the fifth floor. Florence hadn't wanted him to take the gurney into the rec room, because patients started showing up there about six, and she didn't want any of them to get the idea that they could sleep there.

She was adamant, and he didn't feel like arguing. He was exhausted, and he wanted to get a little bit of sleep before day shift found him a new room—probably on a different floor.

He was just starting to doze when the sound of boots against linoleum snapped him awake.

The beautiful detective was standing over him.

"Ezekiel Darby?" she asked quietly.

"Yes," he responded, as if he had done it a thousand times. Then an ache pierced his brain. He had answered to Ezekiel Darby, but he wasn't Ezekiel Darby.

Ezekiel Darby had been his cover name. His deep cover name. He'd used it for two years, with the Fighting Patriots.

Christ.

His real name was Ronan Ghent, and he was an FBI agent assigned to the federal interagency Fighting Patriots task force. All of the information about that, about his life, about himself, flooded in.

He sat up, feeling dizzy, overwhelmed, and grateful.

"I'm not Ezekiel Darby," he said.

She smiled at him. "I know," she said.

He took her hand, callused and strong, and resisted the urge to pull her down to kiss her. That would be wrong. But Jesus, she had just helped him figure out who he was. The joy of it made his eyes fill with tears.

"I'm Ronan," he said quietly.

"Pleased to meet you, Ronan," she said. "I'm Lita."

And then she grinned. He laughed, feeling a happiness so pure he doubted he had ever felt that before. And he now had the memories to sift through to see if that thought was accurate.

He patted the side of the gurney. He wanted to tell someone about himself. Screw that, he wanted to tell *her*.

But she was no longer looking at him. Instead she was looking down the hallway, a frown on her face.

She put a finger to her lips.

He didn't hear anything. Then there was a thud, which sounded like a body falling.

She glanced at him, then at the opening to the hallway. "Stay here," she whispered.

He swung his legs off the gurney. "No. You need me."

She shook her head. "I can't take care of you. You need to find somewhere to hide. The Fighting Patriots aren't done with you."

"I know that," he said.

"Wilkins tried to kill you spur of the moment," she whispered. "When he figured out you were undercover. Then he called someone."

Wilkins. Idiot Boy Wilkins. They had worked together just once, back when Ronan was in the good graces of Boyd, one of the leaders of the FPA, and Ronan had demanded that he never work with Wilkins again. Wilkins was a hothead, impulsive, difficult.

They had sent him here to find out where Ronan had hidden the cane. The cane had come with him, from the hospital to his room here. It was, the medical staff said, the only clue to his identity, but it had never triggered anything.

Because it hadn't belonged to Ronan. It had belonged to Boyd. He used the blade hidden in the cane to threaten people. He also used the small storage container, hidden under the knob, to save SIM cards with photos of possible places to attack as well as data from other fringes of the FPA.

Ronan had taken it the night he tried to leave. He hadn't thought his cover was blown, but the trust he had had from the group was completely gone. He had shown weakness, questioned the attacks planned for some of the FPA family members who had gotten out.

He shouldn't have questioned. He should have just left, and reported it. And now, those warnings were probably much too late.

"You know Wilkins," she whispered.

Ronan nodded.

"Then you know what kind of deep trouble you're in," she said. "So find a place to hide."

Another thud, and a moan. He wasn't hiding. He wasn't hiding anymore.

"You got an extra weapon?" he whispered.

"No," she whispered, following procedure, even though he could see the ankle strap near her boot. She had already drawn her weapon.

He didn't blame her. He was injured, unstable, and had a brain injury. He wouldn't have given himself a weapon either.

That only made him respect her more.

"Stay here," she whispered, and hurried toward the sounds of the thumps.

Staying behind was the sensible thing. He could barely stand.

But he wasn't going to be sensible tonight. Everyone in this facility was in danger because of him.

He glanced behind him at the bathroom, and the door directly across from it. The supply closet—not the one for drugs. That was on a lower floor. This one was basic. Paper products. Cleaning supplies.

He tried the door, and was happy to discover that it was unlocked.

CHAPTER EIGHT

The lights near the nurse's station made Lita blink rapidly. Her eyes had adjusted to the dimness of the hallway, which was not a good thing.

As she quietly moved toward the station, she saw booted feet. Simon was down. Dammit. She hoped he was just unconscious, not dead.

Behind the station, the nurse was also sprawled on the floor, her hand still clutching the phone. She had pulled it down with her, but it wasn't bleating, probably because she hadn't chosen a line.

Then Lita heard a *whump* from one of the rooms, followed by the sound of ringing metal. The ringing metal was accompanied by an *oof!* and warbly elderly voice.

"Get *out!*"

A blue light went on over one of the doors. The help-me light.

Someone who shouldn't be was in that room.

Lita held her weapon, not wanting to use it. The walls here were thin enough that Wilkins had pushed his way through one, which meant that a bullet could go through as easily as if it were going through paper.

If she shot her gun in the wrong direction, and missed, she could hurt one of the patients.

There should be another deputy on this floor, but she had a hunch he was incapacitated too.

So she hoped that there was only one attacker, because she would only get one chance at this.

She opened the door, saw a man holding an elderly lady to his side, arm wrapped around her neck. That woman looked like she weighed eighty pounds soaking wet. If he handled her wrong, she would break.

They were against one of the interior walls. Lita did not have a good shot.

"Let her go," she said.

"Nope," the man said. "You tell me where the cane is, and let me out of here, and maybe I won't hurt her. Although I owe her. She hit me in the face with a dish."

"It was a tray," the elderly woman said. Her voice didn't even tremble. "And don't worry about me. I'm old enough—"

"Shut up!" He shook her, and her head wobbled.

Lita did not like that.

"I don't know anything about a cane," she said.

"Ezekiel stole it," the man said. "We need it back."

Lita let out a small breath. The man was here alone. He was Wilkins' partner, and had probably been hiding through all the turmoil. He was here to finish the original job, recover the stolen item.

He had no idea that Ronan had been undercover.

"It's probably in his room," she said.

"I looked," the man said. "The fucking place is torn up. I didn't see nothing."

"Because it's in my therapist's office." Ronan stood just behind her, a thin man in pajamas, with his feet bare. What was he thinking coming in here like this? She didn't need to protect him too.

"Therapist? You go for that crap?" the man asked, and Lita almost smiled. The FPA strikes again. They always sent the dumb ones for what they thought would be the easy jobs.

"We can talk therapy all you want later, Jedidiah," Ronan said. "Right now, you need to let the old lady go."

"I ain't doing that," Jedidiah said.

"Then I'm not taking you to my therapist's office," Ronan said.

Jedidiah nodded toward Lita. "You make the monkey drop her gun."

Her cheeks flushed. Dammit. The insults weren't supposed to get to her.

The old lady poked Jedidiah in the rib cage with a single finger, an old school-teacher trick. He bent slightly, and Lita took a step forward to try to pull the old lady away.

"Mrs. Tucker," Ronan said as he took three large steps across the room. "Look away!"

She did just as he commanded. He raised a spray bottle and squeezed the handle. Liquid streamed out, into Jedidiah's face. The stench of bleach filled the room. Jedidiah screamed.

The old lady collapsed on the floor, her hands over her eyes.

Ronan put one hand out toward Lita. "You got cuffs?"

She didn't answer him. Instead she pulled them, and grabbed the screaming Jedidiah, cuffing his hands behind his back. He was bucking and trying to grab his eyes.

"Calm down," she said. "You're in a medical facility. If you're calm, we'll help you."

He didn't calm, though. He kept screaming, his eyes red. Blood was coming out of his nose.

She'd seen chemical burns before and this one was bad.

"Mrs. Tucker," Ronan asked, as if nothing had happened. "Are you all right? You need to get in the shower, in case some splashed on you."

The old lady looked up at him and grinned.

"Young man," she said, "I am not getting naked for you, no matter how much you ask."

He let out a small laugh, then helped her to her feet. He led her into the hallway as Lita continued to struggle with Jedidiah.

Another officer came to the door, wearing a Three Fires uniform. He looked in, startled, then immediately helped Lita with Jedidiah. He had stopped screaming and was now just moaning in agony.

"There's more FPA assholes coming," she said.

"No," the officer said. "We got them as they were leaving the compound. They're not coming here tonight."

Ronan was handing Mrs. Tucker over to one of the nurses. Then his legs buckled and the nurse had to catch him.

Lita felt her heart stop for a half second, hoping he would be all right.

He used the nurse's strong arm to brace himself, and then stood.

"I'm okay," he said to Lita.

"No, you're not," Lita said. Then she couldn't help herself. She smiled. "But you are damned impressive."

And for the moment, she had to leave it at that.

CHAPTER NINE

August 10, 2015
8:33 AM

R onan had graduated to the sixth floor. His own one-bedroom apartment, not that he had anything to put in it. Two years undercover, six months in limbo, he didn't have anything of his own anymore.

He wasn't even sure he would be staying here. The leader of the task force told him that the government would be paying his medical bills from now on, and that might disqualify him from staying at the Recovery Center.

Something new to worry about, not that he had many worries. He was going to argue that he needed to stay. Consistency of care, and all that.

He had a hunch no one would quibble with that.

No one thought the FPA would come back for a third attempt at him. They had to figure he had given everything up now—and he had. The cane had already gone to the head of the Detroit FBI office, a man Ronan had met several times in connection with the task force.

They needed to debrief him, but not right now. Not as exhausted as he was.

And if the FPA wanted revenge on him, well, Brody was smart enough to know that going after the Recovery Center would be the wrong way to do it. They would need to make him into a lesson, and taking out a bunch of injured and indigent people would be the wrong message.

And it would bring the full wrath of the federal government on them.

Ronan was safe, the facility was safe, and Mrs. Tucker was joyous. She was going to be a media star in all of this, because no one wanted to plaster his face all over the local news.

He sank into the overstuffed armchair across from the small TV. Someone had promised him breakfast—told him he could have whatever he wanted, and he'd ordered the biggest meal of his life. Eggs, waffles, pancakes, donuts, whatever they had. He hadn't been this hungry—well, since he got here.

After that, he was going to see if the bed in the other room was as comfortable as that gurney.

There was a knock on the door. It took him a moment to realize he had to invite the person in. He wasn't in a hospital room any longer. He was in one of the apartments.

"Come in," he said.

The door opened, and one of the rolling carts came in first, bringing with it the smell of fresh coffee, newly baked bread, and well-cooked eggs.

He looked up and saw Detective Montillo pushing it inside.

"I hope you don't mind," she said. "I need breakfast too."

"I thought you'd have to go back to the department," he said.

She pushed the door shut with her foot, then stopped the cart near the small dining table in front of the half-kitchen he hadn't inspected yet.

"Your task force took my prisoner away from me," she said.

"It's not my task force," he said.

"I beg to differ," she said, and put the food on the table. "We're eating over here, because it's clear you can sit upright."

He smiled at her. "Are you here to debrief me, Detective?"

She stopped setting the plates on the table, and turned toward him, a frown on her face.

"I think you have me confused with someone who is at work," she said. "I'm off duty right now. And my name is Lita."

"Lita," he said. "I'm Ronan."

It felt so good to say that.

She smiled at him and said, "You're quite the man, Ronan."

He shook his head. "I'm a mess."

"Yes," she said, "but a fascinating one. One I wouldn't mind getting to know."

His heart pounded hard, not from exertion, but with—oh, hell, he had no idea. Disbelief, maybe? His life was changing again.

"I'd like to get to know him too," he said. "While I get to know you."

She returned to the table, and poured coffee into one of the white mugs the center used.

"Then let's get to it," she said. "Although this is not the usual get-to-know-you conversation people have over breakfast."

"Unless they've had a special night together," he said.

She laughed. "It was a special night. But maybe at some point, we can have a more traditional kind of special night together."

He walked carefully to her side. "I'd like that," he said. "I'd like that very much."

SAFE LIKE CEDAR

LISA SILVERTHORNE

Lisa Silverthorne has "always admired romance writers that created satisfying romances within suspenseful storylines, packing all of that romance and suspense into a compelling seasonal setting. Like summer. And not just romance. Steamy romance that gives off sparks. And heat—lots of heat. So I loved stretching my writer's wings with the challenge of bringing all of these elements together into a short story."

Her story "Safe Like Cedar" hits all of those notes and several more. In some ways, it's a romantic companion piece to her most recent Fiction River *story, "Traffic Stop," which appeared in our latest Special Edition* Spies.

Lisa often has an element of romance in her Fiction River *stories. Her strong short fiction has appeared in eleven of our volumes, as well as two of our special editions, with more appearances to come. If you like the romantic element to her fiction, find our* Christmas Ghosts *issue (which I edited) or pick up the recently released* Feel the Love, *edited by Mark Leslie.*

Or look up the more than 100 short stories she has published in other venues, including Pulphouse. *Her novel* Isabel's Tears *appeared a few years ago, and her second book,* Rediscovery, *just came out. You can find information about all of her work at lisasilverthorne.com.*

Like "Night Moves," "Safe Like Cedar" takes place in the Midwest. But from there, the similarities end. Enjoy the lovely summer festival that Lisa chose as the setting for this breathtaking tale of suspense.

Chalk bombs exploded across the crowded, small-town street festival, startling Ava Harris. Through the haze of purple and turquoise smoke, she saw him. Standing beneath the street-lights. At the festival's entrance.

Searching for her? Her stomach somersaulted, dropping into her feet.

She froze, the night muggy and sticky against her skin. Five years of pain and healing rushed back. Gary Burke was back in Indiana. She shuddered. Back in Sapphire.

Why? To terrorize her for testifying against him? Sending him to prison?

Her heart raced, fight-or-flight screaming flight. For a moment, she couldn't breathe.

Five years ago, he'd gotten a decade in prison after raping and almost killing her in an alley during Sapphire's Starlight festival. Before Burke, the festival had been her favorite part of summer. She'd intended to reclaim the hometown festival for herself tonight.

Until Burke showed up.

Without so much as a text to warn her.

She backed away, puffs of orange and yellow and red chalk clouds rising in her wake, desperate to fade into the crowd. She had to find a way out of here.

Scent of fresh-cut grass was sweet against the smell of hot asphalt and sunscreen as she moved deeper into the crowd, bursts of colored chalk filling the expanse.

The street dance was starting. Behind her. At the other end of the street.

Ava turned, slipping through the rabbit warren-like holes in the crowd and ran.

Before he saw her.

Sandals clapped against pavement, her breath ragged, fear twisting the old knots in her stomach and bubbling up the memories she'd tried to bury.

No, it wasn't supposed to be like this! After five years struggling back to normal (whatever that was now), this was her night. Her hometown. Her recovery.

Local police assured her she'd be notified when he was released from prison. That she'd be the first to know. That he'd be arrested if he came near her.

Didn't someone know he was here? Back in Sapphire like

nothing happened. Like no one remembered what he'd done to her.

That he was a monster.

The Indiana heat wrapped around her like a wool coat. Stifling. Sweltering. Taking her breath.

She swiped at her face, bangs trickling purple and blue rivulets down the sides of her face, onto her pink tank top, jean shorts damp and clinging to her legs.

Thunk!

Ava jumped.

Another burst of chalk, yellow and green, misted the hot night with colored smoke.

She glanced around for a safe spot, gold lights twinkling overhead, expecting him to be right there. At six-two, he'd towered almost a foot over her, long thin face twisted and leering, stony brown eyes wild.

She shuddered, pulling in a breath. A chill rippled across her skin, turning it to gooseflesh, the memories still so visceral that they ached through her.

Big, sweaty hands like embers against her skin, tearing off her halter top, pushing up her skirt as she fought. Kicking and clawing. Screaming. The sweet stink of Jovan musk cloying against alcohol and sulfurous bad breath as he smashed a clammy hand over her mouth. And whispered in her ear.

I'll kill you if you fight me.

Those overpowering, muscular arms like anacondas choking the fight out of her as he ripped off her panties.

Forcing her to submit.

Shaking, Ava glanced back toward the streetlight at the corner of Main and River Streets, to keep him in sight. In front of her so she could escape.

A cold wind blew across her heart.

Gone.

She bolted between two embracing couples dusted in layers of colored chalk, sandals scraping pavement. Her breaths came in hot gulps, triple-digit heat still battling the night and cool sliver of moonlight rising above the Wabash River.

Weaving in and out of the crowd, she struggled to hold back the panic and fear.

Why had he chosen her? Why?

The cops treated her like a suspect that night, insisting on knowing what she'd worn to the festival. As if a miniskirt and halter top at a hot summer street dance was just asking to be assaulted.

Like it was her fault she'd been raped. Like she'd somehow asked for it.

The one exception had been a handsome blond Sapphire cop who rode with her in the ambulance that night, holding her hand. He'd given her the only safety she'd known that night. Before the numbness set in and claimed the rest of her emotions. Her parents had been out of the country on business, leaving her to face all of it alone. But Officer Hawk Davis stayed by her side through the whole ordeal, through the investigation, arrest, and trial. She'd gotten to know him. To care about him—and maybe something more.

Until the sentencing.

Then he just vanished from town without a word. She never saw him again. She never got to thank him for being there. Or to find out if she'd just been another assignment.

Ahead, she rushed beneath the gold lights twinkling under swaths of gossamer fabric draped in arches across the street that ran behind the hardware store and in front of the row of gingerbread artisan shops facing the Wabash River Walk. A winding trail ran parallel to the river and the street.

She'd managed to finish her counseling degree, but it took five years to come back to the festival she loved. To face her demons and take back her sense of security. To stir awake that scalded sense of joy the lights and plumes of colored smoke once brought.

She shuddered, glancing through the crowd at the alley that cut between artisan shops.

Where that monster had dragged her, with a huge crowd of people right there, oblivious to the assault.

No! She balled her hands into fists. She wouldn't let him shove the memory of that night back into her head. She wouldn't relive it again.

Fairy lights glimmered along the shops' gabled roofs, reflecting off the dark river water like Monet's water lilies. Softening her panic.

She took a breath. Held it. Released.

Each store, painted a pastel color and trimmed in white, had their doors open wide and candles flickering in the windows. Pottery and paintings. Wool scarves and woodworking. Ceramics and jewelry sparkling against the warm haze of candles and lights.

Every summer, people came to the festival from all over the state, swelling Sapphire to three times its size. Indiana's best-kept summer secret.

Like Gary Burke's release from prison.

Past the shops, dozens of people gathered under the fabric arches and twinkling lights as stars appeared in the humid night sky. They used to shut the lights off downtown to see the stars better, but they stopped five years ago.

The street dance was starting.

Relieved, Ava pressed into the closeness of the dance crowd.

There was safety in numbers.

The band, four bearded guys in shorts and ragged T-shirts, began to play, drums thumping as a steel guitar whined a tinny melody that gave way to guitars thrumming their best Southern-rock anthem into the sultry night.

The crowd cheered and sang along as more chalk bombs hissed through the thick heat, settling against sunbaked asphalt and people dancing in the flush of colored chalk dust. Sidewalks steamed against the tangle of sweat-slicked bodies flailing in the wash of colors.

Fury burned through Ava's flushed face, splattered vivid blue and purple, throb of bass echoing beneath the frenetic drumbeat swirling the crowd into a frenzy of sweat and bodies and classic rock, everyone moving together as one. Ava tried, but all she wanted now was to scrunch flat and fold herself into the sea of faces that Gary Burke didn't recognize.

Colored chalk dust clung to her dark hair and face as a comforting mask. Maybe it would keep her out of that monster's reach?

Breathe, Ava. Just breathe.

Tang of cold beer mixed with the smell of sweat and chalk and hot pavement. The triple-digit heat had barely cooled as she glanced up at the stars filling the night sky. Wanting to wish on them again. To look ahead in her life instead of always looking back. Except for Officer Davis. She couldn't get him out of her head. What happened to him? Did he leave the area? Moved to the big city? Found a wife? She'd asked about him around town, but got no response.

Lightning bugs flickered in the dark, rising like bonfire embers as fairy lights twinkled against the translucent fabric arches.

In front of the alley.

Fear spiked cold through her chest, the ghosts of that night rising as she glanced around the dim lit street. Through the tangle of people dancing and clapping. In the sweltering heat burning her face as the bass riffed out "Bad to the Bone."

She surveyed the festival's perimeter again. Sidewalks. Sawhorses blocking off the street. Gray-and-white beer tent at the end of the block. Rush of the Wabash whispering through the short bursts of silence.

That's when she saw it.

Flash of stringy black hair. Long, lean shadow twisting across the street. Stretching toward the band.

Burke!

In dark pants and a long-sleeved dark shirt. Tapping his foot to the music as he leaned against a trash can. Staring into the crowd with empty eyes like a shark stalking seals.

Heart pounded against breastbone. Mouth went dry, hands shaking—the old fear rising.

Ava moved with the other dancers, sliding close, folding herself into the dark pockets deep within the crowd.

Don't give away your location, her sweltering brain screamed as she danced deeper into the crowd, moving away from the band.

She crouched. Head down. Around her, feet thumped the steamy asphalt to the beat. Cicadas chirred a steady buzz above the music and the din of the crowd.

Someone grabbed her arm.

The scream bubbled up, but she swallowed it back as the hand clapped gently against her shoulder. She closed her eyes, recoiling, willing Burke away from her.

"Ava Harris," said the buttery-warm voice. "I'm here to protect you."

As her breathing slowed, she opened her eyes, turning to stare at the man at her shoulder.

Her heart fluttered, then skipped two beats.

Hot enough to evaporate the words right off her lips. Sweltering enough to melt a bra clasp in fifteen seconds. Officer Hawk Davis. The cop from the ambulance. Back in Sapphire?

He was out of uniform, in tight jeans, checkered Vans, and a black muscle shirt. He had the body of a surfer, his curly, summer-blond hair, crooked smile, and devastating blue eyes hotter than River Street in August. Much more attractive than she remembered.

For a moment, she almost forgot about Gary Burke. Almost.

"It's...you," she said, grabbing hold of his arms, feeling that stab of attraction sparking inside again.

Did he feel it, too, or was she just another job to do?

Hawk's smile was bright, but distant.

"Ava," he repeated in that low, warm voice. "Been searching all over Sapphire for you. Glad I found you."

She shook her head, the memory of his kind face and sizzling blue eyes coming back to her from the ambulance ride. So patient. Staying beside her at the trial. And the sentencing.

"You remember me?" he asked above the music and the crowd, a hand on his chest.

"Of course, I remember you," said Ava, her voice sounding small and shaky. "And your kindness. Why are you here?"

"To catch a monster," he snapped.

Her stomach dropped. "He's here. I just saw him."

Hawk moved closer, the emotion leaving his face. Hawk's gaze flitted through the crowd, around the edges of the street dance.

"Burke told his cellmate that when he got out, he'd return to Sapphire to finish the job. Lawyer got him early release on some trial loophole." His gaze returned to her face, the corners of his mouth flattening into a straight, determined line. "I'm here to close it."

Ava winced, the old sour fear washing over her again. Five years of watching over her shoulder, looking for egress at every party, in every restaurant and every store. Five years of jumping at every unexpected touch.

From anyone. Including Hawk five years ago. Back then she'd been so sure he was as attracted to her as she had been him. Throughout the case and the trial, he kept his distance, except for his eyes. Until he just disappeared. Like he'd never been in her life at all.

"Is it me he wants?" Ava asked, voice quivering, a sudden chill against her skin.

Hawk nodded. "He's a serial rapist and worse, but you're the first woman to testify and send him to prison."

"Why haven't the others testified?" Ava asked, wide-eyed, watching the detective's eyes for emotion.

Hawk's eyes were blue flames. "Because the rest of them are missing. We just haven't found the bodies yet."

The hair on Ava's neck stood up. She pulled in a breath. "He's close, detective," she answered in a shaky voice as he leaned in closer to hear her. "I saw him at the festival entrance.

I'm afraid to leave. Thought the street dance would be the safest place."

"It's Hawk, remember," said Hawk, with those beautiful pale blue eyes and crooked smile making her a little dizzy.

Of course she remembered.

Ava watched a hint of pain wash across his eyes. "I tried to contact you," she said. "After the trial was over, but you never—"

"Don't worry," he said, ignoring her statement. "There are undercover cops all over the festival. The moment Burke gets near you, we'll take him down. You have my word."

So, she'd have to see him again. Up close. The thought nauseated her.

But Hawk's determined gaze and confidence burned in the summer heat, sweat-soaked bangs pressed against his forehead, face damp with sweat and flecked with colored chalk as he stepped closer. She trusted this man with her life. And she wanted him in her life like he'd been five years ago.

"I won't leave your side," he said, flashing that crooked smile again. "You have my word."

Ava nodded. "Thank you."

But there was something in the way he looked at her, just a little longer, a little deeper.

"Let's blend into the crowd," said Hawk, and he began to dance beside her.

Dancing with a cop. She smiled, hoping his proximity kept Burke away.

She exhaled, letting some of her fear and apprehension dissipate as she swayed beside Hawk. She tried to focus her attention on him, but with Burke out there, her skin crawled.

How many other cops danced or stood nearby? Watching. Waiting. Maybe their presence would keep her safe?

"You have a nice smile, Ava Harris," said Hawk, a grin on his face. "It's nice to finally see it."

"Thanks," she said, her smile widening into a grin.

It was nice of Hawk to notice.

"Why did you disappear right after the sentencing?" she asked.

The grin faded from his face, a far off expression replacing it, his eyes darkening.

"I got called back to—other cases," he said, his voice unconvincing.

Had he gotten too close? Stepped over the line? She sighed. *Like she had.*

As they danced beside each other, she watched Hawk's gaze still on the crowd, focusing on the perimeter, on people moving around them. Then he'd glance at her and smile, his gaze flitting around the perimeter again. Always on watch.

His focus made Ava relax a bit, feeling that little hint of safety again. Like she didn't have to be on guard with Hawk on watch again.

Abruptly, the band's lead singer announced an old 80's ballad. Something from a band called Meatloaf. Meatloaf—really? Two out of Three something or other.

A keyboard plinked out a soprano opening, sad and haunting until the lead singer picked up the melody, lamenting about his dying relationship.

People in the audience sang along as the ballad rolled across the muggy street. They coupled up and slow danced together. Some held up their phones, pale blue lights twinkling like starlight against the slow rhythm.

Hawk slid his arms around her, pulling her close, tight against his bare shoulder. He smelled warm like leather. Safe like cedar. God, she remembered how good he smelled.

Stay in character, she told herself, but his closeness and intoxicating scent left her knees a little weak, the song taking her back to her first high school dance and the boy that broke her heart that summer.

And that night in the ambulance.

She'd been terrified of being touched, but around Hawk, something just—let go inside her. Pushed back the trauma and fear of five years, blurring her focus on Hawk. And the feelings she'd buried after he disappeared.

She swayed with him, his body against hers, his clean-shaven face soft against her cheek. The deep rumble of his voice as he sang along was hotter than the state fair in August. God, she'd missed the heat of another body against hers, the gentleness of someone just wanting to feel connected. People shouted out the ballad's haunting lyrics, but Hawk singing them in her ear made her sink deeper into his warmth and comfort, lose herself in his arms. But even now, at the back of her memory, the cloying sweet stench of musk drowned out any other smell. She'd hated the stink of it, gagging her that night in the alley.

"Is this just part of the job?" she whispered in Hawk's ear.

He lifted his face from her shoulder, his eyes sad now. "Not this time," he said, brushing colored powder off her cheek.

He gripped her shoulders, staring so deeply into her eyes that she thought he might see past the damage and into her soul, but something else played across his eyes.

Pain. He was reliving something that cut him deep. Something that had scarred him as deeply as her own ordeal.

She enfolded him in her arms, wanting to comfort him like he'd done for her.

"I left suddenly, I know," he said, laying his head against her shoulder, his face hot against her bare skin. A soul-rattling sigh escaped his lips as his gaze returned to Ava, his eyes wet with tears. "See, my sister—"

The first *pop, pop, pop* rang out like firecrackers. Like fireworks.

It took several moments to register even as Hawk's body stiffened against the first loud bang. Already moving into action.

He pulled her down, underneath him, against the hot, oily blacktop that gouged her knees and smelled like tar.

Only when the string of sounds pealed above the band a second time did Ava realize they were gunshots.

Around them, people screamed, running and darting like frogs on an interstate. The band dropped down behind the stage, huddling behind amplifiers and cases.

Hawk sheltered her, gun drawn as he scanned for the shooter.

"Stay down!" Hawk shouted, waving his arm at the dissipating crowd. "Stay down!"

People fled in all directions.

Something whizzed past Ava's face, almost grazing her nose. With the crowd out of the way, Hawk pivoted, finding a clear line of sight to the shooter. Still protecting her, he returned fire. Toward the dark image crouched beside a trash can.

Hawk covered her again as a hail of shots crackled across the street.

Piercing squeal of police sirens drowned out the screams and the running.

A dark figure lurched onto the street, rifle slung over one shoulder, pistol in his hand. He passed under the gossamer fabric arches, lights flickering against his hard, lined face.

Disappearing into the clouds of colored smoke.

Hawk turned.

Out of the haze, a pistol lowered to his chest, firing off three rounds. All three struck Hawk in the chest.

Whump, whump, whump! Like a sack of potatoes hitting the pavement.

Hawk fell backward. Into the street.

"Hawk!" Ava cried, sliding toward him. "Hawk! You can't be dead—please!"

Arms shot around her, throwing her into a headlock, dragging her backward. Out of the street.

"Miss me, baby?" Burke sneered, smashing his rough, unshaven face against hers in a savage kiss.

The sweet stench of Jovan musk made her gag as he dragged her toward the alley.

She fought. Struggled. Kicked and gouged at his face.

He just laughed. An overconfident, acerbic sound that made her skin crawl.

"That should keep all those fucking cops busy for a while," Burke said with a grin. "Now, you're gonna pay for my prison time, you little bitch. And this time, they'll never find your body. Just like your cop boyfriend's little sister."

"What?" Ava cried, wide-eyed, struggling against Burke's hold.

"You think he's here for you?" Burke shouted, laughter rumbling through his chest as he hauled Ava deeper into the alley that ran north, halfway through town.

Far from any help.

"He was just using you as bait. Telling you there were cops out here protecting you. Bullshit! It was only him! He's the only one who returned fire."

Her head swam. Was that true? Is that all Hawk wanted here tonight? To bait the man who killed his sister?

And now, he was probably lying dead in the street. Her eyes filled with tears, the sickness rising.

Burke slung her like a ragdoll into the red-brick alley wall caked with chewing gum, spray paint, and dirt. Bricks gouged her legs and arms. The stench of sour beer and urine mixed with the heat and stink of his musk cologne.

She gagged again.

He leaned back against the other wall, pistol pointed downward as the wail of sirens and screams swirled through Sapphire's dark streets.

Ava bolted, lurching left, sandals smacking the squishy alleyway floor. She pumped her legs hard, trying to get some distance from him.

"Goddammit, stop!"

She shifted out of Burke's reach, shoulders rolling right, and hit the sidewalk on Lafayette Street (in front of the hardware store) running for her life.

An ambulance whined from the distant interstate, moving closer.

Ava tried to make it around the block, but Burke was faster, cutting her off before she got to First Street.

Grabbing her hair, he jerked her backward, dragging her by hair and arm. Back into the alley.

With police on both sides of the alley, turning the street dance into a blockade, Burke tore open her tank top.

No! Her brain screamed. She wouldn't be his victim a second time.

He moved toward her, rifle at his back, pistol in his right hand.

She backed away until the brick walk was at her back.

He leered at her, grin twisting his thin, angular features until his brown eyes turned cold. Stony.

Her life meant nothing to him. She saw it in the blank, almost bored stare of his eyes. Empty.

He motioned at her with the barrel of his pistol. "Take it all off or I'll beat it off you."

With slow, shaking fingers, she took hold of her torn tank top and slid it off, revealing her black sports bra underneath.

Burke shoved her into the wall again. "All of it! Now!"

Rustle of footsteps whispered all around them.

Burke turned toward the sound as she twisted the tank top in her hands. Stretching it long and thin.

Taut.

A shout echoed through the alley, rising in layers. Faint flutter of sobs reverberated from the street somewhere behind her.

She took a step toward him.

Burke still looked toward River Street.

Another step, a smile rising above her fear. Her rage.

Shadows rushed past the alley. Where the street dance had been. Burke lifted the pistol toward the sounds.

She was close enough to see his cold, hateful eyes. Smell his sour, alcohol-laced breath. Hear the sharp hiss of breath as his nostrils flared, teeth grinding as the rage ignited inside him again.

He whirled around, leveled the pistol at her chest.

"Burke!" Someone shouted.

He twisted left, toward the voice, shoulders hunching as he aimed the pistol toward the voice.

With a swift, fluid stretch, Ava wrapped the stretched-out tank top around his neck and yanked it tight.

Twisting. Pulling. Garroting.

Shadows rushed down the alley toward her, rustle of metal against fabric, shoe soles crackling against the damp alleyway as Ava pulled the tank top tighter until the monster dropped to his knees, face paper white and gasping.

Someone grabbed the gun from Burke's hand, but she held on tight, not giving him one more chance to destroy her.

The warm palm sizzled against her bare shoulder. Hawk's face swung into view. Her eyes stung. Back from the dead!

"It's over now," he said in a soft, comforting voice, Burke's pistol in his fist.

She kept her grip tight until Hawk's hands enfolded the tops of hers, his voice soft in her ear.

"Let it go, Ava," he said in a half-whisper, buttery voice soothing. "You're better than him."

When Hawk's warm cedar scent punched through the musk and her rage, she eased her grip on the twisted fabric around Gary Burke's neck. Burke fell forward and Hawk pounced on him with handcuffs. Another officer then another was on the scene, one taking the rifle off Burke's shoulder.

As consciousness returned, Burke's gaze swiveled back to Ava, the hatred in his eyes renewed.

"Never again," said Ava, glaring down at him.

On his knees, he looked small and angry and pointless. She crossed her arms over her chest and stood her ground. She would never let anyone take from her what this monster took. Never again.

As the officers marched Burke out of the alley and into a police car, Hawk returned to Ava's side.

Gently, he took off his tank top and slid it over her head. Instead of bare chest, she saw the bulletproof vest he'd worn.

"I thought you were dead," she said, voice shaky.

That crooked smile burned through her as he patted the vest. "Had to protect you any way I could."

"What about the people at the dance?" Ava demanded. They mattered, too. "Were they just collateral damage to you?"

He shook his head. "Of course not! No one knew he'd shoot up the place. There are lots of injuries, but no one died tonight."

"What about your sister?"

His expression darkened, eyes misting as sweat beaded his face. "Was I the bait, Hawk?"

She had to know.

His eyes widened and he shook his head. "Bait? No way I'd use you as bait to smoke out a killer. Much less a monster like Burke. I came here to protect you, Ava. You're the reason I'm back in Sapphire."

"Burke said—"

His eyes narrowed. "He was taunting you, Ava! Like he's been taunting me from prison, emailing me about my sister. Mentioning the clothes she was wearing. The necklace. Hinting at where he buried her."

Hawk fell silent, his blue eyes shiny in the soft wash of moon-light overhead.

"Is that why you—"

"Left Sapphire?" he said, reaching out to brush a purple-caked strand of hair out of Ava's eyes. "I went to Indy. Where they found her burned-out car and purse." His voice hitched. "I had to go."

Ava slid her hand into his and squeezed. "I didn't know, Hawk. Why didn't you tell me?"

He put his hand over hers. "You didn't need that image in your head," he said with a sigh. "Not with everything else you were dealing with."

"Was Burke lying?" she asked.

"I checked out his taunts," he said, his voice catching, turning shaky. "Nothing but old riverbed. I won't stop looking, though. Someday, I'll bring her home to Sapphire."

Ava slid her arms around his waist, hugging his body into hers. Into his warm, soothing scent. She put her hand in his, squeezing.

"Let me hold your hand this time, Hawk," she whispered against his ear, her lips brushing his downy soft earlobe. "It's my turn."

He smiled, turning his body into hers. "I'd like that, Ava."

Leaning down, he found her mouth and pressed his lips to hers. She kissed him back, knowing he'd be at her side when this hot summer faded to autumn and beyond. Into next year's Starlight festival. For now, she'd be at his side, settling into the heat of his embrace. Safe like cedar.

FLYING ABOVE THE HINDU KUSH

a Night Stalkers 5E romance story

M. L. BUCHMAN

No romantic suspense volume would be complete without a military romance short story. Fortunately for us, M.L. Buchman writes a lot of military romance at both the long and short lengths.

He has made quite a name for himself with his Night Stalkers romance series. Three times Booklist *has placed one of his novels in their top ten romance novels of the year. Barnes & Noble and National Public Radio have also listed his novels in their top five romances of the year. His most recent novel,* Target of One's Own, *appeared in January.*

In addition to the fifty novels he's published, Matt has written more than seventy short stories. Some have appeared in Fiction River, *including the lovely romance short "The Ghost of Willow's Past" in* Christmas Ghosts. *For one week every month, he puts up a short story for free on his website, mlbuchman.com.*

Matt says he focused on the word "heat" to write this story. "Summer heat, the heat of what our internal past brings to a boil inside, the heat of hatred, the technical challenges of heat to flight, and several other aspects. I wanted to burn through those layers to forge something new and better from that fire...and found this story."

CHAPTER ONE

O
kay, taking bets on who hates us more?" Captain Tyra
Walker sat in the left seat of her MH-6M "Little Bird"
attack helicopter and ran through engine start-up checklist called
out by her copilot.

External power
Key switch
Generator Switch on
Confirm audible alarms
Gen Switch off
Auto Re-IGN Test switch to Test

"Command. Definitely," her copilot, Herman Geller, voted.

"For planting us in the suck-high desert during an entire
Afghan summer or for giving us the short straw of tonight's
mission?" She confirmed fuel level and system-failure warning light
functionality.

"I'm generous. I'm believe in Command's willingness to punish
us in multiple ways. Though I'm leaning toward the latter—did
you see that performance profile on this flight? *Air filter clogged
warning indicator.*"

"Check." Of course she had.

Typical Command: they were loading her helo heavy, then

sending her up to the theoretical limits of high-and-hot flight. Command loved the outer edge of the performance envelope. Helicopters didn't. Thin air—which only grew thinner with more altitude and the unremitting heat that made sweat pour down the back of her neck like a tropical waterfall—gave the rotors nothing to bite on. Their Bagram Air Base hangar was almost a mile high to begin with. Where they were headed tonight was nearly double that. Heavily loaded helicopters didn't like that—not even the ones specially modified for the Night Stalkers.

"What's your vote?" She turned to her left to face Norm as he was loading his dirt bike into the helicopter's side carrier. She confirmed the cyclic-trim's motor operation, working the control beneath her right thumb and listening for the soft hum of the actuators. As always, he looked a little surprised when she addressed him directly. Maybe it was because Delta Force operators were so used to being invisible that he was uneasy at being seen.

Tonight he was the reason for an infiltrate-exfiltrate mission: deliver Norm deep into very unfriendly territory at night, hide out during the day, and then make sure he got back out the next night.

Major Norm Lawrence was anything but invisible, at least to her. Maybe because he absolutely looked the part, once she knew who he was. Delta operators weren't generally big boys like SEALs. She'd dated a SEAL or two and certainly didn't mind the way they were built one tiny bit. But Delta selected for more the wiry-but-tough type. The Major matched her own five-ten, and wore one-eighty of pure muscle that looked damn good on him. His light tan let him blend in almost anywhere.

"My vote on what?" His voice was low and gruff, as if he rarely used it—which, being Delta, was true.

"Who hates us most tonight? We have one vote for Command, I'm in favor of the Pakis who keep supporting the Taliban while they take our aid money." She should really shut up on occasion. It sometimes felt as if she was channeling Tyra Banks "Talk Show Host," as if there hadn't been enough comparisons because they were both tall, black, and shared a name. But the other Tyra's embodiment of strength had seen Tyra herself through the toughest times so perhaps a little channeling was a good thing.

"It's just a world of joy out there," and Norm strode back toward the table to fetch more gear.

"Did a Delta just make a joke?" Geller looked up from his checklist and leaned over to stare past her at Norm's back. "He must really like you."

That pulled Tyra out of her normal routine and made her miss her reach for the collective control to lock the throttle twistgrip on Full Open.

She'd noticed Norm from the first day his small team had hit Bagram Air Base north of Kabul three weeks ago. He was impossible to miss.

Her company had flown in the day before on a huge C-5 Galaxy transport along with five of their Night Stalker helicopters. The 160th Special Operations Aviation Regiment was back in Afghanistan. They'd dragged their machines out of the plane's cargo bay and prepared them for a six-month tour. This was her third with SOAR—before that she'd flown for the 10th Mountain in Iraq. Cleaning out the Taliban and ISIL was never going to happen, but it was her job to do what she could.

The message on how painful this tour was going to be came the next day when a half dozen Delta Force operators, embedded with a platoon of fifty US Rangers, hit the pavement. In three weeks of nightly missions, this was the first time the head of the Delta team was on her bird.

Even among such a collection of fine specimens, Major Norm Lawrence had stood out. People simply made room when he walked by.

There was a buffer of respect that moved with him and few could enter it.

Over the last few weeks, they'd both taken to never passing each other without some form of acknowledgment. There was something very attractive about his self-contained nature. They'd spent an entire meal once talking about the ups and downs of being an Army Special Operations officer. Looking back, Tyra realized how exceptional that was for him. And, even more curiously, how much she'd like to do that again.

She was rarely comfortable around men—which made it God's little joke that she had ended up in the almost exclusively male world of Special Ops.

CHAPTER TWO

N orm double-checked his gear, then hauled on his pack. Only forty pounds, it felt strangely light—but tonight was recon, not assault.

Just a world of joy out there?

Shit, man!

That was the way to smooth talk a woman when she gave you an opening? Mumble something cryptic then beat ass before she had a chance to respond? He didn't want to face her response to his lame-ass remark.

He had his pick of women back Stateside. Delta bunnies were thick on the ground all around Fort Bragg, North Carolina. But Captain Tyra Walker came from a whole different class. He hadn't even known that the Night Stalkers had women pilots until he stepped off the plane and saw her. She spoke like New England Ivy League and carried herself like a runway model. As tall as he was, ballet-dancer posture, and a skin color that would get his white ass beat back home in Arkansas but looked incredible on her. There was an impenetrable reserve to her that men seemed to just bounce off—he sure as hell had.

He shifted another five pounds of ammo for his sniper rifle into his pack to have something to do—then he dumped it back out because he really didn't need it. At last the engine was fully wound up and he could see her finishing the run-up.

At the last possible second, he crossed to the Nightmare dirt bike—custom-built to Special Operations' specs—that he'd latched into the Little Bird's side carrier and climbed astride it. He snapped a line from the D-ring on the front of his vest to the helicopter's frame and pulled on the headset.

"Delta ready."

Tyra didn't even answer—which told him too much of what she thought of him. She just lifted the skids up a foot, scooted out of the hangar, and took off into the night. Within moments, the high desert terrain began shifting into the rugged foothills of the Hindu Kush Mountains. The lights of civilization were gone within minutes and the land lay black below.

He liked riding out in the wind, usually. At this temperature it was more like being desert roasted. Once Tyra hit cruise speed, he leaned against the side of the helicopter to get into the slip-stream and out of the hundred-and-fifty mile-an-hour blast. He couldn't fit in the tiny rear cabin because it was filled by the ammo cases for the Minigun mounted on the tiny helicopter's other side.

His kind of ride—one with real teeth.

Like the woman at the controls—Special Operations tough.

He'd really enjoyed talking to her about serving as an officer. He could hear how deep it was in her bones despite her fine upbringing. She had ideals and had thought hard about things he'd taken for granted. She'd forced him to reflect on some of his major decisions. He'd have still ended up in the same place, but he might have done it more purposefully.

She was the first woman who'd ever forced him to think with anything above his waist.

All the Delta bunnies—actually Special Operations bunnies because the last thing a Unit operator did was admit to being in The Unit—didn't understand that all the low-cut dresses in the world couldn't make them soldier-hot.

At the top of his soldier-hot list was Tyra Walker, and that was before she started talking in that thoughtful way of hers.

The Little Birds flew without doors. The big windows in the doors didn't offer all that much protection and the tiny cockpits got claustrophobic fast. Plus it offered better visibility for the pilot. He could just see her left elbow as she flew. That's when he realized that he was using up the batteries in his night-vision goggles and switched them off.

Darkness descended. The thin crescent moon would be down before they reached the landing zone, only the stars lit the night—the Little Bird was blacked out. The Hindu Kush continued climbing. He'd fought in the Kunar Province before. He'd spent far too much time down in that brutal landscape and wasn't looking forward to returning. In the distance, where the Hindu Kush became the Western Himalayas, he could see the glint of snow-capped peaks—too far away to ease the pounding heat of an Afghan summer.

What would it be like to sit with Tyra, away from all this? Someplace cool and quiet where he could perhaps just talk about... That's where he ran into trouble. He was only one thing, a Unit operator. What else could he talk about that might interest a woman like her?

As if she heard him thinking about her, she spoke over the intercom.

"'A world of joy,' Major? That's a pretty cheery view for a man headed into unfriendly territory." Her tone was light. Perhaps he hadn't offended her and she'd merely been busy.

"Technically it's friendly territory. Pakistan is an ally."

"With allies like that..."

"...who needs enemies," he finished the old saying. She'd been thinking about his cryptic remark, which was more than he'd done before making it.

"Where's home, Major?"

"I'm not supposed to have a past. Unit operator. Man of mystery and all that."

She actually laughed.

He'd never heard her do that and it was a strangely bright sound to accompany flying into enemy country.

"Leaving a line of broken hearts behind you."

"Sure. Just dump 'em by the side of the road when I'm done. That's me. It's in the training manual."

The dull thud of descending silence shouldn't have been audible, but it was. Now there was only the high whine of the Allison T-63 turboshaft engine, the heavy pounding of the blades, and the rush of the wind.

Shit! Teasing wasn't his style, so why did he do that? He wasn't even sure where it was coming from. Clearly it was up to him to restart this conversation—*not* one of his strengths.

"No broken hearts that I know of. And I'm from nowhere fancy. You know the movie *Winter's Bone* with Jennifer Lawrence, rural Ozarks?"

After a long silence, she came back with a careful. "I know it." Maybe she was busy with some navigation, though there was no cross-chatter with Geller.

"From there. No relation though. Jennifer Lawrence, Norm Lawrence." And though it tasted drier that the dust in the Afghan air, he mentioned the name of his hometown. Long gone and no reason to go back.

This time the crashing silence shrouded them for over a hundred miles, crossing above the soaring peaks of the Hindu Kush Mountains to the landing site.

CHAPTER THREE

D amn you, Geller!" Tyra was almost thankful for the sudden problem as a relief from her own whirling thoughts.

"What did I do?"

"You were right," Tyra fought the controls but every time she slowed, the helo lost altitude. "Command is the one who has it in for us. What's the outside temperature?"

"One-one-five."

"How can it be a hundred and fifteen degrees at eleven at night? That's ten degrees over predicted. At present loading, that places stable hover almost a thousand feet below where I need to be." And she'd be damned if she was going to crash.

That's what had happened to the stealth bird in bin Laden's compound. Five degrees Celsius, nine Fahrenheit, *over* the predicted temperature for the raid at four thousand feet above sea level—with the helo right at its load limit including fourteen SEALs and a dog. When the air in the compound turbulated in the rotor's downwash, there was no extra lift in the rarefied air, and they went down.

And Command still hadn't learned their lesson.

"Major." It took all of the control she'd built so carefully over the years to keep her voice even. "I'm going to drop you lower down the trail and then retreat to higher ground once we're lighter."

"Roger that."

Yeah, set him down and spend who knew how many hours trying to digest an awful truth. The place she'd barely managed to escape alive, the one she'd sworn she'd never have anything to do with ever again, was the place Major Norm Lawrence called home. She was so sure she was over it, then—*bam!*—every horrid memory slammed back to life.

Had he been friends with the guys who'd attacked her? God forbid, had he been one of them? Or the buddy who'd laughed with them afterward about the "nigger bitch" they'd nearly raped to death? Every time she heard that word now was like being thrown back into the pit.

She would *never* be ready to hear it again.

Tyra found a clearing that fit her fifty-foot minimum clearance requirements. She'd barely touched the skids to Pakistan dust before Norm—no!—before Major Lawrence was racing away. He had shed his helmet and the intercom headset for a turban and night-vision goggles. His dual mode—electric and gas—bike brilliantly illuminated the trail with an infrared headlight visible only through the NVGs.

On the ground for less than five seconds, she pulled the Little Bird up and back. Over five hundred pounds lighter, she managed to retreat and land in the planned cul-de-sac high in the mountains. She resisted the urge to fly away and leave the bastard there—barely. Within minutes, she and Geller had a camouflage net stretched over the Little Bird.

To find them now, someone would have to be hunting for them.

CHAPTER FOUR

Norm was in position long before the pre-sunrise prayers.

Both the Khyber Pass far to the south and the river crossing a hundred kilometers to the north at Arandu were too well patrolled now for the munitions smugglers. It was summer, so the Pakistan merchants were desperate for safe ways to ship munitions to the insurgents in Afghanistan. During the harsh winters, the high passes were closed and there was little money until trade and crops returned each spring.

There were rumors that a new route had opened over the backbone of the border halfway between the other two crossings: from Khar, Pakistan, down the hard cliffs and into Mangwal, Afghanistan. Khar was such a small place, he easily found a position high in the hills overlooking the square.

He unpacked and assembled his sniper rifle and wrapped it in burlap so that it wouldn't catch the light when the sun rose. His mission was strictly recon, but he needed the best view possible, which was through his sniper scope—well steadied by its attachment to the rifle. He slid on the silencer out of habit.

He lay for an hour wondering what had brought down that second comm silence during their flight. But the more he thought about it the less he understood.

Fine. He would compartmentalize it until he could ask.

Except Tyra Walker didn't compartmentalize very well. She kept sliding sideways into his thoughts in ways that were very pleasant...and horribly distracting.

After the prayers, there was movement in the square. Small tables in front of a cantina. Four men came to sit around a table.

Four men who—

Holy shit!

Three of them were Alpha targets. He'd studied the "baseball card" biographies of all the "knowns" in the area. Sitting down for morning coffee were the leader of Kunar Province Taliban, the Number Two in Afghanistan's branch of ISIL, and a Pakistani general known to be corrupt as hell. The last, whoever he was, was not likely to be a good guy. Guards lounged around the square, their AK-47s on clear display. Any villagers with an ounce of common sense would be far away.

Recon only.

But they didn't train Delta to make decisions slowly or fail to modify plans as needed. This was a kill-list opportunity like few he'd ever heard of. He'd didn't have the forces to take them prisoner and get intel, but he could certainly damage the beast.

He eased out his satellite radio and called Command. Was a drone available? Yes there was one in the area. Authorization? Answer promised in five minutes. Good thing it was still early evening in Washington DC.

He kept his eye on the target. If they started to leave, he'd take them down. Twelve hundred meters, three quarters of a mile, but within range of his weapon...barely.

CHAPTER FIVE

Tyra sat among the boulders on the dirt. She had to get away from the helicopter. Even from Geller, whose turn it was to be on watch. She and Herman had flown together for over a year now, so he knew that her silence was out of the ordinary and she damned well wouldn't be explaining herself to him either.

She had left the past behind. Far behind. After all, it was a decade ago. She'd been with men since then and congratulated herself on being clear of the baggage. How had it followed her through time and halfway around the world? The therapist had warned her all those years ago that it might and she'd set out to prove him wrong. What did a *man* know about rape survivors? Apparently too much.

Tyra had made it a mission to redefine herself, her life...and she had the perfect image to use. *Tyra Banks, Supermodel of the Year.* First African-American on the cover of *GQ* and twice *Sports Illustrated* swimsuit issue cover. Smart too. Her own show. Her own everything.

Tyra Walker had done the same, except it had been her version. She'd—

A sharp crack of gunfire sounded behind her.

She spun and raised the FN-SCAR rifle that always hung across every Night Stalker's chest and sighted back toward the Little Bird just as Geller's body tumbled out of the helicopter to the ground. No living man would fall in such a way.

Not the time to think about him.

The assailant was on the far side of the helo, but she could see his legs under the belly.

She didn't hesitate to kneecap him.

He didn't fall—she'd have killed him if he did—though his scream was very satisfying. A quick scan. Only one. Some lone scout who had heard her when she'd flown too low last night and had come looking.

Then something came flying over the helo in her direction.

A grenade, headed right for her in a perfect lob. There was no way to dive clear, no rock to get behind that wouldn't expose her to fire.

She counted seconds.

A trained soldier holds a grenade long enough so that it explodes as it reaches the target. The average person wants to get rid of a live grenade as fast as they can.

Out of choices, Tyra bet her life on the assailant being average.

One one thousand.

Two one thousand.

Three—

She caught it high and, spinning her arm, winged it back low and hard. It wasn't her best pitch, but she'd been a top softball pitcher before...well, before.

Four one thousand.

It bounced once in the dirt beneath the helicopter and arrived at the assailant's feet just at fi—

She dove behind her boulder as the grenade blew. A few bits of shrapnel pinged the rocks around her.

Then she peeked around the side of her shield.

Big mistake!

She saw the leading edge of the fireball and barely managed to escape it.

A Little Bird's fuel tanks were crash-rated not to leak. However, blowing up a grenade right below a tank had been too much.

The fuel touched off and blew the shit out of her Little Bird. No little pings of shrapnel—this time whole chunks of her helicopter crashed around her.

Pilot's seat.

A piece of the motorcycle carrier.

A twist of composite that might have once been a rotor blade.

Her helmet, that she'd left on her seat, ricocheted off multiple rocks like a pinball in a life-sized game.

The fireball roared aloft as the helo burned.

Then the ammunition for the Minigun began exploding. Most of it wasn't going anywhere, but eight thousand rounds of 7.62x51mm ammo went up far faster than even a Minigun could fire them. All Tyra could do was cover her ears and pray.

CHAPTER SIX

Norm heard the thump even though he was a dozen kilometers away. At first he thought his airstrike had arrived and somehow hit behind him. Then he turned and saw the roiling tower of smoke far back in the mountains.

There was only one thing up in those hills that could explode like that: Tyra's helicopter.

A scathing, whispered curse didn't make him feel any better. He couldn't leave until—

Authorization for an airstrike or not, time was up. He lined up the shot, then had to wait until he could get his racing pulse rate back under control... There.

One, two, three—the radio squawked—four.

Four bullets in flight before the first one had time to arrive.

He sent four more, bracketing their targets' likely movements as the first rounds drove home.

He grabbed the radio.

"Strike authorized. Lase target." He didn't have time for this, but he also didn't have a choice.

He flicked on the infrared laser that hung under the barrel and held it on the center of the table. Three were down, one was crawling away.

He shifted his aim, but there was no need.

A Hellfire missile slammed down and obliterated the village square. The buildings to all sides lost roofs, two even had their front walls blown in.

The guard details were all down as well. Any civilian casualties would be up to the village and the news media to deal with. Delta Force, as invisible as always, had nothing official to do with this kill.

The radio was squawking at him, but it wasn't Tyra so he ignored it.

He sprinted the three hundred meters back to where he'd stashed the bike, moving faster than any Super Bowl running back.

The electric engine gave him a near-silent departure for the first kilometer. Then he fired off the gas engine and opened the throttle wide.

CHAPTER SEVEN

Tyra was lost. The black hole had swallowed her.

Once again she was face down in the ditch. Naked. Broken.

That horrific night she hadn't seen anything except the headlights of the truck that pulled up behind her. She'd run out of gas while trying to get home from the Running Start program at the community college during her high school senior year. Nothing but the flashlight in her face when the bad Samaritans came up beside her car.

Later, afterward, Tyra had crawled along the ditch to escape the blazing heat of the car they'd torched. Her mother's car. Vague memories of lying in the hospital bed while her mother screamed. Blaming her for not watching the gas gauge. More upset about the destruction of her eight-year-old Dodge than of her daughter. Even half-conscious, Tyra had known she herself was done with her past.

The rape kit testing had revealed five men's DNA, none on record. She'd lost count, but it had seemed like more. Maybe the test was crap.

Tyra could only cower as the cop had found her, lost and broken beside her mother's precious burning—

A hand touched her and she screamed.

CHAPTER EIGHT

I t's okay, Tyra. It's me."

The look in her eyes told him that she had no idea who he was.

"It's Major Norm Lawrence. It's okay. I'm here now."

He reached for her again, but she scrambled away.

"Don't you dare touch me!"

Then he was staring down the wrong end of an FN-SCAR combat assault rifle. She knelt in a textbook firing position. The safety was off, her finger was inside the trigger guard, actually on the trigger. It was rock steady in her hands—her response time was worthy of a Unit operator. At ten feet there wasn't a chance she'd miss.

Norm backed off. Held his hands open.

"It's okay. We have to get out of here. Now."

"Not. With. You."

Had she blown up her own helicopter? Gone somehow rogue, or insane? That didn't seem likely or he'd be dead already.

He glanced at the still-burning wreckage. The whole upper part of the helicopter was gone, shredded, but parts of the belly still remained upright on the skids.

Beyond it, he could see a body...no, two. One wore a Night

Stalkers survival vest even though he was burned beyond recognition. The other was a native, or at least parts of one—as attested to by the half-melted AK47. A quick scan of the surroundings, but they were alone for now. Just one local fighter. It wouldn't stay that way for long.

Moving as fast as he dared under Tyra's tracking aim, he circled the wreckage.

Nothing to salvage.

Even the Night Stalker in the vest was unrecoverable except for a femur here and a hand there. He grabbed a bag from the bike and collected what he could, which was little enough. He did find the dog tags blown twenty feet away, but if the man had a "last letter" in his pocket, it was long gone. Norm couldn't even remember Geller's first name.

"We need to move now." He circled back around to Tyra who still had her rifle up. Her finger outside the trigger guard now, but he still wouldn't be able to outdraw her.

"I repeat: not with you."

"You know who I am?"

"Yes, and I know where you're from. And I was almost killed there by a bunch of your Ozark buddies. I'm sure they told you grand stories in the bar—it's not that big a town." Her voice sliced through the heat with a chill deeper than a Hindu Kush winter.

"When?" He could see her breathing rate. If she didn't slow it down soon she was going to hyperventilate, even at this altitude.

"Ten years ago."

"I left fifteen ago. I've never been back."

"Do you swear?" Tyra's voice was still brittle.

He laid his hand on his heart and the sudden move made her flinch. Bad choice. "On my honor as an officer."

Norm counted ten beats of his heart beneath his hand while she stared at him with those dark eyes, gone almost black. She finally shifted her aim aside, but remained on her knees.

Then she hung her head and sat still as death.

"Tyra?"

She nodded once, twice. Then using her rifle like a crutch, she managed to reach her feet, but her shoulders remained hunched, cringing as if the world would strike her at any moment.

No, as if *he* would.

Unsure what else to do, he pulled his sidearm out and held it out to her butt first.

She stared at his weapon, then slowly, finally, looked up at his eyes.

"Take it. If it will make you feel safer, take it." He felt strange offering it. He'd fired tens of thousands of rounds with this weapon in training. It had been his companion through hundreds of missions. Yet he couldn't think of what else to do.

She studied the weapon again, then shook her head.

He reholstered it, slowly. "Can we go now?"

Tyra looked up and scanned the horizon as if aware of her surroundings for the first time. She nodded. He led her to the bike. It wouldn't be long before someone came looking to see what had happened here.

He dropped the bag of Geller's remains into a saddlebag. From the other, he took a trio of breaching charges—each big enough to take out a heavy steel door. A second explosion wasn't going to draw any more attention. Besides, this one would be small and smokeless.

Hurrying now, he arranged them around the last of Geller's gear. He tossed a few bits and pieces of the helo, those that had survived total destruction, on top. He trotted back to the bike and flipped a trigger.

There was a hard thump—nothing bigger than his palm remained. That was the best he could do.

He swung onto the bike, then looked at Tyra who stood just two paces away.

CHAPTER NINE

C limbing onto the back of the dirt bike and lacing her hands into the sides of Norm's vest might count as the hardest thing Tyra had ever done.

Every place she touched him—and it wasn't that big a bike— had her twitching with nerves and cold sweat despite the heat.

Thankfully he didn't ask if she was ready, because there was no way she could have answered.

The ride was a blur.

The rear wheel skidded along the trail as Norm laid hard into corners. He took them south and west into the depths of the Hindu Kush.

The packed-dirt road thinned to a porter's trail, probably for mules. Norm turned off it onto a goat track, and then led them deeper into the mountains until they were making their own way across bare rock and weaving between boulder fields.

Somewhere along the way, finally feeling she was safe, she lay her forehead against the back of his vest and wept.

For Herman Geller, who had always been a bright spot in any mission.

She wept for the innocence of the girl who'd been driving down the road singing along to country-western on the radio when she ran out of gas.

She wept for the past that hadn't been purged. Could never be purged.

And finally she'd wept simply because she'd needed to.

She was barely conscious of Norm carrying her out of the heat and into a shallow but blissfully cool cave. While she sipped from the bottle of water he'd put in her hands, he radioed in their location. A helo would come for them after dark. The drone was retasked to keep an eye out for anyone approaching their remote position.

Finally, he settled beside her, his back against the same cave wall as hers. His rifle lay in his lap, pointing at the entrance. Their view was wide and covered the only possible approaches across the rocky ground.

"Why did you leave your home?" Tyra's voice was barely a whisper.

CHAPTER TEN

Norm had been starting to wonder if she'd ever speak again.

"It was a small town. Didn't like it much. My dad was a big man who spoke with his fists. Which had taught Mom not to speak at all. Even at school I was the misfit. Didn't care enough about any of it to learn much from the teachers, too small for football, did okay in baseball. I liked third base, a real action spot. But never got close to anyone. After high school, I simply walked out, hitched a ride to the nearest recruiter's office, and asked to be let in."

It all seemed so simple now, even if the steps hadn't been nearly that orderly. He told her about going Rangers, Officer Candidate School, then Delta tapping him—one of the great honors of his life, even if he hadn't fully understood that until now. The Unit only recruited the best.

It was like that one dinner they'd shared, explaining things to Tyra brought them into focus.

"The Unit is as close to home as I ever imagined."

"And now?" Her voice still too quiet to even echo in the cave.

He shrugged. "Told you. I'm not that much of a thinking guy. Except when you're around, it seems. What about you?" And then

—"Shit! Sorry. Ignore that question. I'm thinking you've had enough of the past for one day."

"I've had enough of the past to last a lifetime." Her laugh was a scoff but, however rough, it was still a laugh. Then a deep sigh. "You probably need to know, I was a victim of rape, in your"—her voice nearly strangled with tightness—"in *our* hometown."

"Did they catch the bastard?" A fury surged through him worse than watching his father beat his mom, he himself already too battered to fight back.

"No. And I don't think they ever will. The cops tried, but I never saw their faces."

"'Their'?" *Shit!* If he ever found them he'd—

A cool hand rested briefly over his. "Thank you for that."

"For what?" He couldn't keep the snarl out of his voice.

"Over the years I've learned the hard way that some guys are put off by a woman who's been violated. Some sickos are turned on by it. Still others go blank as if I never spoke, as if it didn't matter. You're pissed. That emotion sustained me for a long time...once I climbed out far enough to get there."

"Climbed out far enough? Tyra, you climbed out so far the hole filled in behind you and a forest grew over it. I had you pegged for some hot model with a Princeton education or one of those other posh schools up north. Just couldn't figure out why the hell you were a Night Stalker instead of off somewhere being famous or something."

"I'm a Night Stalker because it's important. I discovered that I like to fight back and I'm damned good at it."

Which he'd seen for himself. They sat in silence for a long time while Norm tried to shift his view of the woman beside him. He just couldn't make Southern girl fit. But now he couldn't make her Northern fit either.

She was...herself.

And that was truly incredible.

CHAPTER ELEVEN

Is that why you wouldn't talk to me? Thinking I was all stuck-up Ivy League?" Tyra often was told that she was, but it was wrong. She was protecting herself. Holding up a shield against a past. One that maybe—*please let it be true*—couldn't touch her anymore.

"No." Norm smiled. "No. I didn't talk to you much because you scare the shit out of me. So goddamn beautiful and smart. Then add being a SOAR officer on top of that...You are an amazing package."

"I'm an amazing *woman*." And she felt an utterly womanly sigh at the way he saw her: as the person she'd spent so many years trying to become. Maybe the past was truly over—No! Maybe the past was, at long last, truly *in* the past.

"Right, that's what I meant." Norm finally turned away from the scorched landscape beyond the cave's mouth and looked at her.

"I forgot that for a while after the explosion." And she could still feel the hole and knew it would always be there. But Norm was right. It *was* filled in and grown over. She'd finally flown high enough to climb clear of it, even if she could never be wholly free.

She couldn't leave the past completely behind, because that too was a part of who she was.

"You *are* an amazing woman." His face suddenly Delta-serious. "You better keep remembering that. Every day!" Like he was handing out marching orders.

"I do." And those words echoed strangely inside her. Not because they were foreign, but rather because one day, with this man, they could be so very right.

He raised an arm in question and she didn't hesitate to answer by sliding through his protective shield just as he had slipped through hers.

That feeling was itself an answer. Whatever her past, Norm was an amazing man who wasn't a part of it. Now their mutual protective defense wrapped them together rather than driving them apart. They sat hip to hip, their rifles in their laps, and before them an incredible vista of the jagged Hindu Kush Mountains. But they were the brutal past.

Beyond the cool warmth of their cave, the achingly blue sky beckoned her ever upward.

When Norm kissed her on the temple, their course shone as clear as a flight plan. Together they were going to fly so high.

LOVE ON THE RUN

KELLY WASHINGTON

If I tell you much about Kelly Washington's "Love on the Run," I'll spoil the story for you. I will mention that one of the protagonists, Callum, also appears in the powerful "One Ballerina Dancing," which appeared in our second Special Edition, Editor Saves.

In fact, Kelly's work has appeared in six regular editions of Fiction River, *and two of our four special editions. Her short story, "The American Flag of Sergeant Hale Schofield," which first appeared in* Fiction River: Hidden in Crime, *was selected as one of* The Year's Best Crime and Mystery Stories 2016.

To find out more about her work, visit her website , www.kellywashington.com or on Twitter at @kellywashwrites.

Callum

For most of his life, Callum McCauley relied on one person to unfuck his life: Joanie Miller. When his loser dad beat the shit out of him, Joanie wiped away tears and blood, staining her own shirts in the process.

In grade school, when the principal expelled Callum for destruction of property, nine-year-old Joanie proudly took the rap, a gleam in her angel-devil green eyes.

At seventeen, when drugs and alcohol grabbed him by the throat, Joanie's *Jesus-now-what?* attitude pulled him out of the gutter, cleaned him up, and pointed him in the right direction—which was a shove toward the high school so he could get his dipshit act together long enough to earn a diploma.

And at nineteen, when he was busted with heroin, eleven thousand dollars in cash, and three semi-automatic military-grade weapons, while speeding in a stolen vehicle, Joanie's adult-like mannerisms and a strongly-worded letter convinced the judge to go lenient.

Callum's sorry ass to transferred from the Texas State Penitentiary system to the United States Army.

It wasn't so bad. They shaved his unruly reddish-blond hair, gave him a gun, a paycheck, and called him a grunt.

Either way he was going to get a uniform and three squares a day, and it turned out he was good at pointing weapons at other people. The Army put this skill to a lot of use.

He used to keep a list, but Callum stopped counting when the confirmed kills surpassed the misses.

He and Joanie were as different as they were inseparable. Trailer park trash has a way of doing that to hungry gutter kids. Runt-size Joanie's ambition was as large as her imagination could conjure within in the pages of a book; Callum's was doing whatever he could to stay out of juvie while simultaneously reaching for what was most likely to put him there in the first place. Fighting. Drugs. Weapons. Whichever was easiest at any given time.

On days where Joanie wasn't pissed at him, she'd read at her window, her words loud enough for him to hear from the trailer next door. Didn't matter that the dumpster sitting in the back made it nearly unbearable, the smell of rotten eggs biting the back of his throat, with roaches by the thousands milling about, Joanie's earthy, laughing voice was his salvation.

His *only* salvation.

He'd know her voice anywhere.

He might have been the older of the two, but she was the strong one; the one who owned a compass that pointed true north. Even if Joanie's true north led to a pile of dog turd, it was good enough for him.

Of course Callum loved her.

Always had, and always would, but when she got a college scholarship and moved away, his moral compass evaporated when Joanie left him. She kissed him on the cheek after he walked her to the bus stop, so that helped, and she promised to write even though he couldn't read worth a damn.

At boot camp, and the years following, he'd find a letter waiting for him. As he read her words, he'd fantasize about being her hero. He'd be the man of her dreams.

Of course that never happened.

Clever and beautiful, Joanie Miller was her own heroine, saving herself from abuse and neglect. One of her last letters, which came when he was stationed in Germany, mentioned she was getting married, and could he get his dumb ass back to the States to attend the wedding.

Did he? Of course not. Instead he volunteered to redeploy, and found himself in the jungles of South America, hunting FARC criminals while Joanie hunted for the perfect wedding dress to wear down the aisle and marry a man not named Callum McCauley.

That was thirty years ago.

Sometimes he wondered about her, which did him no favors. He'd chase away memories with a bottle of whiskey or a dozen lines of coke, or both. Women helped, but not usually. They tried to fix him but gave up when it was like trying to repair shattered glass. Not that it was their fault. He was amazed anyone wanted to try.

A man can change in thirty years, and men like Callum who owned mercenary instincts honed by years living on the edge usually turned to gristle and bone, lean with hard experiences, surviving on a heart that was more mechanical than sentimental. He worked for whoever paid him the most: the good, the bad, and the in-between, which was most folks.

It was best this way. Maybe one day he'd get a dog, take it easy for a while. Maybe after the current job.

He was in Miami to talk about an immunity deal, earn a few bones, and meet up with the DA to rat out a slew of dirty cops when he figured he'd all but forgotten about Joanie Miller, and Callum was okay with this.

But when his burner cell phone rang at 1:32 on a Saturday morning and he heard her voice on the other end of the line asking him to unfuck *her* life, he knew it couldn't be good. He didn't have another thirty years to get over her again.

Joanie

Joanie Miller Bretton put down the knife and picked up the phone. Manicured fingers tapped the numbers and she wondered how many rings would it take before the call was answered.

She wasn't alone in the kitchen, but she was the only one standing, and it was quiet. Very quiet. It wasn't unnerving just yet. Give it a minute or two, and Joanie knew she might freak out. Especially if it went to voicemail.

It was a Friday night, the air was stiflingly hot. She'd focus on the heat, instead. Her eyes swung to the wide-open French doors, revealing an amazing view of the Golden Gate Bridge. It was the property's main selling point. She and Teddy bought it back in January and were looking forward to the upcoming fireworks show.

The sun had just set, but the bridge was lit and it captured her attention while the phone made its outbound call. Her other hand drummed the countertop. Inches away, a handmade pottery bowl held two apples, an orange, and a browning banana.

Beside this was a black briefcase, which she glanced at, but her eyes zipped back to the banana.

She should throw it out. Only Teddy ate them.

Four rings in, the line answered.

"Go." The voice was cigarette-gruff and hollow. Even thirty years later, she physically responded to that voice.

"Callum?" Joanie asked, shaking.

She pressed her hand flat against the countertop, waiting to see how he reacted. They hadn't spoken since she married Teddy Bretton, an up-and-coming lawyer right out of college. But by doing so, she burned the unstable bridge that led back to Callum McCauley. Not her finest move, but a necessary one.

As a child, the desire to survive fueled Joanie's unquenchable hunger. That hadn't changed in the years since. Even after all their financial success, it never seemed to be enough because every time she closed her eyes she was back in that roach-infested trailer.

Back then she was a journalism major itching to travel the globe and Teddy was the best solution to satisfy that itch. It wasn't a loving partnership, but it worked for them. They were a handsome couple and she thought they had a decent marriage.

Of course she was wrong.

Tonight, their secrets collided, which was why she found herself needing Callum.

"No names." A heartbeat later she heard a sizzle-click. He must have lit a cigarette. Then he asked, "Where are you?"

She knew he'd recognize her voice. If anyone could help her, it would be her childhood friend, the gangly, slouching boy with the inquisitively sad, bruise-filled face who lived on the other side of the dumpster.

Of course, he was none of those things now.

As a journalist, her contacts had contacts, and she kept tabs on Callum. He could make people and things disappear. Their history would serve her well, but this wasn't just any situation, and Joanie had no choice but to trust him with this one. In truth, there was no one else she *could* go to.

"San Francisco."

"I'll be there in seven hours."

Joanie expelled a breath and wiped the sweat dotting her upper lip. The banana was beginning to bother her, so she tossed it in the trash.

"Okay," she answered automatically even though the shaking got worse. Seven hours meant he was on the East Coast. Would he get here before things got worse? She eyed the bloody knife, then the briefcase. "You don't want to know why I'm calling?"

"No."

There was no hesitation in his voice. It terrified and soothed her.

Callum gave her additional instructions on where to meet him and ended the call after that. Wrist flicking, she placed the phone on the counter, and the click sounded like a gunshot, jolting her out of a fog. The urge to move, to run, hit her hard then.

God, it was hot, but she was freezing.

Perhaps she should close the French doors, but that'd mean stepping over Teddy.

Head angled as if he were enjoying the view, his distinguished, prone profile seemed larger than life. Any second now he was going to get up and accuse Joanie of embezzlement, blackmail, and a host of other infractions, not to mention murder.

Considering it might be one of the last times she looked at the bridge from this vantage point, it struck her as ironic that she found the view rather dazzling. It would have been better if Teddy were on the other side of the kitchen, but some things couldn't be helped.

She needed to get going. She needed to follow Callum's orders.

Some things change, and some things don't. If anyone knew what to do, it would be Callum, the boy she'd been in love with since she was a brassy seven-year-old girl.

Marta

It was unlike Teddy to avoid Marta Epstein's phone calls, even late into the evening. He was her top attorney and a damn good one. The best, in fact, though she admitted she wouldn't want to be on his bad side.

As she picked up Teddy's case files and reviewed the evidence for the tenth time, Marta began to doubt that their office needed anything further to convict the mayor of tax fraud and embezzlement. It was all right there, in black and white.

Whatever this new lead was, it prevented him from taking her phone call, which meant it was bad. She flipped through the file again, page by page. Nothing.

She'd go to his house, instead. They were not losing this case.

Marta jumped in her SUV and drove to Belvedere.

Callum

Bag already at the ready, he called in a few favors while leaving a note for the Miami District Attorney. A *Family Emergency* didn't mean a damn thing to a man like Callum, and the DA would see through the lie, but an extra day or two wouldn't kill the cop case, and if the immunity deal fell off the table, Callum would slip away.

It was summertime and people go shit crazy when it's hot. Humans were the stupidest species on the planet. Callum had met his fair share of them. The DA would be busy.

Besides, Callum needed a few minutes to process what just happened.

He wasn't often caught off guard, but his forty-seven-second phone call with Joanie torpedoed his usual even keel. Under thirty seconds would've been better, but he chalked it up to needing a cigarette before he could continue the conversation. He'd ditch the phone, but that was easy.

Joanie needed his help and he'd fucking scoop out his insides to get to her on time. Didn't matter what the problem was; his feelings wouldn't change. She could have slaughtered an entire family and he'd be there to pick up the pieces. He'd seen a lot worse. Fuck, he'd done a lot worse.

His fifty-three-year-old heart thumped like a junkyard engine that hadn't been kicked in decades. It made him nervous, and a man who killed others for a living rarely got nervous. It was always, *One more job and I'm done.* He'd been saying that for a decade. Each job promised more money—money to retire.

He was an old dog with a few barks left in him. Joanie, then the Miami job, and *then* he'd be done.

After a line of coke and a developing tick under his eye, he boarded a friend-of-a-friend's jet and flew to San Francisco. He needed more than seven hours to prepare himself to see her, but that was all he had.

Joanie

When you're fifty-one, it's good to have friends who remember what you looked like at eighteen. Callum's memory of her would place her back when she was a constantly tanned, freckle-faced teen with crooked teeth and aggressively furled eyebrows due to the sheer number of times she yanked him out of trouble.

In Texas, kids don't do things halfway. Callum's personal version of trouble would fill a high school football field and Joanie's oversized persistence in worrying over him was loyalty touched with insanity.

Strangely, it worked.

Perhaps she was a worrier by nature, but she liked to think of it as hypervigilance mixed with planning. Early on, she and Teddy decided not to have children, but it was mostly at her insistence. Joanie never had a good mother figure and presumed she'd be a bad mother herself. Childhood treatment begets adulthood behavior. It was fine and she never regretted their decision, especially now as she stood in her closet and packed.

No need to conduct an emotional conversation with nonexistent children, and after stepping over Teddy's body to lock the French doors, she didn't have the mental capacity to talk to anyone.

The only person who might come around was Teddy's boss, Marta Epstein, the state's Attorney General, and that was because he discovered new evidence on a high profile case. If she could keep Marta away for another twenty-four hours, Joanie'd be long gone.

She showered, changed, and in the night's folding darkness, she used Teddy's car to pull cash at an ATM. She knew not to withdraw too much; it'd raise red flags over the next couple of days, so she removed a paltry eighty bucks. She'd miss the house for its view, but no doubt she'd envision Teddy's body lying in the kitchen, forever ruining any other enjoyment from the property.

But old worries reveal fresh ones, and Joanie was prepared to leave the country for good, only Callum told her not to leave until he did damage control.

She left the windows down as she drove three hours north toward Timber Cove. At the boat landing, she took out the pre-paid phone she bought last week, which was what she used to call Callum, and threw it in the water. Her personal phone was on her nightstand.

Foamy white crests crashed rhythmically, the spray dampening her already sweaty skin.

She loved the sound of the ocean. Joanie was thirty when she first saw the Pacific Ocean. Teddy, a West Coast native, mentioned that you don't *see* the Pacific Ocean as much as *experience* it, and he was right.

The waves' cadence matched her beating heart, as if it were communicating with her, and there was a moment where she wanted to walk into the water and let the ocean keep her.

When they were young and broke, they spent a weekend in Timber Cove, sailing, and when you're married to a sailor, you become a sailor, too. Otherwise you never see your spouse.

She smiled at the memory. Joanie wasn't the sentimental type, but she'd forgotten about Timber Cove until tonight. She came here because Callum said to get rid of the phone at a location she'd been to before, and now she was glad she did.

Maybe that's how this would all end: sail away and let the ocean keep her.

As she turned away, she felt crushing guilt. It didn't last long, but it was enough for the furrowed eyebrows to return. Joanie spent the drive back to San Francisco questioning whether her actions were worth it, and by the time she picked up Callum, her conscience was in the clear.

Marta

When Marta was a block from Teddy's house, his Lexus pulled out of the driveway, and she decided to follow. If she'd had known it would be a six-hour trip, Marta would have turned around and returned to the office.

But in Timber Cove, when Joanie emerged from car and Teddy was nowhere in sight, Marta's interest was piqued.

So she waited to see what happened next.

Callum

From the airport, he walked to Chubby's Fire Pit BBQ food truck, which was parked near the Coyote Point Marina. The weather favored their rendezvous location. The water was gray and choppy, and it'd probably rain in less than an hour. Only diehards would be out this morning.

Given the time of day, it was deserted. The fish-scented wind buzzed in his ears. To his left, docked boats creaked and moaned in a calm swell. Seagulls squawked their morning displeasures, and on Bluff Trail, which led deeper into the recreational park, a jogger wearing earbuds zipped by without looking up. Not even the jogger's dog noticed Callum.

Dressed like a bum, Callum McCauley easily blended into every background, which was how he liked it. No one paid attention to the homeless, but they were his most valuable resource. They saw everything. The amount of money he paid them over the years to gather information for him was in the tens of thousands.

Knowledge was a commodity he frequently exploited.

A few minutes later, Joanie's car pulled in.

From beneath a crappy baseball cap, Callum watched Joanie's car idle for ten minutes, which were his instructions, before he limped over and slipped into the passenger seat of her sleek car.

Of course his breath caught.

Her hair was black with threads of gray, and her clever green eyes were not quite as bright as he remembered, but otherwise she hadn't changed. Oh sure, Joanie Miller polished up like a million bucks, and she smelled so-goddamn-amazing, but deep down she was still that petite, tough as nails eighteen-year-old he walked to the bus stop.

"Callum," she whispered. Both hands were white against the steering wheel, and on the left hand he spotted the matted sheen of a well-worn wedding band.

He had seven hours to daydream—fuck that, no, he had *thirty* years to daydream—but that wedding band was like warning tape winding around his heart, over and over. It was a bitter taste, but he'd get over it.

"Joanie." It came out in a croak. "Keep driving."

He removed the cap and became conscious of his rumpled, and withered cigarette-smelling appearance. A haircut might've been nice if he had the time, and perhaps a quick shave, but Callum McCauley didn't clean up for anyone.

Joanie wasn't just anyone but it might be best if he considered this a quick job, the type that filled the gaps between big jobs. He smelled her stress. It wasn't godawful or anything, and for the first time since she called, he wondered just how much trouble she was in.

"Thanks for coming," Joanie said as she drove north on Highway 101.

"Tell me what you want done, and then I'll tell you what will go down." It was how he always started these things. What they *thought* they wanted, and what they truly needed were often very different things.

She didn't look at him when she said, "I killed my husband last night. I want you to get rid of the body and make it look like someone else did it."

Well now.

This job just got a helluva lot better.

Joanie

The drive itself was a blur, but it didn't take long to reach the house. At the red lights, Joanie stole glances at Callum's distinctive profile. He was never a handsome boy, and he wasn't now, but to look at him was to be mesmerized. She adored his shaggy reddish-blond hair and his striking face.

Sitting in Teddy's car, Callum was tall and gaunt, but he still slouched. He probably woke up drinking whiskey before ever getting out of bed, and his face was what she called seasoned. Cigarettes, hard liquor, and plenty of fistfights created an interesting asymmetry, like an abstract painting that made little sense up close but from a small distance it all came together.

Somewhere out there there'd be a woman waiting for him, her voice as rough as his, yelling at him to stop pestering her and get his own goddamn dinner. They'd fight and fuck, and still hate each other but go on as always.

In a way Joanie envied that life. It had passion, and in the deep blue swirls of Callum's eyes, she saw the raw passion residing there. He couldn't hide that from her, even though he was trying.

Holding her breath, she turned down her street. No cop cars or news vans. No blaring sirens or nosy neighbors clamoring to say how they barely knew her but that she seemed nice enough.

She thought she'd freak out when she pulled into her driveway, but she was as calm as ever.

"Do you know already who you want the crime pinned on?" he asked casually as she drove into the connected garage, closing it when they were inside. "If you don't, there's plenty of assholes around here for the picking."

Joanie was right to call him. She loved him because of how she felt around him. Full. Complete. Free. She never had to prove herself to him, and frankly she enjoyed taking care of him when they were younger.

"The mayor of San Francisco, or someone who works from him."

His hand froze at the door handle. After a tense pause, like maybe he was running through his options, he asked, "Why?"

"I have nothing against the man, but Teddy was investigating the mayor for tax evasion and embezzlement. It's a logical choice."

Callum shrugged. "Okay."

"Okay," she repeated, feeling better already.

Joanie got out of the car.

Callum followed her without saying another word.

Marta

At 5:12 in the morning, Marta took a photo of the man who climbed into Teddy's car and sent it to her FBI field office. Though with the lowered baseball cap, she knew it would be a long shot.

"Find out who this is," she said when Eric deLong called her back.

"Looks like a homeless guy," he said conversationally, which meant he wasn't taking this seriously. "Maybe Teddy's offering him breakfast in exchange for information. We do it all the time."

Eric was probably at home drinking coffee and reading the newspaper while she'd been tailgating Teddy's wife all night. Marta was tired and on edge because Teddy had yet to return her phone calls. If they lost this case against the mayor, she might kill Teddy.

Marta didn't reveal that Joanie was the driver, but Eric had a point. A sliver of doubt crept in. Did Teddy ask for Joanie's help? Instinct told her no, and that Joanie was up to something. Thing was, Joanie was one of the nicest people she'd ever met. Two and two did not add up.

She followed them from a distance when they left Coyote Point Marina. "Just see what you can do. It may be related to the mayor's case."

"It'll take twenty-four to forty-eight hours, Marta. Photo's not that great."

"When we're fired for losing this case, I'll sign up for photography class. Until then, process the photo."

Eric chuckled. They'd all worked together for so long that sarcasm was the norm. "I'll see what I can do, Marta."

When Joanie pulled into her residence, Marta kept going. With all the trees, and the way their driveway curved up and over, she'd never see anything once the gate closed. She grabbed a cup of coffee and parked down the street, waiting.

Waiting for what, she wasn't sure, but until Teddy showed up it was on Marta to figure out.

Callum

It wasn't going to rain after all. Standing in Joanie's metallic-scented kitchen, Callum took in the view from the French doors. The sun had burned off the gray fog and the Golden Gate Bridge held him captive. It wasn't the most interesting thing to see in the kitchen, but a close third. Joanie was second, her husband the most.

If there was no husband, and no bridge, then the house itself might count. Joanie lived in a fucking mansion. In a little bit he'd ask where the money came from, but it wasn't important right now.

At least there was a garage. Getting the body to the car wouldn't be a problem.

Callum looked down at Joanie's husband. The man was handsome, in his mid-fifties, clean-shaven with a strong jaw, silver hair, and a tall, trim physique. His head was at an odd angle, which was probably how he fell, and his mouth was open, a trickle of dark blood staining the side of his lips.

He studied the torso. The white shirt was a canvas of red; beneath him, coagulated blood formed into an oblong circle, burgundy and matte. So far so good. It was a classic scene he'd come across many times.

Twelve stab wounds, if his count was accurate. There was passion here, but not balls-to-the-wall out-of-control passion. It seemed a little too clean, but not planned.

Joanie probably wanted to kill him at some point and last night it all came together, just not like how she would have planned it. If he knew anything about his childhood friend, it was that she'd been a planner since the age of seven.

"He did the first one himself," Joanie said from the other side of the kitchen. A black granite island separated them. She played with an orange, alternating peeling and rotating it. She'd put it down, pick up the apple, and do the same thing but it was messier as her nails dug out small apple chunks. Mostly she focused on the bloody knife and a briefcase, both on the island's countertop. "I can make coffee."

Callum hated coffee, but he'd drink it nonetheless. She needed time and he needed whiskey, and both were luxuries at this point. Personal questions would have to wait.

"That'd be nice, thanks. I take mine black."

Marta

She was beginning to think it was a lost cause when Eric called her.

"We found something," he said. "You were right, he isn't a bum. He's James Caul, the thirteenth most wanted man in America. Murder, kidnapping, mob connections, you name it. Caul is an alias. He's got a dozen names, but his real name is Callum McCauley. He's a former Army sniper. Twenty years ago he was allegedly recruited by the CIA, so there's fifteen-year dark spot. After that, he went independent and has been underground ever since. He'll pop once a year or so, but no one's ever caught up to him. Word is the Miami DA, working on behalf of the US Attorney's Office, is looking to cut him a sweet deal if he reveals thirty years of information, to include sources, dirty cop shit, and covert operations."

Teddy's disappearance now meant jackshit to Marta. The prize was Callum McCauley. He was fifty fucking feet away and there was nothing she could do.

"Fuck me. Lemme guess, CIA has denied he's in their system?"

"Yup."

"Standard. Teddy's case has nothing to do with any of this, unless the mayor is mixed up in it somehow."

"Teddy might not even know. Get this, McCauley and Teddy's wife grew up together. They were best friends."

Joanie

Stressful situations were always better handled while holding a cup of coffee. Joanie handed Callum his mug. "If you're thinking Teddy was a bad husband, don't."

"I wasn't." Instead of drinking it, he placed it on the counter, and asked, "Do you think you're capable of helping me move him?"

Relief spread through her. "I think so." She didn't want to touch him, but the sooner he was out of the house the better.

He walked to the kitchen's entrance and dug into a duffle bag he placed there when they first walked in, removing rolled-up plastic tarp, the kind used to protect floors while painting. Additionally, he pulled out a resealable bag, a lidded plastic cup, and a spatula.

On the way back he picked up the knife and placed it in the pocket of Teddy's shirt.

"That's his name, Teddy?"

"Theodore Bretton, San Francisco's District Attorney."

Callum grunted a non-response. "Do you have his cell phone?"

"Yeah, here." It had twenty-four missed calls, three of which were from her, wondering when he'd get home.

Using gloves, Callum smudged a small amount of Teddy's blood on it before placing it in the resealable bag. "It'll make it look like a struggle occurred," he explained.

Together they began to roll his body inside the plastic, the blood smearing both the inside and outside of it. Thankfully Callum took the top half of the body, which meant he dealt with the blood.

They did this until the outside roll wouldn't smear blood in the trunk. The constant sound of snapping plastic made conversation impossible. After that, they carried Teddy's body to the garage, placing him in his own trunk.

"Now what?" Joanie asked, breathing heavy. She was in shape, but fuck it if carrying a dead body wasn't serious work.

Callum barely looked fazed and she wondered how many bodies had he carried in his lifetime. Probably best not to know.

"I'll collect some blood in this." He held up the cup and spatula.

That made no sense to her. "To do what with?"

"Frame the mayor." Joanie nodded, understanding. He continued. "Before we leave, we need to clean the kitchen. I have everything we need. Then we'll dispose of the body. I know a place."

She knew her love wasn't misplaced.

Marta

While she waited for something to happen, Marta called Teddy's secretary to have his last three cases sent to her tablet. The first was a standard embezzlement case, and in the second, for some reason Teddy was dabbling in a missing persons cold case, which was fine. But the third case, which wasn't a case, but more of an informal inquiry, was where Marta struck gold.

In recent weeks, Teddy was corresponding with the Miami DA's office regarding the McCauley agreement. Nothing seemed finalized, but Teddy's verbiage indicated the Miami deal could be turned into a trap to take McCauley into custody. Teddy claimed to have leverage to make the trap more successful.

She whistled. Teddy was willing to use Joanie to lure a wanted felon. What an asshole. Her esteem for Teddy took a dip. That said, intuition told her Joanie wasn't altogether an innocent accomplice.

Marta called Teddy's phone again. It went straight to voicemail. Where the fuck was he?

She put the tablet away when Teddy's car drove away from the residence. Joanie was driving. McCauley was in the passenger seat. Marta needed to take a monster piss, but she sucked it up and followed. She was in too deep by now to quit.

Callum

The same car had been following them for a while, but he wasn't worried. He could tell it wasn't a cop.

Northeast of San Francisco, near the Mare Island Naval Shipyard, Callum did a job for a gal named Dozzier who wanted to eliminate her competition. He flew in and took care of the problem. Now, three years later, she was a successful business owner in Vallejo.

It was time to cash in that favor, which he did when he called Dozzier to let her know they were coming.

When he hung up, Callum decided it was time he got answers.

"Talk to me, Joanie. Where's the money coming in to pay for your house? I didn't know district attorneys made that much money."

Joanie laughed. "They make a decent income, but I'm the one who allows us to afford houses like this. I'm the type of journalist who has a knack for digging up salacious dirt on people. When they find out, they are willing to pay me not to write about it. I graciously accept their kind gifts."

Callum grinned. "You're just doing them a favor." He knew all about favors.

"Typically I'm not looking to expose someone, but I'm inquisitive. I like seeing what makes people tick, and finding out what happens when you nudge them ever so slightly."

"Did it ever backfire?"

They crossed the Bay Bridge. On either side, boats skimmed across the sparkling blue water. Maybe on the day he got a dog, he'd get a boat, too. He didn't know shit about dogs or boats, but he could learn.

"It got tense a few times, but nothing serious. It's a skill, black-mailing. The more you do it, the better you get at it."

"Did Teddy know?"

"Yeah, but not until recently. He brought it up last night while threatening to expose me."

Obviously there was more to this story because that reason alone wasn't a twelve-stab reaction on anyone's part. But he had to ask. "Is that why you killed him?"

"No, but his anger was exciting. Teddy was a kind but placid person and feeling his hatred directed at me was rather exhilarating."

Joanie was not a typical client for someone like Callum. She wasn't scared or afraid, though she might be experiencing mild shock, and she sure as hell wasn't expressing remorse at killing her husband. Most tried to convince him it was an accident. Joanie wasn't doing that. She was doing everything but that.

"Then why did you kill him?"

"To protect you."

Marta

Marta knew criminals like the back of her hand. She'd been putting them away for forty years, and most of them behaved the same. So when Teddy's car drove in the direction of the naval ship-yard, she wondered if there was a certain something they needed to dump. It was a risky move in broad daylight, but she counted on criminals being stupid.

Marta knew one thing for certain: McCauley wasn't stupid.

Joanie

Callum laughed and Joanie joined him. "To protect me? Haven't heard that in thirty-odd years, Joanie. Pull in here, but go around back."

It was a generic but busy shopping center you see in every town. The plaza was named after the largest space occupier: Dozzier Plaza, which was the name of the veterinarian clinic situated in the center. She was familiar with the name as one had opened near her house. Joanie hooked the first right, passed the dumpsters, and drove slowly down the slim access way.

When Joanie left Texas, the only criteria she had when searching for apartments was that the dumpster be nowhere near her residence. She didn't want to see it. Didn't want to smell it. Didn't want to know it fucking existed.

Did Callum have a similar requirement, or did the past not bother him as much?

In the center-back of the plaza, a short woman wearing a white lab coat walked out, waved them down, and directed them to pull into an open warehouse. The sign on the door read Dozzier loading entrance. Behind them the woman closed the heavy metal doors, shutting them inside.

Perhaps Joanie should have felt nervous, but she was perfectly at ease. The warehouse itself was on the smallish side, with enough room for a larger loading van and maybe one other car.

On the far end, industrial shelves held various sized boxes. Along the other side Joanie spotted offices filled with files, and in the center was a large oven-looking furnace.

It made sense now.

He jumped out. Joanie did the same. The place was steal-your-soul hot and a pit stop for Satan when he was away from hell.

The woman shook Callum's hand and called him Caul, but didn't address her, which was fine. She couldn't breathe anyway.

"Need access to your animal incinerator, Dozz."

"Already fired it up for you, Caul. It'll hold up to two hundred pounds. You do the heavy lifting and I'll do the rest."

Thank God Teddy was one-ninety.

Maybe someday she'd look back on today and wonder if she was out of her mind as she helped Callum remove her husband's body from the trunk of a car and shimmy his corpse into a pet incinerator.

Dozz closed the hatch and answered the unasked question. "Takes a couple hours. Five on the safe side."

They left when Dozz made it clear she'd take care of the rest, no questions asked.

Marta

Marta lost track of them when they entered the shopping plaza, but gained sight after she lapped the parking lot. They left the plaza and headed toward downtown San Francisco. Maybe this was a lost cause. Teddy probably had a good reason why he wasn't answering calls. She'd probably have a message waiting for her when she got to the office. Once she crossed the Bay Bridge, she'd return to work.

Except Teddy's car did the same thing.

It was a bizarre feeling as Marta followed their car into the Attorney General's parking garage.

Callum

They crossed the Bay Bridge and turned onto Fremont Street. It was time to frame someone else and keep any and all suspicion away from Joanie.

"So tell me what you meant when you said you killed Teddy to protect me."

"I grew up protecting you, Callum. It was my job. Last night, when Teddy was already angry about the blackmailing, he quickly shifted into rabid-mode, and his entire goal was to hurt me."

"What happened?"

"He knew I had a friend named Callum from childhood, but he didn't know it was *you*, or at least he never put two and two together. When Teddy said he was going to get you arrested, I grabbed the kitchen knife. I promised to use it on him if he touched a single hair on your head. He rushed forward, grabbed both my hands and forced the knife to pierce his stomach. It wasn't even that bad of a cut. He was so crazy."

That still didn't explain why she stabbed him eleven more times, but he didn't have time to ask. They entered the garage.

"Which one is the mayor's car?" Callum asked, and she pointed. "Slow down as you get closer, but don't stop. Loop around and pick me up."

He rolled out of the car, crouched low, and crawled to the mayor's passenger door. Using a wide, flat tool, he worked the lock, opened the door, and planted Teddy's phone and the blood. He was quick but maybe not quick enough.

Callum heard the rushing of feet headed in his direction.

Marta

Teddy's car crept along but it wasn't until a few minutes in that Marta realized Joanie was the sole occupant. McCauley was somewhere in the garage. She called security.

Joanie

When she circled back, her stomach dropped. Callum was gone, but security officers were very much present. One tapped on her window. "Pop the trunk, ma'am," a guard instructed, and Joanie was happy to comply. It was searched and she was free to go.

She smiled. "You haven't seen my husband, have you? Teddy Bretton? We were supposed to meet for lunch but he's probably upstairs working his butt off."

Naturally the security officer would not have, and he was apologetic all the same.

At the elevators, someone yelled False Alarm.

She left the garage, scanned the streets, and recognized a homeless man sitting on the sidewalk. His sign read, "Pennies for Vets."

It wasn't a lie. Callum McCauley was a veteran. Joanie stopped and he climbed in.

"I was so worried. All good?" she asked.

"All good, but let's finish the conversation. Why the hell did you stab your husband eleven times?"

She liked seeing him flustered. Perhaps they could make this a more permanent thing.

"Is that how many it was? I couldn't tell you. Teddy knew about your Miami deal and was able to convince the DA there to arrest you rather than give you complete immunity. The only way I could protect you was to kill my husband so you'd come here and help me get rid of his body."

For a moment, there was total silence in the car.

"You might be the most amazing woman I've ever met, Joanie Miller."

Joanie smiled. "I was hoping you might say something like that."

Marta

After she exited the ladies room, Marta checked in with her secretary. There was no news of Teddy, or his whereabouts, but the secretary put a call through to voicemail ten minutes ago.

"Thanks, Becca."

It killed Marta that she lost her lead on McCauley, but she wouldn't stop investigating the connection, even if it took years. She didn't make it this far in her career by giving up. Priorities were priorities and today's priority was the mayor.

Marta closed the door to her office, intending to nap, but instead listened to the voicemail.

Adrenaline kicked in as she listened. "No fucking way," she muttered after the third replay. McCauley and Joanie were good. Very good. Evidence would never point to them, but she knew Teddy was most likely dead and that they did it. Unbelievable. Her hands were tied.

She called Eric deLong. "Get a forensics team on the mayor's car."

Callum

He had no idea where she was headed, but it wasn't back to the mansion in Belvedere. She pulled into a marina near her house and left the car idling. In the backseat, she pointed to the suitcase and the black briefcase.

"Run away with me, Callum," she said, her tone playful yet serious. "We'll sail to Santa Cruz and watch the fireworks from my boat."

Looking at her earnest expression, Callum found himself in an unusual predicament: undecided on what to do next.

The Joanie job was done, and the Miami deal had gone sour, which happened from time to time so he wasn't all that surprised.

It was time to get a dog and a boat and relax a while.

"You own a boat?"

"Two, actually," she answered casually. "*Brassy Pants* is an old school sailboat that barely floats, and *Love on the Run* is my

Monte Carlo power boat. We'll be comfortable on her. I'll teach you to sail. Weathered as you are, Callum, you already look the part."

His heart thumped. He was entering unfamiliar territory. "Being on the run is not a glamorous life."

"It is if you have money." Her angel-devil green eyes sparkled. That explained the briefcase, which meant Joanie always planned to leave. "I didn't touch Teddy's stuff. Which reminds me, I need to call in a missing persons report."

Her calmness nearly undid him. She was absolutely perfect for him.

Was he actually considering this? Hardened criminals in love and on the run? The more the thought about it, the more he figured they could make it work. He already knew how to navigate the ins and outs of living on the edge, and his network was extensive.

Callum had to make sure she understood what she was asking for.

"This *will* catch up to you," he stressed. "Eventually, this will catch up to both of us."

"I'm willing to take my chances if you are. Besides, if anyone messes with us, we'll kill them."

Of course he fell even deeper in love.

She leaned over and placed a gentle kiss on his lips. "I've loved you since I was seven, Callum. It just took me a very long time to say it."

Jesus, he might cry.

"I love you, too, Joanie." He kissed her in return and couldn't believe she was finally in his arms. "I'm in. Show me this boat of yours."

They left Teddy's car idling. It'd either run out of gas or someone would steal it, adding to law enforcements' confusion. Didn't have to outsmart them, just confuse them for a while, and most times that was all he needed to slip away. As long as they were one step ahead, they'd be fine.

Joanie readied the boat, which was like a five star hotel room floating on water. There'd be plenty of room for a dog.

It didn't take long before they were under the Golden Gate Bridge and out to sea. Hugging the coastline, Joanie sailed south. The ocean had nothing on Joanie. She looked amazing behind the wheel.

That night, they made love while Santa Cruz put on a crazy fireworks show. However, Callum thought the fireworks happening inside the boat were more his style.

One day it all might end, but not right now, and he was fine with that.

NEED TO KNOW

SABRINA CHASE

Now for some much needed levity.

"Need To Know" isn't humor per se, but its tone is much lighter than most of the stories in this volume. In addition to writing romance and suspense about the summer, Sabrina Chase manages to create an entire charming world in fewer pages than the other stories in this volume.

Sabrina has great control over her voice, as evidenced in her first Fiction River *appearance, "Our Man in Basingstoke," which showed up in the previous special edition,* Spies. *Two of her short stories have appeared in our magazine* Pulphouse *as well.*

She has published eleven novels, spread over three different series and at least two different genres.

The story's inspiration comes from one of the masters of the romantic suspense genre. Sabrina writes, "I've always loved the Elizabeth Peters books featuring smart, funny heroines, exotic locales, clever heroes, and derring-do mixed with witty repartee so I thought it would be fun to write something in that vein myself."

It's fun to read as well.

There wasn't enough wine on the ship to hide the awful truth —my formal-length evening dress was not designed for athletic escape attempts.

I put my empty wineglass down and leaned over the polished teak railing of the lounge balcony, hoping to see a rope, a ledge, anything that could get me safely down to the deck below. It was a beautiful Mediterranean night with balmy breezes, brilliant stars, and the fresh tang of saltwater in the air but I was in no mood to appreciate it. The ancient Greeks had learned the hard way about free gifts, and with my background I should have known better.

"It's a history cruise!" my aunt had gushed. "Everyone on board will have the same interests you do!"

Tempted by copious amounts of free food, sun, and avoiding

the drudgery of a summer job I forgot that I would be trapped on a boat with my retired aunt and her gaggle of elderly friends who considered matchmaking a blood sport. I also hadn't known most of the other passengers would be a combination of chic, serious, European, and at least thirty years older than me. Not what I would have expected for a luxury history cruise.

Maybe I could sneak out another way. I turned back to the balcony door, an arch with vines and pots with plants all around it and a fluttering banner draped over a rod. And froze. My aunt's best friend, May, was weaving her way through the crowd and the elegantly displayed antiquities, talking a mile a minute and closely followed by a stunningly handsome man with bronze skin and black, curling hair. Dmitrios was supposedly assisting the lecture program in some capacity, most likely as a paperweight.

Strangely, he had been paying considerable attention to my aunt and her friends even though there were several supermodel-level women on board. I had only agreed to come to the party because I assumed—wrongly—that he would not be here.

"...lovely girl, and studying for her masters in history, I'm surprised you haven't met her yet."

Matters had become desperate. They hadn't seen me, but they would soon. I darted to one side of the balcony arch with olive trees and some other kind of shrub in terra-cotta pots. There was just enough shadow in the branches to hide me. Keeping an eye on the elegant crowd in the lounge, I stepped back slowly and silently into the leaves—and came to an unexpected stop when I hit something that was clearly *not* a tree or part of the ship.

Solid, but resilient. Warm. And with rather strong arms that grabbed mine. Utter shock held me immobile, then furious resentment that someone else had taken my hideout.

"Shh!" I whispered, and wondered why it sounded strange until I realized the other person had done the same thing. OK, we had something in common. The mysterious stranger and I remained completely motionless until May and Dmitrios moved away from the balcony entrance.

I edged around a tree, sighing when I saw they were still on the prowl for me.

"Suppose you tell me what you are doing?" The voice was male and didn't sound overly friendly, but he was speaking low enough nobody inside would hear.

"Trying to escape." Maybe I could climb the vines and get on the lounge roof?

"Why?"

"My aunt's friends are trying to set me up with any man with a pulse. They mean well, but..."

A slight rustle of leaves. "What's wrong with him?"

"Dmitrios? He's a walking statue. I heard him inform another passenger that Marathon was named by the Greek government after the race, to attract tourists."

The man made a small choking noise. "Fair point. How about I help you escape, and you forget I was here?"

"Deal." I couldn't really point fingers at him for hiding when I was trying to do the same thing. Odd, but I was desperate.

I saw a hand reach up to the long cloth banner on the rod and tug it down. The next thing I knew, he had wrapped the cloth across my back and under my arms, swept me up, and carried me to the railing, somehow managing to get his hands on pretty much all of me except my feet. Startled, I struggled but then I was dangling over the rail, held by the cloth as he lowered me down to the deck. I ran off without looking back.

The next morning I inhaled half the pastry buffet, resolving to forget what had happened and enjoy myself, but I couldn't. It just didn't make sense. For one thing, when I was flailing about I definitely felt something hard along his ribs, under his arm. It had given me a bruise. And then there were the wandering hands that didn't feel like groping. More like a search.

A gun. He'd been wearing a gun, and thought *I* would have a weapon too. But then he let me go. After getting me to promise not to tell anyone he'd been on the balcony. So what was he? That required another chocolate croissant to ponder. Lazy bodyguard? International jewel thief? Mall ninja?

Then my aunt's gaggle showed up and any further thought became impossible.

"Which excursion did you pick, Sarah? We'll be in port soon," my aunt said.

Sitting in the sun reading a book was not an option, I knew. I was supposed to Have Fun. "Probably the ruins." The other choice was shopping and I had no money.

"This is so exciting!" her friend Alice gushed. "How fortunate you found that group rate through your old job! I can't imagine what this would cost if we went on our own."

That was the other odd thing. "You know, Aunt Ilse, I don't recall where you worked," I said. I had vague memories of strange, exotic gifts when I was young but nothing extravagant. Not at the level of taking five people on a luxury cruise.

"Oh, it was a global insurance firm," she said brightly. "Anybody going snorkeling with me?"

There were no lectures today, so I watched Aunt Ilse snorkel off the special low deck on the back of the ship. For a woman in her seventies she was rather athletic.

"I'd better hurry and get lunch before the trips start," she said as she came up the stairs from the water, which was crystal-clear and not even that cold. The bay we were in had lovely craggy white rocks and even some submerged columns. From the deck I couldn't even see the port. Paradise. Only my paradise seemed to have some snakes in it.

Ilse had done a lot of world travel. Maybe she would know. "Aunt, do these ships have armed guards?"

That got me a look. "Not usually. Why do you ask?"

"I, uh, think I saw someone with one."

Aunt Ilse sat on the wood bench to towel off. "Don't worry, Sarah. There are some fairly important people on this cruise. Government people like Jacek Stanishev and Sofia Danti. Probably a bodyguard."

Lunch was another gastronomic orgy. The crowds flocked around dishes with strange and trendy ingredients like kohlrabi and stringy seaweed, but I headed for the table in the corner with the traditional Greek food. The little round chef was so authentic he didn't speak English, but with every return visit to load up my plate his beaming smile widened. The next time I went up he waved his hands for me to wait, darted to the kitchen and returned with a plate of shish kebab. The metal skewers looked exactly like small swords.

"Oh, that was *great*," I sighed after the last chunk of meltingly tender lamb. Maybe this was a preview of dinner. All I had to do was survive the trip to the ruins. As I handed the plate back to the delighted chef one of the skewers fell, and I bent to pick it up.

"Yes, I'll take care of it." That same quiet voice from last night! I sprang to my feet and glanced wildly about. A man was just turning away as a group left the room. I got a brief impression of intense gray eyes and cropped reddish hair—and then crushing pain in my wrist. I looked down, seeing the kebab skewer I was still gripping and a muscular hand grabbing me. I remembered that grip. "What are you doing here?"

Really amazing eyes. His face was more rugged than handsome, but maybe that was because of the death glare. I realized he was waiting for me to say something.

I tend to resort to sarcasm under stress. "Hi, we haven't met, have we? I'm Sarah. I'm a *passenger*. You?"

The glare abated and now had a flicker of uncertainty. "Andrew. I...I'm assisting Jacek Stanishev."

Oh yeah. One of the dignitaries Aunt Ilse had mentioned.

The ship intercom announced, in the requisite five languages, that the city shopping tour would be leaving from the dock in five minutes, and the tour of the ruins in fifteen. "If you'll excuse me, I have to go admire ruins." I managed to pull my hand free and return the skewer to the only man on the boat that truly valued me, the little chef.

"Oh, of course you're going to the ruins! We are too!" May

gushed. My aunt and the rest of the gaggle were behind her. And so was Dmitrios, looking extremely *GQ* in an open black shirt and tan slacks. Damn. I had to think fast. If there was a way I could get everyone, especially Dmitrios, to think I was somewhere else....

"Actually I think I will go into town. I ate too much to climb around ruins for hours. Take lots of pictures!" And then I ran off in the direction of the crowd leaving the dining room, merging with them and keeping my head down until I saw my chance—a side corridor. I hid in a cramped and musty utility closet until I was sure both tours were well away from the ship and drifted as unobtrusively as I could to my true destination, the snorkeling deck.

I had my ereader in my shoulder bag already, the requisite sunblock, and a snagged bottle of water. The door to the deck was closed, but the handle turned and I heaved a huge sigh of relief, closing it silently behind me.

The view was just as peaceful and beautiful as I remembered. While shaded now, the wooden benches had been in full sun for hours and were quite hot. The efficient staff had already cleared away any towels and the storage under the benches was locked. As I was looking I saw a flash of color. A blue-and-white shirt lay discarded on the deck right next to the water steps, hidden from view by a storage locker. A folded towel peeked from underneath, and I pounced on it with glee. Comfortable, I stretched out on the bench, started reading Thucydides, and forgot all my troubles.

A splash made me look up. The light had changed to a golden honey, and the sun was lower in the sky. I checked the time. The tours were due to return in less than an hour, and I should get in position to merge back with the returning crowds. I gathered up the towel.

A hand reached up out of the water. Andrew heaved himself up with easy grace, slung something like a small, hard plastic backpack off his shoulders, then froze when he saw me. The backpack had a black tube coming out of it, and he was wearing blue swim trunks and a diver's knife. He'd been scuba diving?

The glare was back, so I looked elsewhere, and that view was very nice too but not exactly what I would call relaxing. Defined muscles everywhere but not bulky. And...scars. A long one on one shin, and two small, round blotches at the edge of his ribcage. Not surgery scars. He glanced at the towel in my hand, grimaced, and picked up the shirt and put it on.

"You're not supposed to be here." Definitely a growl.

I swallowed. "Neither are you."

He started moving toward me. "You said you were going on that tour."

"I lied. I prefer to read a book." I waved the reader at him while reaching for the door handle. I didn't know what was going on or exactly why I felt like running, but I did. I wrenched open the door and darted through, hearing him right behind me.

The corridor to the snorkel deck and the cross-passage had glass panels along one side for the ship's gym, tastefully etched with *kore* and other classical figures. Horrified, I glimpsed a man in a black shirt moving stealthily down the cross-passage and stepped back, slamming into Andrew. Again.

Dmitrios. He'd skipped the tours too. I was trapped with no way to escape—and I panicked. All I could think of was somehow persuading Dmitrios to leave me alone. I turned, wrapped my arms around Andrew's neck, and kissed him. I heard something hit the floor next to me.

As soon as our lips touched I realized how insanely stupid I was. Dmitrios was not going to believe we were lovers when Andrew shoved me away in disgust. I had just horribly embarrassed myself for nothing.

Only Andrew didn't move away. The kiss became intense, edging into fiery, and his arms wrapped around me tightly. It was comforting, and terrifying, and I didn't want it to stop. Dmitrios *had* to believe this.

Dmitrios. I pulled away, gasping for air and remembering where I was. I was on a cruise ship in the Mediterranean and the man I had just been passionately kissing kept showing up in the oddest places, usually with a weapon. I had no idea why, but as long as the possible explanations involved criminal activity it was dangerous to get involved.

I checked. No sign of Dmitrios.

Andrew's eyes were still closed. I pushed harder to get free, and when they opened there was no trace of glare. "I, ah..." He took a deep breath. "Thank you for your help. That was close."

I blinked and waited for my brain to start working again. Then I looked down. I had dropped the towel when I launched myself at him and it had nicely covered the little backpack scuba kit he'd dropped. I'd probably hidden his unconventional attire from Dmitrios as well, the way I'd been wrapped around him.

Somehow I found my voice. I was too embarrassed even to blush. I just wanted to die. "No problem." Wait, he wanted to hide from Dmitrios too?

He grinned, and I died again. It was a crooked grin and I realized I had been terribly, horribly wrong. He was the most handsome man on the ship. "You've been very well trained, I must say. But they didn't tell me you were going to be here too. Who are you working for?"

"I am *just a pass—*"

"You don't need to keep that up for me. You are clearly not a civilian; your reactions give you away. Besides, I *did* get a briefing on your principal." He hesitated, then gently touched my cheek. "You know how hard it is to meet someone special who...understands what people like us do. We've both got to get back to work, but...I'd like to see you again when this is over." All I could do was nod. He gave me that devastating crooked grin and went back to the snorkel deck, allowing me to admire his splendid physique from another angle.

I wandered back up to the main deck in a fog, not even thinking to hide from the returning tour groups. It was just my luck. I finally meet a man who tasted better than chocolate, and he was either part of the mafia or a mental case.

"Sarah! How was the shopping?" Aunt Ilse and her gang crowded around me, bright-eyed and chattering.

"Um, I think I got a bit too much sun," I stammered. Not that anyone listened, but it would hopefully excuse me acting like a stunned fish. "Should lie down."

"Nonsense! You're probably just hungry," May said, dragging me off. "I know I'm famished, I climbed the entire amphitheater! Come on, it's time for dinner."

Dinner was conventional table service, as opposed to the breakfast and lunch buffets, so I couldn't run around with a plate and then leave. I smiled and nodded as the gaggle discussed their day and the sights, letting their voices wash over me. It was strangely soothing to my troubled mind. The wine helped too.

"A tree full of goats. Quite festive, actually, but one does wonder about droppings...."

The thing was, Andrew didn't really act like a criminal or a mental patient. But he *did* seem to think I was something I wasn't. Something like him. Something that casually mentioned briefings and principals and civilians and had specialized equipment and weapons. Something like a spy then? But why have spies on a history cruise?

That night I lay in my bed listening to Aunt Ilse's gentle snores, completely unable to fall asleep because every time I closed my eyes I saw Andrew's. Finally I got up, desperate for a distraction, and picked up the leather-covered folder with the room service menu. Fantasizing about food in the moonlight might calm me.

There was no point in getting my hopes up. *People like us,* he'd said. He wouldn't have any interest in me when he found out I wasn't a spy, but a boring history graduate student. I ignored the tear that trickled down my face and landed on the dessert list.

A long, thin shadow flickered across the sliding glass doors to the narrow balcony, followed by a larger one descending. The shadow moved stealthily to the side. I heard a faint rasping noise, then a breeze of warm, salt air as a masked head pushed past the sheer curtains.

I was in a very bad mood. I didn't have Andrew and I didn't have *crème brûlée*. I backhanded the intruder with the room service menu. He fell back with a grunt—which turned into a scream as he toppled over the railing, followed by a loud thud.

"What's going on?" Aunt Ilse was surprisingly coherent after waking suddenly.

"Someone just tried to break in," I said, moving to the glass doors and looking down. The intruder was lying on the deck and standing right next to him was Andrew with his gun in his hand. He saw me and grinned, then blew me a kiss before kneeling down and pulling off the intruder's mask. It was Dmitrios.

"Come away from the window, dear. He might have a friend with a rifle." That startled me enough I stepped back quickly. Looking in the reflection of the glass, her face was completely calm. Glancing down, I saw she had something silver in her hand, but when I turned around it had vanished.

Now there was shouting and flashing blue lights on the dock. I couldn't resist one last look to see Dmitrios being hauled off by the local cops.

"Well, I doubt I'm getting back to sleep after all that excitement," Aunt Ilse said briskly, and saw the menu in my hand. "Excellent idea. We'll have an early breakfast."

"I don't want breakfast, I want explanations! Why was Dmitrios, of all people, trying to break in to our room?"

"Not hungry?" Aunt Ilse felt my forehead. "You don't seem to be ill... but you were out of sorts at dinner. We all noticed."

A brisk knock sounded on our door. Aunt Ilse moved quickly to one side of it, and there seemed to be something in her hand again. "Who is it?"

"MacKensie." I recognized that voice....

She opened the door, and Andrew slipped in. He nodded to me. "Nice work again, Sarah. Ma'am, we've already ID'd him. Alexandru Vidraru, Serbian secret police. He must have identified you from their files. We'll be changing the prime minister's schedule to—"

My aunt coughed, and glanced at me. Andrew looked back and forth between us, confused. "What?"

I sighed. Much was becoming clear. "She's trying to warn you I'm not cleared for that information. Unlike her." My aunt, who never did say who she had worked for, and traveled a lot. I gave her a skeptical look. "Global insurance, huh? You should have told me the latest cruise ship fashion trend was firearms, Aunt Ilse. I feel very underdressed."

Andrew shook his head. "But you always...she's really your aunt?"

"Yes, *really*. I kept telling you but you never believed me. I'm just a passenger..." My voice cracked, and I had to look away. "Sorry. I'm not a spy or anything. Just a history grad student."

Aunt Ilse shrugged. "You're not a spy at the moment, but they generally prefer on-the-job training. My degree was in English literature. Shakespeare." She smiled. "You might consider it. You meet such interesting people."

"Is that why you invited me? To meet your spy friends?"

Her smile widened. "Among other things. We needed a large number of completely trustworthy but unknown people to populate the ship to make the...event seem innocuous. So they brought me back, and naturally I thought of my childhood friends and my lovely niece who really should get out more. I insisted it be a history cruise for you, you know." She turned to Andrew. "Do you think they'll give you some time off now that Vidraru is caught? Sarah never got to see the ruins. You were quite clever, dear, but *never* wear white for surveillance or covert operations. It draws the eye. I don't think anyone else noticed, though."

And there was the crooked grin again. "I did, when I found her after doing the underwater security sweep. I'll ask Stanishev."

"If he gives you any trouble, remind him he *still* owes me several favors," Aunt Ilse said darkly. "We'll expect you at breakfast."

"Wouldn't miss it for the world." Andrew gave me a very adroit kiss before slipping out again.

My aunt observed my reddening face with one upraised eyebrow. "Oh yes, definitely a talent for spycraft. What have you been up to, Sarah?"

"Need to know, Aunt Ilse." I grinned at her. "Need to know."

BRIBING GHOSTS

LEAH CUTTER

Leah Cutter has lived all over the world. Her time in China, in particular, has influenced her fiction. The summer part of this anthology made her think of Ghost Month, which usually falls in the seventh lunar month of the year.

The story itself weaves Ghost Month traditions with romance to create a tale like no other in this volume.

Leave that to Leah, whose award-nominated novels include Paper Mage *and an urban fantasy mystery series that she calls the Kickass Cassie novels. For a list of her books, go to leahcutter.com.*

There you'll also find information about her short fiction, including her eight Fiction River *appearances, and her appearance in our previous Special edition,* Spies. *She also edited our previous volume,* Stolen, *and will edit another volume in the near future.*

F u Ran knelt in front of her father's grave. At least she'd remembered to bring a rough, red-and-black checked blanket so her jeans wouldn't get too dirty kneeling on the ground. The August sun beat down on the back of her head from the clear blue sky, making her wish she'd wrapped her long black hair up in a bun, getting it off her shoulders and neck. She wore a short-sleeved white blouse that her father would have considered scandalous as it didn't cover her up to her neck, but it was far too warm to go around completely swaddled.

She also didn't wear any makeup—something else her father had always associated with the corrupting Western influence creeping into the mainland.

On the ground in front of Fu Ran sat a paper boat, about the size of her two hands held together. It had been cleverly folded out of bright red-and-gold "Hell" money—*joss* paper to be burned as an offering for the dead. Between the boat and the unassuming gray tombstone a few feet away, Fu Ran had stuck nine rows of incense into the ground, three sticks per row, twenty-seven total: the same as her age, hopefully a lucky number that day. Sweet smoke curled up from the lit ends, hazing the clear air.

Earlier, that spring, during the *qingming* festival, her entire family had gathered to clean the front area of the grave: her mother, her two older brothers, her grandfather, as well as one of her aunts and three of her cousins. No weeds remained, and the grass in front of the grave marker stayed short.

Now, Fu Ran knelt all alone. No one had dared come with her to visit a graveyard during *gui yue*—Ghost Month.

According to tradition, Judge Yama opened the gates of Hell on the first day of the seventh Lunar month, setting all the wild ghosts free to roam the earth. On the fifteenth of the month, there would be many celebrations and events to feed and entertain the ghosts, who would all (hopefully) leave by the end of the month.

Though Fu Ran's family had made offerings on the first day of Ghost Month to appease any hungry ancestors who came to visit, bad luck had struck them hard. Fu Ran's mother remained in the hospital after the car accident that had claimed the life of her middle brother. Her eldest brother had lost his job. And her youngest aunt had come down with the flu and was still bedridden, the doctors worried and ordering more tests.

Obviously, some angry ghost (or ghosts) were angry with Fu Ran and her family. She'd decided that making an offering in a temple wasn't good enough. The incense and the Hell money she burned there might get lost among all the other offerings and not go directly to her father.

Her family needed an intervention in the spirit world. Who better than her strong, calm, overly principled father? Who'd died only three years before from cancer?

So on the eighth day of Ghost Month, Fu Ran took the hot, stinky bus all the way to the outskirts of her city, Fuzhou, to visit her father's graveyard. The bus's air conditioning had been overwhelmed by the sheer number of bodies, with mothers and their sisters holding two children each in their laps, sullen teenagers crammed together, even ancient grandmothers stoically standing, their arms wrapped around each other's waist to hold them up.

Though her parents had given her an auspicious name—*Fu Ran* basically translated into English as lucky—Fu Ran considered herself the unluckiest girl in the whole world.

She had excelled during her college exams and had gone on to get an advanced degree in chemistry, however, no job awaited her. With the death of her father, her family had lost their Party connections. No sponsor had come forward to advocate for her.

As a result, she could only get a soul-crushing job in one of the numerous factories that lined the coast, making cheap shoes and clothes to be exported to America, but that wouldn't be putting her education to use. Plus, those jobs didn't pay well at all, and too many factories still had deadly accidents.

She didn't have a boyfriend—not even a secret crush—though her girlfriends teased she must like *someone*, even if she didn't.

Bills were mounting up. Fu Ran wasn't sure how the family would pay not just for her brother's cremation and burial expenses, but for her mother's hospital stay as well. (It was just too inauspicious to conduct the funeral during Ghost Month, so the ceremony couldn't occur until the following month.)

Fu Ran didn't know if praying to her father would help. She'd found a paper boat because he'd always loved to go fishing on the Min River. He'd told her stories of poling a flat-bottomed boat as a boy, going upriver to where it widened out and a small pool formed where he could almost always find fish.

Fu Ran didn't know what else to do, where else to turn. Her father's old boss, the family's primary Party affiliation, had disappeared out of their lives when her father had died. None of her professors had taken her on as an assistant, despite her high grades. The loss of her brother tore at her chest like an open wound; no amount of fancy surgery could seal the hole.

After she finished her prayers, imploring that not just her father but any and all of her deceased relatives needed to help her family, she set the little boat on fire.

Maybe the boat would delight her father and get him to intervene with the ghosts targeting them.

Or perhaps he'd be dismayed at her whimsy and send more devils to haunt them.

Fu Ran defiantly stood up. The heat of the flames washed across her legs. The scorching sun beat down on her head, making her sway in place. The smell of incense swelled up and made her cough. Dark spots formed in the corners of her eyes.

She blinked.

All but one of the dark spots went away.

She turned to look at the now-moving shape.

It was a man, not a ghost. Definitely not her imagination, either. White shirt, black pants, black hair, dark eyes, tanned skin.

He walked to the tombstone closest to him, then knelt down, looking around.

Then he stood and walked quickly to the next.

Who was he hiding from?

He spotted her standing. He paused and stared hard at her.

Fu Ran resisted the urge to wave at him, just to prove that she wasn't a ghost either.

He shook his head, then changed direction and came directly toward her without pausing again.

His dark eyes drilled into her very soul, holding her captive.

"It isn't safe here," the man said as soon as he drew near. He had a very cultured accent, possibly from Beijing.

He wore his black, glossy hair super short and cute. He had rolled the sleeves of his white shirt up above his elbows, showing off nicely muscled arms. Both his well-made black dress slacks and black leather shoes were scuffed and had streaks of dirt on them.

"Why isn't it safe here?" Fu Ran asked, not wanting to be chased off. This was *her* father's grave, after all. She had every right to be there. "Are you afraid of the ghosts?"

He gave a sharp, barking laugh. "Ghosts?" he asked, looking around. He spied the rows of incense almost burnt to their ends sticking out of the grave. Then he looked at her strangely. "You are a brave woman to make offerings to..." he paused, glancing at the tombstone "...your father, I'm presuming, during the middle of Ghost Month."

"Someone had to," Fu Ran explained. That was all she was planning on saying about the matter. As her aunt always said, wear your broken arm *inside* your sleeve.

The man nodded and bowed his head low to her. "I can only hope that when I have a daughter, she will be as dutiful. But for now, we both need to get out of here."

"Why?" Fu Ran asked, stubbornly crossing her arms when the man reached out to touch her, perhaps hurry her along.

The man glanced over his shoulder. "Spies," he hissed. "Taiwanese spies."

Fu Ran gasped. All her life, the Party had warned about Taiwanese spies. Fuzhou sat directly across the strait from the renegade island. She'd had nightmares as a child about Taiwanese soldiers swarming out of their boats and taking over the city, killing everyone in her family.

She looked past the man, in the direction he'd come from.

She stiffened, shock holding her very still.

Four men stood at the very edge of the cemetery.

"Too late to run," Fu Ran told the man. She reached out and grabbed his sleeve, tugging on it. "Come. Kneel with me. They will believe you are being a dutiful son."

The man glanced over his shoulder, then back at Fu Ran. Relief flowed across his features. The smile he gave her was as dazzling as the sun overhead.

Really, it was just the summer heat that made her knees feel so weak, not his look.

"You're right," he said, gracefully kneeling down on the blanket. "They're just following a man. They don't know me by sight. I'm Zhong Di," he said, putting his hands on the ground and lowering his head.

"Fu Ran," she said as she knelt and did the same.

They each prayed in silence as the last of the smoke from the paper boat rose up into the clear sky.

Just as the men grew closer, Zhong Di reached into the breast pocket of his shirt and took out two more pieces of Hell money. He handed one to her, set his on fire with a lighter and then gestured for her to do the same.

The men abruptly swerved and walked past them.

Fu Ran felt her shoulders drop with relief. Finally, something was going right!

It wasn't until the cemetery was completely empty that Fu Ran spoke. "Why did you have Hell money with you?" she asked.

Zhong Di gave her a carefree grin that made him look even younger and more handsome than he had initially appeared. "It's Ghost Month," he said. "And I've always believed in carrying the appropriate bribes. Who knows when you'll need them the most?"

Fu Ran nodded. A very practical answer. Though the Party decreed that this was the Worker's Paradise and everyone was equal, somehow it generally took bribes to get anything done.

Maybe that was why the Party allowed all the sacrifices during Ghost Month: they saw it as bribes for ghosts.

Both of them rose. The sun was finally hanging lower in the sky, the heat of the afternoon passing. Loud choruses of cicadas sprang up. Zhong Di helped Fu Ran first shake out her blanket, then fold it up.

"Where will you go now?" Fu Ran asked, not willing to let Zhong Di disappear like a ghost.

He sighed. "I could lie and say that I was going back to my apartment, but they might have it staked out by now."

"My middle brother just died. My mother's still in the hospital. My aunt is very sick," Fu Ran said all in a rush. "You could stay in our living room, and sleep on the sofa, but it would still be very unlucky."

She knew that it wasn't proper to invite Zhong Di home. She'd just met him! She didn't know his family or any of his friends.

Plus, he wasn't safe. He was running from Taiwanese spies. Maybe he was a spy himself.

However, she couldn't help herself. There was something about him, maybe how he held himself, or the look of confidence in his eyes, or perhaps even the strong muscles of his arms, that made her throw caution to the wind.

Then again, she'd started the day rashly, making the decision to go to a cemetery during Ghost Month. Might as well continue down that same path.

Zhong Di gave her a smile that matched her reckless feelings. "I accept, but you can't ask too many questions. That wouldn't be safe for you or your family."

Fu Ran considered his statement for a moment. Again, he sounded very practical, an attribute both her mother and her father would approve of. "You will tell me what you can of your troubles?" Fu Ran asked. "Then, tell me the rest later?"

"I promise," Zhong Di said solemnly.

Fu Ran shivered. It sounded like a vow that he'd honor even unto death.

Who was this man? What mysteries filled his life? And how could she bribe him to make sure that he continued to "haunt" her, to stay with her like an old ghost?

The back door to the apartment building where Fu Ran's family lived had graffiti on it already, though it had just been painted an industrial brown not two weeks before. Black and white stickers with strident characters had been slapped on it. Plus some stupid advertisement for an illegal band.

Fu Ran sighed but didn't say anything. She pulled open the door, gesturing for Zhong Di to walk in. He carried the plastic bags containing their dinner. It had been so kind of him to buy enough food, not just for her, but for three additional people as well.

After he stepped into the dimly lit stairwell, she shut the door after him and locked it carefully. The stairway smelled of concrete and bleach. At least it no longer smelled of urine, as it had the previous month when a homeless man had snuck in and spent the night sleeping there.

"Ready for a climb?" Fu Ran asked. While there was an elevator at the front of the building, it was often broken, always dirty, and it made clanging noises that Fu Ran didn't trust.

"After you," Zhong Di said gallantly.

Fu Ran couldn't help but give him a smile before she turned to the prospect of the six flights of stairs that they needed to climb. While she was young and in good enough shape to reach her floor without being too winded, she always felt sorry for the older people in the building. She'd frequently pass them sitting on one of the landings, wheezing and trying to catch their breath.

With Zhong Di following her, Fu Ran couldn't help but show off a little, climbing the bare concrete stairs quickly. She rarely touched the railing. Though it was painted a happy red, it was often sticky or slimy from who knew what.

The sixth floor looked cheery compared to the plain concrete staircase. Lights in red, green, and blue paper lanterns hung from the ceiling down the center of the hall. Fu Ran's family along with the neighbors had painted the walls a bright yellow. Large windows with green glass (reinforced with chicken wire) stood on the right of each door, supposedly to supply the tiny apartments with more light. Ancient red carpet covered the floor, worn bare in many places. The hall smelled of garlic, chicken, and incense—the smells of home—with a faint undertone of more bleach.

No numbers or names marked any of the apartments, of course. It was too easy for evil spirits to follow a person home if they could easily find their address. All the doors had been painted different colors, though, to make it easier for guests to visit.

The old woman at the start of the floor, closest to the stairway, with the strongest Party affiliations, got the lucky red door. Everyone else had to settle for other colors.

Fu Ran happily stopped in front of the dark blue door of her family's apartment. They lived one apartment in from the far end and just across the hallway from the communal showers and toilets for that floor. She hoped that Zhong Di wouldn't think too poorly of them since they didn't have a private bathroom. However, at least they didn't have to go down the street to the public toilets, which were always filthy.

"I don't know who's home," she warned Zhong Di. She didn't know what kind of reception he'd get from either of her aunts, who frequently stayed with them, or her brother.

"Hopefully we have enough food to feed them," he replied with a smile.

"Thank you," she said again as she unlocked the door.

Just inside the tiny alcove, she saw only her eldest brother's shoes waiting there, a pair of worn brown-leather loafers. She hoped he wouldn't be too hard on Zhong Di. Fu Ran slipped off her shoes and put on her house slippers, then handed a pair of guest slippers to Zhong Di.

Thankfully, he wasn't too "cultured" to be ashamed of wearing guest slippers, taking off his shoes and slipping on the guest pair.

The kitchen ran along the outside wall, with a tiny stove that Fu Ran's mother had always worked miracles with, a sink that was barely big enough to hold a dinner bowl, and shelves that rose to top of the eight foot ceiling, stocked full of instant meals, dried goods, spices, bowls, and chopsticks. It still smelled of rice and pickled fish.

To the left, the apartment opened up into what had originally been one long room. Her family had divided it up to make an extra bedroom for her brothers.

Fu Ran breathed a sigh of relief when she saw the door to her brother's bedroom was closed, with a little placard hanging from the doorknob, showing a red lotus flower.

The sign meant that the person behind the door didn't want to be disturbed. The other side of the sign held a golden laughing Buddha, which, when showing, meant he would welcome company.

Though the concept of spending time alone was frowned on,

both of Fu Ran's brothers, and Fu Ran herself, needed it some-times in order to study.

And now, to grieve.

The living room itself held a low coffee table that the family usually sat around for meals. The white-and-gray top of the table barely had any dents in it from the numerous children who had banged on it over the years. The legs showed more wear, the gold paint flecking off to reveal the steel underneath. Fu Ran often slid her fingertips along them, as if she could gather strength from their sturdiness.

While the floor itself was concrete, Fu Ran's family had bought several colorful rugs to cover it. Her favorite was made from black, blue, and white cloth all braided together. It sat under the table and provided good insulation from the floor.

They had one black, scratchy couch, pressed up against the wall. Lamps sitting on the wooden end tables at either arm of the couch made the room bright. Folded-up black metal chairs leaned against the kitchen wall, ready for guests.

The wall to Fu Ran's left held a few pictures—school gradua-tions, important ceremonies, her father's death portrait.

Her brother's picture would join there soon enough, something Fu Ran didn't want to think about just yet.

On the right wall were two closed doors: one leading to the bedroom her parents had shared, one going to her own tiny room.

Zhong Di put the bags holding their dinner on the table, then gracefully sank down.

Fu Ran breathed a sigh of relief. At least he didn't seem to mind sitting on the floor.

They eagerly divided up the food, leaving two whole bags for leftovers. Soon, Fu Ran slurped her noodle soup, the broth having cooled to the perfect temperature, with just the right amount of tangy onions in it.

By the time she'd finished that and started in on her rice and stir-fried vegetables, she finally felt human, as well as ready to hear Zhong Di's story.

He'd seemed to come to the same conclusion, and started by saying, "I work as an inventor for...let's just say one of the big shoe manufacturers."

"Really?" Fu Ran asked. "Were you working on different rubber for the soles?"

Zhong Di blinked and nodded slowly. "In a way, I was. Why do you ask?"

Fu Ran didn't like the suspicious look in his eye. "I studied to be a chemist," she told him. "With an advanced degree."

"Oh?" he asked, surprised. "Who do you work for?"

Fu Ran looked back down at her rice. She suddenly was no longer hungry. "No one," she said. "I had good grades—the best in my class—but no one would hire me."

"I see," Zhong Di said.

Perhaps he did. It wasn't easy for someone as poor as Fu Ran to be hired into a good paying job. Particularly without Party backing.

"Anyway," he said after a few moments of silence. "I...let's just say I made an interesting breakthrough. When I showed it to my boss, Ya Du, he told me not to continue with that line of reasoning." Zhong Di sighed. He appeared to be choosing his words carefully. "Instead, two men approached me that night."

"Spies?" Fu Ran asked when he didn't speak again right away.

"I believe so," Zhong Di said. "They flattered me. And offered me a lot of money if I would sell them my discovery."

Fu Ran could tell by the way that Zhong Di hung his head that he'd originally been taken in. "What happened?" she asked.

"When it came time to give them the formula, early this morning...I just couldn't do it. I couldn't sell it to them. It was four men. I'd never seen them before. They weren't businessmen. They were goons. I saw them at the end of the street, then just turned and ran. They've been after me ever since." He sighed again.

"Could you sell them a formula that didn't work?" Fu Ran asked. "Alter it slightly?"

"Possibly, but that wouldn't stop them from coming after me,"

Zhong Di said. "And I can't turn in my boss. He has strong Party connections. It would be his word against mine. Nobody would believe me."

Fu Ran shook her head as a plan came to her.

Why did men always think they needed to do everything on their own? By themselves?

She blamed the West for that corrupting idea.

"I may have a plan," she said slowly after Zhong Di had fallen back to eating. "But it will take some careful timing on both our parts. As well as reaching out to our connections."

"Really?" Zhong Di asked, his eyes gleaming. "I knew that traveling to the cemetery was sure to bring me good luck."

Fu Ran couldn't help but giggle. That was the first time someone had found anything lucky in a graveyard.

Then again, possibly Zhong Di would bring good luck, and not trouble, to her and her family as well.

Fu Ran kept her expression professional, despite how she shook like a little girl inside. She wore a somber, light gray blouse and a black skirt—her one, good interview outfit—with her hair pinned up in a tight bun. Tonight, she'd tinted her lips just slightly pink to make her seem younger, as well as used eyeliner to make her dark eyes look rounder and more innocent.

She didn't squirm in the hard-backed wooden chair that she sat on—that might have overplayed her hand.

Zhong Di's boss, Ya Du, sat and looked sternly at her from across the broad expansive of his oak desk. They were meeting after hours at the shoe factory. He wore the light grey jacket currently favored by Party officials, though the top button and standing collar dug into his fat neck. His flabby lips and plump face made him look like a toad, while his black eyes were tiny and full of cunning.

The office stank of burnt rubber from the factory despite the cool air that blew constantly from the vents. Bright neon lights buzzed annoyingly above them, highlighting how dingy the place looked. Sad green paint covered the walls, scuffed and peeling. A huge picture of Xi Jinping hung on the wall just behind Ya Du, framed in bright red matting. Various Party awards hung beside it.

No school diploma, however.

"I'm glad that someone had the intelligence to come to me with this," Ya Du said. "And you're sure that Zhong Di has no idea you're here?"

"He does not," Fu Ran said, her voice steady. She suspected Ya Du was trying to figure out just how alone she was and whether or not he could just make her disappear. "Zhong Di said he was going to *hide* his discovery, instead of sharing it with the People."

Fu Ran made sure that she sounded every bit the patriot. She'd considered wearing a jacket with a red star pinned to the lapel, but it had been too warm that evening, plus it felt like overkill.

They needed for Ya Du to make Fu Ran the same deal he'd made Zhong Di.

"So you brought the formula to me," Ya Du said with relish.

Fu Ran wasn't about to tell him that it wasn't the original formula. She and Zhong Di had altered it slightly so it would be sure to fail.

"Of course I would bring it to you! You are his immediate superior," Fu Ran explained. "If he isn't going to take credit for it, you should." She hesitated, and for the first time, added some sadness to her voice. "My family has had so much bad luck this Ghost Month."

"Really?" Ya Du purred.

Fu Ran pushed down on her flush of anger. He sounded like a cat who'd just spotted a wounded bird.

"My brother was killed in a car accident," Fu Ran said softly. The pain constantly tore at her heart, and she no longer had to pretend to be sad. "My mother is still in the hospital because of it." The doctors had finally said that she might be released by the end of the following week, but then she'd have a lot of physical therapy for her broken leg and hip.

And how was her family going to pay for all of that?

"Ah," Ya Du said, sitting back in his chair. He nodded, as if he'd come to a decision. "I have some people who might be interested in such a formula."

Fu Ran frowned at him. She knew she couldn't just jump at the chance he was offering. She had to make him convince her. "I don't understand."

"Sometimes, it's better to help each other along the path, rather than to bask in the sunshine by yourself," Ya Du said, mangling a famous Party slogan.

Fu Ran blinked. "How can we help each other?" she asked slowly, despite her rapidly beating heart.

Good patriot or not, Ya Du would also believe her to be a practical person.

"Instead of selfishly using this formula to better our American masters," Ya Du said, his face scrunching together on the last two words as if they tasted sour, "we should use it to better everyone. In particular, your family."

Fu Ran nodded as if she understood. "And you can help me do that?"

Ya Du smiled broadly at her. "I can! I can introduce you to some people who would pay you very good money for such a formula."

Fu Ran tilted her head to one side, as if considering the prospect. "Why wouldn't you take it to them yourself?" she asked as innocently as she could.

"I have more than enough!" Ya Du said, his hands spread out as if to indicate the richness of his office. "Besides, I am just a humble servant."

Fu Ran contained her scoffing snort. She'd bet that the Taiwanese agents had paid Ya Du already. And were probably pressuring him to deliver, since Zhong Di had slipped away.

The real reason Ya Du wanted her to approach the agents on her own was so that he could keep his hands clean.

She was about to make sure that Ya Du got his hands dirty, though.

"I couldn't possibly meet with such people on my own," Fu Ran said, shaking her head. "It wouldn't be safe! Or proper," she added, glaring at him.

"You are meeting me here in a factory, after hours," Ya Du pointed out.

"That's different!" Fu Ran said, indignant. "You're a married man, and an upstanding member of the Party."

"True, true," Ya Du said, nodding and preening. "How about this? We'll meet tomorrow night at the Green Tearoom, at eight p.m. I'll make the introductions."

"And this is the best way to help everyone?" Fu Ran asked as if looking for reassurances. "Including my family?"

"It is," Ya Du assured her.

"Thank you so much," Fu Ran said, rising from her chair then bowing lowly, as if Ya Du were a great man.

"With pleasure," he said, smacking his fat lips together.

Fu Ran left, her insides shaking but her hands still steady.

Just one more night, and Zhong Di would be free of his foreign ghosts.

Though the Green Tearoom had been built just a few years before, it still felt ancient, with scarred wooden floors, soft amber walls, and discreet lights. The air smelled of refined green tea and lemony cakes. Beautiful pink and white orchids sat on the front reception desk. The young woman behind the dark-oak reception desk wore the replica of an old-fashioned robe and was so covered up, Fu Ran knew her father would have approved.

A large room opened up to the right of the reception desk. Low tables filled the floor, each with comfortable-looking pillows scattered around them. Many men, and a few women, sat at the tables, drinking tea, eating small bites, and toasting one another.

While only the best people with the strongest influence would be allowed in here, it wasn't a place that she ever wanted to return to. She wouldn't be comfortable here.

Perhaps Zhong Di belonged here, but not her. Even though she wore her "interview" outfit again—same black skirt, with a different white shirt, and a discreet black handbag—and maybe she could pretend as though she belonged, she would never actually fit in here. She'd grown up too poor.

The thought made her heart ache.

When the receptionist heard Fu Ran's name, instead of seating her in the public area, the woman led her down a short, closed-in hallway. At the first corridor, the receptionist took a right. Brighter lights shone down here, and soft green carpet muffled their steps. Closed wooden doors lined this corridor.

The receptionist opened the third door on her left, then waited for Fu Ran to enter.

Fu Ran nearly protested. She didn't want to wait by herself in an empty room for spies to come meet her!

Then she swallowed down her fear. She could do this.

She clutched the black handbag she held a little tighter. She wasn't completely unprepared, either.

"Come in! Come in!" she heard Ya Du's cheerful voice.

Fu Ran straightened her shoulders and marched into the room, knowing full well that it could be a trap.

Ya Du sat in the place of honor, at the head of the table. He still wore his jacket that mimicked a Party uniform.

Fu Ran didn't allow herself to sag in relief when she saw that three other places had been set at the table.

The spies would be here.

Before Fu Ran could ask Ya Du about his day, the two spies came in. They looked like the spies who had first visited Zhong Di, as he had described to her, the main characteristic being that they were both so ordinary that it would be easy to forget them. They wore their black hair fairly short. Their eyes were lighter brown, almost hazel color, and their skin looked more tanned. They'd obviously been well-fed their entire lives: good fingernails, white teeth, no pock marks on their faces. One wore a brown, Western suit, while the other wore gray, but both suits were cheaply made.

After the introductions had been made and tea had been served, Mr. Gray (as Fu Ran had tagged the man in the gray suit) asked, "So, I hear that you're a chemist as well."

"I am," Fu Ran said proudly. Then she remembered her part. "But no one will hire me," she added in a meeker voice.

"We may have need of a good chemist," Mr. Brown said.

"Really?" Fu Ran asked.

She knew she was just playing a part. It wasn't hard for her to sound genuinely excited. She'd looked so long for a real job.

"We would have some tests for you, of course," Mr. Gray said. "But it could be a real opportunity."

"I'd have to think about it," Fu Ran said cautiously, as a good girl would. She didn't add that she would check with her family as well—they didn't need those complications.

Ya Du smiled beneficently at all of them, like a father making a good match for his little girl. "Good! Good! So now that I have made the introductions, I think I should leave."

Fu Ran kept a pleasant smile pasted to her face. He couldn't go. Not yet!

Thankfully, a quiet knock on the door came to her rescue.

"Sir, I—" The receptionist stepped into the room, looking flustered.

Four men stepped in behind her.

Policemen. Wearing olive green uniforms. Not blue.

That meant they were part of the Armed Police Force, who handled security measures, not regular crimes.

"What's the meaning of this?" Ya Du asked, standing and sounding offended.

"We heard there was a meeting here with two Taiwanese spies," the tallest policeman said. He glared at Mr. Gray and Mr. Black.

"These are just two business acquaintances of mine," Ya Du said.

"Right. Business," the policeman continued. "We need to see your papers."

Mr. Gray and Mr. Black reached into their jacket pockets and took out their wallets and their identification papers. Fu Ran meekly handed hers over. Ya Du huffed greatly before he fished out his own.

"What's this?" the policeman asked, waving a five-hundred yuan note, then pulling out a second and a third.

"Just to show my appreciation for the officers of the law," Ya Du stammered.

Fu Ran couldn't keep a grim smile from her face. It figured that such a good Party member would try bribing everyone he met.

"You're all going to have to come in with us," the policeman said.

"What?" Ya Du asked, puffing up his chest like a stupid peacock. "Do you know who I am? I have important friends, you know."

Another man stepped into the room, pushing past the officers.

Fu Ran blinked, surprised.

It was her father's old boss. Another Party official. Gau Wan.

"I do know who you are," Gau Wan said. He sniffed as if he disapproved of all he saw. "And I have important friends as well."

He looked old, much older than the last time Fu Ran had seen him. Gray hair covered his head, wrinkles marked his face with lines of sorrow, and his skin hung off his cheeks as if he'd lost a great deal of weight. He wore a Western-style black suit, well-tailored, with a white shirt and shiny black shoes.

Fu Ran swallowed down her fear. He wasn't going to turn on her, was he?

As part of the plan, Zhong Di had promised to get a highly regarded Party official to come to the teahouse with the policemen. Hopefully, one who couldn't be bribed by Ya Du.

How did Zhong Di know Gau Wan? Though admittedly,

Fuzhou wasn't that big of a city. It wasn't completely infeasible that the two might know each other. Zhong Di was much richer than Fu Ran, and ran in different circles. The same circles as Gau Wan.

Gau Wan had disappeared after her father's death. Other Party officials had taken note and done likewise, leaving her family adrift. What had happened to him? Some tragedy, she could tell. She suddenly felt guilty for all the angry thoughts she'd had about him over the past few years.

"Let's go down to the police station and get this all straightened out," Gau Wan said. Though he kept an easy smile on his face, his tone brooked no argument.

The two spies looked at each other.

They tensed.

They were going to make a run for it.

Everything seemed to suddenly shift to slow motion.

Mr. Gray started reaching inside his jacket pocket.

Fu Ran just as covertly reached into her purse and wrapped her fingers around the cool glass she found there.

Before Mr. Gray could pull out his weapon, Fu Ran brought out the vial she carried. Neon-green, viscous liquid filled it.

She held it up over the table.

Every eye suddenly turned to her.

"You will go quietly with the police," Fu Ran told Mr. Gray. "No heroic measures. Or I'll break this over your head and you'll die a long, drawn-out, *painful* death."

Mr. Gray visibly gulped and removed his empty hand from his jacket, then raised both hands into the air.

Fu Ran turned her head and glared at Mr. Black. "I have a second one in here for you as well."

Ya Du sneered. "You wouldn't dare."

"What do I have to live for?" Fu Ran said, anger rising in her voice. "I have no father. My mother's sick. My brother is dead. One more tragedy for my family would surprise no one."

She knew even as she said the words that she lied.

She had something to live for. The hope of a relationship with Zhong Di.

However, that hope was ephemeral, as likely to disappear with the bright morning sunlight as mist from the sea.

Ya Du didn't say anything more. Mr. Gray and Mr. Black were frisked (and several more weapons discovered) before they were handcuffed and taken away. Ya Du didn't have to bear the embarrassment of handcuffs, yet he was still going to be seen by some of the more important movers and shakers of Fuzhou in the presence of police as they walked him out of the tearoom.

Finally, only Gau Wan and Fu Ran remained. She took a deep breath and sagged down, resting her elbows on the table and dropping the vial.

"Careful!" Gau Wan said, rushing over.

Fu Ran grinned. "It's just a soporific," she said. "It would have made him feel very sleepy, very quickly. Then as if he'd been run over by a bus."

Gau Wan chuckled and shook his head. His smile melted the years away from him. "I need to apologize," he said softly. "For abandoning you and your family. My wife got sick the week your father died and I lost track of everything else. Zhong Di rousted me, finally reminding me of my other duties."

"I'm so sorry," Fu Ran said. And she was, though a small part of her still wanted to yell at him for disappearing years ago. However, he really did look as though he'd gone through hell.

"How do you know Zhong Di?" Fu Ran asked as she stood up. She was still going to have to go to Party Headquarters to tell them about the attempted bribes. As well as give her statement to the police.

"He's my godson," Gau Wan explained. "I fell out of contact with him, as I did everyone else."

That explained how they knew each other, and why Zhong Di had felt he could ask for this kind of favor.

"It was the least I could do, given how I'd abandoned your family," Gau Wan added, holding open the door for Fu Ran.

"I see," Fu Ran said.

And she did. She couldn't hope for anything more, like maybe a job offer or even some money to help cover their hospital costs. Gau Wan had paid his debt by believing Zhong Di's story, by not being swayed by another Party member, and by showing up that night.

"Thank you," she said as he helped her into the back of a police car.

She didn't expect to see either Gau Wan or Zhong Di again.

They'd done their part.

Now they'd slink away into the night like the ghosts they were, and she'd be on her own again.

Fu Ran eagerly strolled through the city park. Water merrily splashed out of the mouths of the stone fish that rose in a tower in the center of the main fountain. The wind carried the smell of the sea. Though no clouds marred the bright blue sky, the breeze cooled everything down.

Just past the fountain, Fu Ran discovered Zhong Di, as the note he'd left her had promised. She told her stupid heart to stop beating so hard. She hadn't seen him for two weeks, not since the night of the police raid on the teahouse.

Ya Du had been publically shamed and now awaited trial for treason and working with Taiwanese spies. Mr. Gray and Mr. Black had disappeared, and would probably never surface again.

Zhong Di looked so gorgeous resting against the tall edge of the fountain. His black hair shone in the sunlight; his dark eyes sparkled at her. He wore a lime-green short-sleeved shirt that showed even more muscles, gray pants, but only sandals on his handsome feet. Fu Ran couldn't help but feel as though all the air had suddenly thinned, making her lightheaded.

She was glad that she'd worn her prettiest skirt, pale green with the outlines of flowers done in thin black lines. It was short too—

her father had hated that skirt, as it showed off her knees. She'd borrowed white sandals from one of her cousins, along with a peach-colored top.

When Zhong Di pushed himself off the fountain and started towards her, she realized that he had a string wrapped around one hand. A bright red balloon bobbed along in the air behind him.

"Hello," Zhong Di said. He sounded shy.

"Hello," Fu Ran replied. She was happy to be able to get the word out despite her desperately dry throat.

"I wanted to thank you, yet again, for helping me," Zhong Di said.

"It was nothing," Fu Ran said, disappointment stabbing her chest. Of course, that would be the only reason he'd want to see her. He couldn't be interested in her. Not like that.

"So I brought you this," he said, bringing forward the hand with the balloon attached.

"What is this?" Fu Ran asked as she reached for the string and tugged the balloon down. Then she gasped. A Chinese junk was painted on the face of the balloon, floating across a smooth sea.

Zhong Di shrugged, seemingly embarrassed. "An offering."

Fu Ran tilted her head at him, puzzled.

"I know it's tradition to burn Hell money for ghosts," Zhong Di said all in a rush. "I thought...I thought maybe we could start a new tradition." He placed his hand on the balloon string, just above Fu Ran's. "Send our offering up into the sky, straight to heaven."

Fu Ran beamed at him. "I think that's a marvelous idea," she said, letting go of the string.

Zhong Di unwrapped the string from around his palm. He pinched it lightly, then held it out to Fu Ran.

Blushing, she reached out and pinched the string as well.

Zhong Di looked up into the clear sky and said softly, "I want to thank all the ancestors who guided me a cemetery during Ghost Month, so that I might find my luck and my love." He turned to face Fu Ran, his look hopeful.

Nodding, Fu Ran turned her face up as well. "I, too, want to thank all my ancestors for prompting me visit a cemetery, even during Ghost Month, so that I might find my luck and my love."

She looked down at Zhong Di.

The smile he gave her might have been brighter than the sun.

They released the balloon together, and hand-in-hand, watched it sail up, up, up, into the clear blue sky.

COME SUMMER, COME WINTER, I'LL COME FOR YOU

REI ROSENQUIST

"Come Summer, Come Winter, I'll Come For You" begins the final section of this volume, which features atmospheric stories that all have gothic influences.

"Come Summer..." marks Rei Rosenquist's first appearance in Fiction River, *but not their last. Rei is a queer agender speculative fiction writer who depicts a wide variety of identities struggling to find a place in a wide variety of speculative worlds. Rei's short work has also appeared in* Heart's Kiss *magazine and the anthology* Enter The Aftermath. *Rei's website ReiRosenquist.com provides links to their fiction and blog, "Zero Ashes."*

Rei set "Come Summer..." in Japan, where they lived for a year and a half "learning the language and engaging the culture as much as possible." Rei traveled to the port town of Otaru, where they planned to write for a month. Instead, they made new friends, and listened to stories.

"One of the most shocking revelations," Rei writes, "was how Western culture had turned a beautiful legacy of community, protection and love into a horror story of greed, murder, and hatred. And from that truth, 'Come Summer...' was born."

Tokyo, Summer 2014.

Through low gray-brown smoggy-looking clouds, the morning sun peeks through. The color, a shockingly dull and far away yellow-orange. The heat is already heavy, damp, absolutely suffocating. A waterlogged wool blanket that scratches at throats, stuffs up lungs, and makes the whole city collectively cough and choke.

As I descend the rickety metal stairs of my ugly industrial cookie-cutter apartment complex, the back of my neck is already wet. Rushing to cross the street before the blinking green light turns to red, my thighs slip slickly past one another. So much for the fresh nylons I unpacked mere minutes ago. The package promised to help with this kind of thing—airing out summer sweat that trickles down your inner thighs like dirty rivers headed to the sea of gross pooling in the bottom of each shoe. A waste of 100 yen.

But then, it *was* in Japanese, so maybe I misread a kanji. Or all of them.

My bad.

I keep on down the sidewalk, sticking to the right side of the raised yellow stripe, dragging myself along at a pathetic pace. Staring down the road toward my destination, Harajuku Station, I sigh wearily. It's so far away and I'm already tired. Long Tokyo hours of bland web design work will do that.

I blink a few times, trying to see through the thick haze all around me. No use. Humidity clings to my eyelashes and eyebrows. It covers the city in a not-quite-sheer film of misery. If only I could find something exciting. Today is a shot at that. A better life.

A drop of sweat trickles from my hairline, a slow snake slipping across my forehead, and drips into my eye. I wipe it away with the small square towel with cutesy trees that smile at me. I keep forgetting to change it out. I don't know what's wrong with me. It smells of mildew. Just like the rest of my clothes, my closet, my apartment, all of Tokyo.

One more reason to hate Tokyo's summertime. "Tsuyuu" they call it, which can mean either "plum season" or "season of mildew and mold" depending on which kanji is used.

Unlike loads of other kanji, I understand the reason for this variation perfectly.

I stuff the nasty towel back in the front pocket of my oversized fake leather handbag as I arrive at the front of the station. Finally. I peep in with my green penguin pass card, climb the stairs, and huff as I see my fate laid out before me.

The clock overhead reads five o'clock p.m., dead.

Rush hour.

And, like a typical Monday, the place is jam-packed. Sweaty bodies wall to wall on the platform, crammed against one another's moldy raincoats and damp suit jackets. The train's headlamp strikes the platform through the mist, diffuse and powder pale.

But I, unlike the masses, am not headed home from work. I'm headed out from my home office for a date. With you.

As if cued by the light, the rain starts. A rushing gush like a faucet's been turned on. The train hisses into the station. Wheels whine and scream like angry children as the conductor hits the brakes. Metal wheels grind against the suddenly wet tracks, stuttering to a halt.

I sag. Inside the train, window to window, it's more bodies. Last in line, I pack myself in by grabbing the roof of the train with my fingers and pressing my back against an elderly man and a couple of young kids in school uniforms. Nobody can move.

The doors close across my nose, and I feel like a dead fish in a sealed can. I release myself to the pressure of bodies pressing against me. Conditioned air blows from the maxed-out "airkon" overhead, but by the time it hits me, it's already rank with the tang of sweat. It wraps me in the top of my head and fills my mouth with stale air. The taste of Tokyo in the summertime.

The train lurches into forward and the bodies all sway as one. For the next five minutes, we are all stuck in whatever position we chose. Accidental or not. I distract myself by watching outside as drenched strangers duck under ruined umbrellas turned wholly inside out. Someone discards one with a black handle and clear plastic top into the gutter where it clatters down to join the graveyard of many an umbrella that shared its fate. Broken by Tokyo's relentless summer.

I feel that umbrella's pain.

Everything is soaked from head to toe, down to my underpants. My bag is dripping from the bottom, pitter-patting against my bare ankles. Low pumps and a skirt. What was I thinking? Poor choice for typhoon season. But then, in the torrential downpours of Tokyo's mid-summer, everything feels like a mistake.

Don't even try. Just throw the drenched mildew-ridden towel in.

Finally, the train pulls into my destination: Shibuya Station.

My spirits rise thinking of my sole reason for braving the weather today. Meeting someone genuinely interesting from that wretched dating site my friend dared me to join. I try not to get my hopes up high. A short fling would be nice. Momentary end of isolation. Something new and exciting to mix up the daily humdrum of web design. That'd be a good change.

I disembark and push through the crush, looking out for the yellow 出口 sign that reads "Hachiko" in big fat Roman letters. It's the most stereotypical place in all of the twenty-three wards we could have met, but when you said you wanted to meet, I'd have jumped for anything.

I come up the long set of dripping stairs and out into the open air. The typhoon is still dumping its worst and there's water everywhere. Hachiko Plaza has become a pond. Nobody is there, aside from you.

I instantly recognize you from the picture you texted me. Small and slight, dressed in a long black coat, dark gray and cream lace decorating the hem and sleeves. Knee-high chunky lace-up black boots. A big floppy black hat dripping in more lace covers your face; a strip of pewter-colored chiffon shrouds you in mystery from me.

Very early 1990s Goth. Adorable.

You look my way and wave a gloved hand. Then, you do something crazy. Rip off your hat, crumple it in your hand, and dash toward me. By the time you are at my side, you are drenched from head to toe. Just like me. I bet your underwear is soaked, too.

Not like that, I chide myself and step out, umbrella-less into the day.

You rush up so quick I can't look at your face. Your hand slips effortlessly into mine. A soft round nose nuzzles against my neck and your high, light voice purrs above the roar of the rain.

"Let's go have fun, love!" you say in a shockingly un-Japanese way and I find myself doubting that you are a native-born Tokyo resident.

My blood boils. My stomach goes cold. "O-okay," I stammer helplessly.

You pull me along. By the time we duck out of the rain, we look like two swimmers who've finished a triathlon but forgot to change their clothes. Everything clings. Might as well be naked, I think, and turn red-hot. I try not to stare. You smile like you know my struggle and slide open the narrow glass door to a restaurant whose name I can't see for all the rain and haze.

A tuxedoed maître d' comes rushing up, speaking in high polite Japanese. You don't hesitate to take the lead and ramble back something I have no hope of understanding, which reaffirms your citizenship. Japanese without a question mark.

The maître d' bows low at the waist and lead us to seats. White table cloth. Rose in a crystal vase. Multiple forks of multiple sizes for multiple purposes. I stare not at the table of this ritzy ordeal, but at you.

Your eyes are watch catch me. Black opals steal the light of the room and swallow it, spitting back only mysterious unknown. Your face is softly round, your cheeks high, your lips a thin red-painted line. Mascara exaggerates the upward swoosh of your long, luxurious eyelashes. I could get lost in there, a mysterious forest of black bamboo.

I open my mouth to attempt something clever, but all I can think of is the weather. Then, I recall we've been calling each other by Line user names.

"I'm Sammy," I say. "It's nice to finally meet you...."

"Mikata." You grin devilishly. "And you are far more beautiful than your profile pics."

My blush deepens and all the discomfort of the typhoon melts away.

You reach a thin, delicate hand across the table and take up mine, made of callouses and big bones. You squeeze my palm with impressive strength. "I like you. Let's stick together."

"Okay," I reply without hesitation.

You smile in a way that says my answer means something big.

"I like you, too," I say partly to fill the awkward silence I can feel coming on and partly, I realize, because I mean it. You are something rare, and I don't want to let go.

We polish off our meal and bottle of wine in what feels like the passing of a thought.

My heart sinks when you stand. "Time to go?"

You head shakes, locks of silky black hair dancing about. "No. Tonight is Hanabi."

My eyes light up at the mention of Tokyo's famous summer fireworks show. "I've never seen it."

"I know a place we can get in. Let's go."

I jump up excitedly. "Okay."

Outside, the sky has cleared, but the sun is already slipping below the horizon. The light is turning blue-gray. Post-storm humidity hangs on the horizon, a thin film of the golden light stretching across all of central Tokyo like a dome. We walk the city hand-in-hand while that band of color in the sky turns from gold to orange. The blue dome of the sky deepens toward black, and the handful of city-visible stars come out.

"The fireworks start soon," you say, and duck into a subway station.

I follow blindly, led by the arm. We come out at Kite-sando and head up the crowded street.

Across the city, rooftop pop-up restaurants are jammed wall-to-temporary-wall with people waiting. All of them are standing room only. For the early-comers, there are tables spread with white tablecloths and glasses for wine. As the evening wears on, waiters dressed in long dress-like aprons bring small dishes of a variety of meats, grilled vegetables. For latecomers, there is hours' wait and maybe standing room only.

We didn't come early by any means, yet here we stand inside a ruby-red velveteen rope. Along the far edge of the building where the rope ends, people shift against one another's backs. We lean our bare arms lazily against the concrete ledge of the roof facing the direction the fireworks will come from. Optimal view, this.

From the distant fans, a low breeze sweeps across the roof and attempts to dry our sweaty legs. It catches the edges of both of our short skirts and sends them swaying.

The smell of food is in the air, savory and sweet. A tray of mini pizzas swings by, held high by a waiter dripping in sweat. I feel bad for the staff in this sweltering head. You cock your head at me and beckon the waiter over. I grab two pizzas and pass you one. The waiter wafts off like a melting ghost.

We prop half-full glasses of wine against each other's arms as if we've been together for years. You sip yours just as the first red burst of light fills the sky. Then blue and white. Then, sparkles like a hundred stars. The lights dance across your face lightly, and I see you are frowning instead of smiling.

"What's the matter?"

"I want to tell you something."

"Go ahead," I sip my wine as purple light pops to life and dies out in a stuttering snap of silver and gold.

"I want to protect you, Sammy."

"No need," I say, feeling completely safe beside you on this rooftop.

You darken, leaning against me. "It's a family thing."

"Hm?" I say, distracted by the fireworks and the warmth of the wine.

"We're protectors," you say in a sly way I pretend not to notice. "Some people think we're gangsters, but in reality—"

"Gangsters? Like what, Yakuza?" I joke lightly, popping pepperoni into my mouth.

Your mouth opens but what comes out is swallowed by one of those big loud whizzy screaming hanabi go off. I don't bother to bring the question up again. It was just a joke and I'm having too much fun. You lean your head against my shoulder instead of my chest because we are the same height. I chuckle at how you can't feel my thundering heartbeat, but rather the unshaken structure of my bones. As if I'm holding your head up.

"I'll always come for you," you say, lift your head, and snog my face before I can say anything. And right then, the massive booming finale begins. We get lost in it, in each other, in the night and the tacky summer heat.

Everything is bliss.

Otaru, Winter 2016.

On every surface, snow is piled at least a meter thick. The air is aflutter with big chunky snowflakes. A wind howls and blows snow from nowhere to collect on the already heavy laden branches, walls, ledges of buildings and tops of roofs. Overnight, the small, huddled town of Otaru has been fully converted. The gentle powdered-sugar dusting has become an impenetrable tower of solid ice. Blocks of snow build up mountains out of shrubs, steps, and curbs. The landscape outside the window is treacherous, yes, but beautiful. Washed clean.

Maybe the snow could wash me too. Clear out the clutter of my heart. Clear the past. Make magic happen and let me find you today.

I open the hostel door, take a tentative step out into the entranceway, and am instantly covered in a downy snow. Clumps of snowflakes flutter by my nose, stick to my clothes, and get caught like dewdrops in the exposed locks of my hair. I come back in, slide the ancient wooden door shut, and stand in the semi-warmth of the entranceway thinking of how warm we were two years ago in Tokyo during the hottest, wettest, stickiest summer on record.

"I want to protect you, Sammy," you'd said.

And stupid me threw that away.

I don't even know why I ghosted you. It was so good, the weeks we spent together in your fancy high-rise apartment. Too good. I panicked. And the slow fade-out was all I could think to do to get away.

A blustery gust of wind carries flurries of snow across my face and over my shoulders. I tuck in deeper to my fluffy polyester scarf, knowing full well that as I nestle my nose deep in its warmth, the aging material is abrading into my lungs. Things I try not to think too much about.

Like how childish I was at the end of that summer.

I should have called you. I could have messaged, at least. Explained. Things were moving too fast. My job sucked. I had no money. I wanted to go back home to Hawaii. I didn't see how we could last.

But I didn't know how to say any of that, so I said nothing.

Then, right before summer ended, you messaged me. Said you were going north to escape the heat. You, honest and blunt, told me the truth. This was a test. To see if I loved you or if I had no guts.

You gave me all the details. The day you flew out and how Otaru was the last stop on the only train line that heads from New Chitose Airport. The address of the single hostel in all of the tiny port town would not have been hard to find. The name of your favorite café.

I should have gone. Met you at the train station in Otaru when you arrived. I should have taken the information, bought a ticket, and been there waiting.

I should have saved us.

But, I didn't. Out of some selfish desire to protect myself. At the time, I was less aware than that. I simply didn't respond, bought a different ticket, and shipped off to Hawaii, tail between my legs. Not running but mildly stepping away from the ledge you offered to jump off with me, hand in hand.

Truth? I was scared to death that if I jumped, I'd get swallowed up to my heart and head in love. The real deal, burning bright, the hottest on record in my life.

And then, I sat on the beach in Hawaii for two years and the mistake ate me alive.

So, I'm back now. In Otaru, not Tokyo. And it's winter, not summer.

But I'm trying to do things right. To find you and fix things. Like I should have.

Leaning my forehead against the windowpane of the entrance-way, staring out at the fluttering snow, I find resolve in this little pep talk to myself.

I puff up my chest, shove my hands in my pockets, and slide open the door again. It sticks halfway open and a bluster of snowy wind slaps me in the face. I crystallize against it. I have to get to the Owl Café. It's lunch time and if what you said two years ago is still right, you will be there.

It's worth a shot.

I step out. The chill wind sneaks its fingers under the edge of my coat and tickles my waist. Ahead of me, caught in updrafts from a vent, snow tussles about and drifts back lazily to the ground. My feet make soft crunching sounds as I trudge across the street and down a series of stone steps that have become a steep slope indented hundreds of times with the hammers of boots and dogs' feet.

Up ahead, the red glowing paper lantern of where I'm headed. Painted in wide black brush strokes is the shop's name in kanji, which I can't read. If the shop's name were something easy to memorize like 田 (ta) or 山 (yama), I'd stand a chance. But "owl" is a complicated series of harried strokes my eyes can't make heads or tails of.

If asked, I'd describe the big paper lantern instead. The doorway made of uneven sanded-down logs, and the rope-wrapped glass orbs lined up. The wrinkled and peeling laminated paper menu tacked up to the wall of rough logs.

Outside, the café has a hodgy-podgy look. It seems popular here in the rustic, down-to-earth port town. Whether it's a lack of resources or indigenous influence that creates the differences, I haven't figured out. But from what I see in photographs, all the buildings around Hokkaido are mottled, pressboard and clay, pasteboard and exposed screws. Logs, some sanded and some with the bark on, make up the majority of small mundane things. Door handles and toilet paper holders.

Owl Café is no exception.

I put my hand on a pale, knotty, sanded log and push open the waxed pasteboard door. In the entranceway, there are blue glass orbs of a variety of sizes balanced on trunks of the same pale wood, more set about at random on the floor, and still more hanging from dusty ropes overhead. I slide open the inner door of glass and blackened wood.

Inside is a cozy room with six well-used wooden tables and chairs of various shapes and sizes. Some are rusty metal, some wooden with crushed velvet cushions. One is subtly curved with a low-rising back that curves ergonomically. A perfect fit. I head for it and the small square table it sits in front of.

At a long, rugged but lovingly used bar, the owner stands dressed in long sleeves and puffy down vest, face hidden behind a white mask. The owner eyes me, then dawdles. Shifting containers of coffee beans, wiping off the bar, arranging a stack of papers. Finally, with nothing left to do, the owner pads over and sets a glass of water before me.

"*Ira shai ma se,*" a high polite voice sings out from behind a white medical mask.

"*Arigato go zaimasu,*" I say in a spot-on accent.

The look of relief is immediate and the shop owner launches into the usual spiel of daily *o su su me* specials and what coffee is currently roasting. I already smell the hints of the Columbian beans caramelizing. It is less the scent of coffee and more like bread toasting. I nod happily, breathing it in and taking the cardboard menu written in ink pens and covered in cartoon stickers. I open it and feel an inward glow as the words come easily to me.

I'm just about to call out to have my order taken when the door chime goes off.

Someone steps in loudly, letting in a flurry of snow with them. I feel a rush of embarrassment for the outsider who's made a silly but rude mistake. I turn to look out of curiosity and my belly fills with butterflies.

"Sammy?" you gasp breathlessly, closing a black and cream lace-covered umbrella speckled with melting snowflakes. Still early 1990s Goth. Amazing.

"Mikata," I gasp back. I'm caught between relief, excitement at the unexpected realization of my dream, and embarrassment that I've just associated you with an outsider who can't figure out how to close a Japanese door.

You rush over to my table, clonking across the floor in the same old chunky high heel boots. I'd have thought you'd break an ankle on these icy streets. Apparently not.

"What are you doing in Otaru?" You pull up a velvet cushioned chair and sit without the hesitation I'd feel in your position. Old ghost of a lover turning up out of nowhere appearing to read a menu in your indecipherable native tongue.

I can't bring myself to say the truth, so I come up with a lame excuse. "Vacation."

"Ha, me too."

"What?" I ask, confused.

"What what?" you prod. Never one for manners, you were.

"I-I don't know. I'd gotten the impression you lived here now."

"No, silly. I still live in the insufferable mess of Tokyo. But lucky you. I'm here for a week or two. My brother is getting married. Finally."

"Makoto? Isn't he younger than you?" I ask, challenging that "finally." A very traditional concept for you. I find that strange.

"Yes, but he's big bother."

I don't really know what that means, but it sounds sexist. I cringe openly to make a point. "Shouldn't you be married too, then?"

You grin bigger than I thought you could. "Yes, in fact. Thanks for asking."

"No, I—" I jump up, knocking over the small low-backed chair. From the bar, the owner looks up, concerned.

"*Ah, sumimasen,*" I blunder. "*Gomen'nasai. Ano...*"

You laugh lightly, waving a hand in my direction. "*Sumimasen. Kyo, kanojo to atta no wa hisashi buri no de hontoni bikurisugimashite, gomennasai.*"

"*Iie iie,*" the shop owner says with a laugh, meaning *Oh, it's all right,* basically.

The two of you ramble in Japanese too fluent and too quick for my ears to pick up. So, I sit back and think. What in hell am I going to do now? Ask if we can spend the day together? Confess my feelings and get that rip-the-bandage-off feeling over with? Say nothing and just see where things go?

I rule that last one out. I've spent enough time in my life drifting. That's how I lost you the first time. Given this outlandish second chance, that's about the last thing in the known universe I'm going to do.

What then?

"So." You turn back to me in perfect English. "I was thinking we could have a snack and then go for a stroll? I'd love to catch up."

"I was going to ask you the same thing."

You laugh and swat at my hand. "No, you weren't, Sammy. You never do things like that."

"I was, actually," I say seriously, and begin planning how to tell you the whole truth in a way that doesn't sound bonkers. That I came looking for you and you walking into this café was chance, maybe, but I had put all my bets on it. I knew in my gut it would work. Even if I had to come back a million times.

You stop laughing, lean across the table, and get your nose close to mine. I almost lean away out of instinct, remind myself why I'm here, and lean in closer so the tips of our noses snog for a brief second. You don't pull away either and we stay like that for a minute without words. Just sitting, connected.

"I believe you," you say in a husky way.

I grin and it pushes our noses closer, making the mash-up a

little uncomfortable. Which gives me a really out-there idea. "I wish we weren't in public," I say.

You sigh, your breath smells like caramelized sugar and it's delicious. "Why is that?"

"Because..." I lick my lips. "Then I would ask if I could kiss you."

"Ask anyway."

"I..." I can't do it. Not in public. Not with the owner who we've both already offended looking on. No way.

"The owner's gone to run an errand. I said we could wait. We're alone."

"Oh..."

"So what are you waiting for?"

"Nothing," I say and lean in, mouth barely parted.

Our lips meet and it's utter blistering joy.

Heat bursts like a bomb inside my mouth, my belly, my heart. I feel as though I'm glowing. Embers of excitement washed in the fuel of relief. I could swear the snow outside is melting and trees are turning green. Flowers blooming. Life bursting forth from every nook and crevice of the room. The summer harvest is coming.

You pull away and the winter crashes back into me. Leaves turn, fall, die in wet gutters. The sky goes from bright white to cynical dark gray. The rain comes. The snow. Ice clings to everything, and I am back in my isolation again.

I look longingly into the black ovals of your eyes. Each is a dancing kaleidoscope of light from icicles, paper lanterns, the glowing woodstove fire behind me. Each light twirls in perfect alignment, following choreographed steps weaving a masterful spell. But I can't tell if it's being cast on me or you.

Which of us is the better liar? Me with my innocence or you with whatever your secret magic is?

Your soft, delicate hand with bones like porcelain reaches out across the worn-out slats of wood. I reach back, my thick hand careful not to crush you. You smile up at me with your stencil-thin ruby-red lips. I smile back, my thick bottom lip pursing and pouting like it does whenever I'm aroused.

Your laugh is the bashful giggle of women in your culture. Mine is throaty and deep, a wave thrashing against a jagged volcanic coast. It becomes the roll of thunder in an oncoming storm tumbling landward off the coast of Kancohe Bay. A crashing clapping boom of mirth from the throat of my people generations back.

You stand. "Let's get out of here."

"But we haven't even ordered."

"So?"

"I..." I don't have an answer to that.

"It seems rude?" You peak an elegant eyebrow at me.

I nod slowly.

"Besides, I already apologized," you explain.

I start, shocked.

"What?" you huff, a hand on your hip as you pull me up from the chair.

"That's not the Mikata I recall."

You blush and run thin fingers through your silken midnight hair. "The Mikata you remember is two years changed, Sammy."

I nod. "And so is the Sammy you knew. It's just Sam now."

You turn toward the door without pause. "I can tell. You look different."

"Different bad?" I pull on a strand of my hair as if tugging it will make it long enough to hide behind. Old habit. Back when I had light brown hair down to my elbows, a place to hide was the only thing that matted mess was good for.

"Not bad. Still beautiful," you say gently.

I blush deeper, tug more.

"Stop it," you say in a firm voice that stills me.

I put my hands in my pockets instead, hunching my shoulders.

"And bundle up. It is winter out there, you know."

"I know," I say and think: yeah, but it's summer in my heart.

We step outside. There is a blast of freezing air that whisks the warmth right off my skin. Below zero Celsius, without a doubt. And despite all the warmth inside, I'm snapped back to reality. To the winter. To the reason I've come "on vacation" to Otaru.

I steal a glance at you. Our eyes meet for a brief second and I realize I have no idea what you're thinking.

The cold is a reminder to be awake and wary. The snow, a reminder of how cold I behaved in leaving you. A warning that I may not be able to melt the ice that could be packed around your heart, for all I know. It's not like I ever asked.

Even now, I've made no mention of my intentions. No motion at apologizing. Nothing. I'm playing cool tourist with a clear record. A block of ice in my own way. It's not on purpose; I just can't help but feel like you already know my heart. But that's not fair. Maybe not even possible. I try to catch your eye again to see what you might be thinking. But you've put your hood up and all I see is fur collecting bits of snow. I tuck my scarf into the collar of my coat and, shivering, pull up my own hood. I think to reach for the crook of your arm, but the wind is sucking the warmth from my fingers like the summer sun strips layers of a Popsicle. So, instead of reaching out, I stuff both hands into my pockets.

You glance my way, eyes hidden under your halo of fur and shadow. But I see enough to see your playful grin as you pull a hand from your pocket, reach out, and tuck your hand into the crook of my arm. The warmth of summer returns, flushing my hands and cheeks. Bolstered by the warmth, I clamp my arm down on your gloved hand, hoping my warmth seeps to your fingers through all our combined layers. I feel a squeeze back and think maybe, in a metaphorical sense, it has. Smiling across at you through a thin wisp of snow, I promise myself again that I'm not going to just drift about anymore.

"I owe you an apology," I say quietly.

You don't miss a beat. "Yes, you do. *Douzo.*" Meaning, *go ahead,* or better translated in this case: *please.*

"I'm sorry."

I feel your fingers tighten through the down and polyester shell of my coat. "I forgave you two years ago."

"Why?" I miss a step and fall behind you ever so slightly.

You pull me back up to speed. "Isn't it obvious?"

"It's not," I admit.

Your laugh is like warm oil poured into my aching, wind-battered ears. "I love you too."

Silence fills the gap between us. It's not uncomfortable and empty, but safe and full. A wholeness that the snow, the wind, the chill can't steal. You move to close the space and lay your head on me. If I were a handful of centimeters taller, it'd be my chest and you'd feel my heartbeat hammering for you. But it's not and so maybe you feel nothing but my bones. The structure that holds me up. I think that's pretty fitting.

"I have my own confession to make," you whisper into my armpit.

"What is it?" I say, unworried.

"The thing about my brother getting married. I lied."

"Your brother isn't getting married?"

"He is, but it's not why I came."

"Then why?"

"Because the hostel manager rang me the day you booked your trip."

"You knew I was looking for you?"

"No. I only hoped."

I breathe out, relieved I wasn't the only one making wildly poor choices based on flimsy thin dreams. "It's okay."

"There's more. I told my brother I'd bring you."

"Hm?" I hum, confused.

"He wants to meet you. All of them do."

"Your family? But...Mikata. The marriage thing—it was a joke. I'm not ready for..." I stammer, the chill of worry creeping in through narrow cracks in my defenses. The last thing I'm ready for is standing up to a traditional family and explaining that their beautiful daughter wants to marry me of all people. Foreign. Poor. Not a man.

You pull away, head shaking. "That's not the reason."

"What then?"

"My brother can explain better than I can."

"Okay." I give in rather than fight. What harm can it do? "Let's go."

We walk to the front of an old ragged warehouse right on the other side of the ocean. Across the bridge to our left, a road leads to the port where boats will be loaded and unloaded in the morning. For now, the town is closing up shop. I glance at my watch. It's barely past four thirty and already the sun is setting. I look up and stare at the warehouse doors. The wood is peeling, the lock is rusted on. On the three floors above our heads, all the windows are boarded up.

"This place looks shut down," I say as if you haven't noticed.

"It's not," you say, and approach a smaller door I hadn't noticed off to the right.

The door creaks open on wobbly rusted hinges. From inside, there is the surprising salty savory smell of yakiniku—grilling meat on an open fire. A gentle, light smoke wafts toward us, sucked outside by the draft our opening this door has created. Across the darkness, there is the sound of shuffling and a jumble of sounds I know must be Japanese. I don't catch a word of it. You go ahead of me, boldly strutting across to the dim orange glow tucked in a far corner. The hard clack of your heavy heeled boots echoes across the room. My shoes, softer soled, tacka-tack along at a shorter, quicker pace. Even from the echoes, I can tell you are confident and I am nervous.

"Mikata!" calls a sharp, middle-range voice. I can't tell if it's your brother or not. We met once in that legendary summer, but both face and voice disappeared from my memory like a photograph left out in the sun for years.

"*Hai! Mikata da. Samu mo iru yo.*" You announce both of our presences.

"*Kuru zo*." Come.

We go hand-in-hand toward the fire, crossing complaining slats of ancient blackened wood. Several soft spots threaten to give out under us. I trip right as you swing gaily into the firelight. It bursts upon your skin like a wave, lighting up every feature with a splash, foaming away in dim shadows. Your hood falls back, face revealed in full for the first time since our mutual confession. Cheeks cherry-red, lips smiling, eyes staring straight ahead.

I follow your gaze to a short guy with long black hair down to the elbows. Rivers of blue-black that end in shores of bleached white-blond. Piercing blue eyes that must be contacts stare ice cold, not at you, but me. I look down at my shoes and notice how dirty they are. How tired and worn.

"You're late," Makoto says in a sharp British accent.

"*Un, gomen'na*," you say in a traditionally mannish way. Claiming strength in the face of Makoto and the rest of these...cronies, I can't help but think.

I feel my confidence shrink even more when Makoto takes a step in my direction. "Sammy, is it?"

"S-sam," I manage to croak out.

A hand clamps on the soft spot of my neck like jaws of a pit bull. I'm worried Makoto will never let go until I've bled out. "Mikata explained?"

"Uh," I say, and look to you for instruction, but you've left my side to grill skewers of meat like we're at a friend's Sunday picnic. I blink, shrink even further into myself, and shift. Makoto's hand tightens on my neck and I inadvertently twitch. Pressure points.

"No. Of course she didn't. Look." Makoto uses the grip to steer me away from the fire. Away from the warmth that had just begun to thaw my fingers, nose, toes. Away from the light and into the darkness of the decaying room.

I sniffle and my nose is filled with mildew and mold. Despite being cold and scared and alone, I'm reminded of that jam-packed rush hour train two years ago from Harajuku to Shibuya the day we first met. The smell is almost identical, and I remember not my disgust at the weather—but my delight at having you in my arms.

"I want you to protect her." Makoto's voice bites my ear, and I'm back in the warehouse again, shivering.

"Okay," I say. That doesn't sound so bad. It also doesn't require a warehouse and secret meetings in the dark. *So what else is going on?* I don't have the bravery to ask.

"It's complicated," Makoto goes on for my benefit.

"H-how so?"

"Mikata's in trouble."

"With?" I'm thinking credit card debt. A bad bet. Things I can't do anything about.

"Arranged marriage."

"I..." I can't believe what I'm hearing.

"So here's the plan. You take her to...where is it you're from? Hawaii?"

"Honolulu, to be exact."

"Good. You take her to Honolulu. You can get married there?"

"Y-yes."

"Then do. After, send her back with the...how do you say...the receipt?"

"Certificate."

"She shows it to her dad. The arrangement is off. Nothing he can do. Then, you two do what you want. Stay here. Move to Hawaii. Don't care."

"I..." I still can't believe what I'm hearing. "You want me to marry Mikata so that she doesn't have to marry someone else?"

"Yes. A real bad guy. You protect her. *Mamoru no tame.* You understand?"

Literally the words mean: *for the benefit of protecting.* "Yes," I say.

"Good. Then you agree?"

I can think of a million reasons why I should say no. And a million reasons why this will never work. But I can also think of a million reasons why I want to say yes—only, I wish it could have been more romantic. Candles and roses instead of a dirty old warehouse and mildew mixed with meat smoke. But here I am and there you are, across the darkness, flipping over little skewers of meat dripping in thick brown sauce. One of them catches fire and your lips, lit from underneath by the blue flame, pucker so beautifully and blow it out like you are kissing the air.

And the flame you kill on the meat jumps to my heart and burns me up. All I want in the world is for your lips to blow on me like that. Like you are kissing my flaming heart. I try to imagine myself saying no, returning to my hostel alone. And in the morning, trudging solo through knee-deep snow to Otaru station, boarding a plane, and stepping out into the tropical balmy warmth of Hawaii without your hand in mine.

And I can't do it. I can't see it. I can't say no. I can't drift off and disappear from your life. Even if it means the most ridiculous situation in all the world—I'd rather say yes than lose you.

"Yes," I say finally.

"Yes?" Makoto repeats with a piercing look. It goes right through me like a blade of blue ice.

"Yes."

"Then you are family." Makoto grabs me and wraps me in a hug that I don't expect. I stumble, foot catching on a loose floorboard, and bring us to the ground. The ruckus stirs the pot of others at the fire cooking. There's shouts in Japanese, and I don't need to know the words to know their angry. Feet rushing. The sound of... is that metal? Chains? Guns being cocked?

And then, it hits me.

"Your family...you are Yakuza," I blather stupidly, thinking only: real bad people.

Makoto laughs, slapping me across the back and pushing off my spine to stand up. "*Dai jou bu, dai jou bu!*" he calls, saying everything is fine. "We are not bad like you think. We protect our own from the bad ones. You understand?"

"Yes," I say shakily, but I'm unsure.

"Good." And Makoto calls out more stuff in rushed (angry?) Japanese.

The ruckus of weapons and feet rushing to kill me stop. More rushed Japanese with loads of slang that I don't catch a word of. Everyone seems to go back to what they were doing. Eating, cooking, drinking, muttering about killing people or something.

I lay there, shivering. Terrified.

Makoto stands over me, reaching down. Beside him, you've appeared in a glowing glory that makes my chest tighten. Gangsters or not, how could I have said no? Isn't this what I came here for? Isn't this everything I want?

"I want to protect you, Sammy," you said two years ago.

Maybe I didn't know what that meant. Maybe I was too scared to ask. But now? I wouldn't have it any other way.

I take Makoto's hand and stand.

"I want to protect you, Mikata," I say, reaching for you.

You come easily into my arms, and we sink deep into an all-encompassing kiss like it's the most natural thing we could do. I can feel you smiling, sly and dark, against my lips. I press into you until I feel your teeth against mine. Our mouths pressed together are wet and hot and we are stuck together. Just like in Tokyo, midsummer.

Everything is bliss.

TOTALITY

KRISTINE KATHRYN RUSCH

I write the bulk of my fiction under the name Kristine Kathryn Rusch. I usually reserve Kristine Grayson for goofy fantasy romance. When I thought of contributing a story to this volume, Grayson tales just didn't fit.

That's okay. I spent part of 2018 finishing a new Kristine Grayson novel, Hidden Charm, *which appears about the same time as this volume. Kristine Kathryn Rusch has a new novel,* The Renegat, *set in her Diving universe that will appear in September. I also write as Kris Nelscott.*

If you find the pen names hard to keep up with, think how I feel. Or maybe go to kriswrites.com to see what's happening next in my life.

Sometimes what is happening in my life influences my fiction. The events of my life certainly influenced "Totality," which takes place during the last full solar eclipse. It hit landfall in the U.S. in the tiny Oregon Coast town that I lived in at the time, and the creepy drive at the beginning of the story actually occurred.

The rest of the story didn't, though, and is strictly a product of my imagination. I think....

They stepped out of the fog like androids from a bad science fiction movie. Regular people, wearing weird glasses, staring up at the sky to the east, the fog ebbing and flowing around them like it did every August morning on the Oregon Coast.

Tia Catrone tried not to look at them, tried not to think about them, but she couldn't avoid it. The highway was mostly empty—everyone was in place for the massive solar eclipse—except her and a black 4x4 with California plates.

The Californians were trying to find a place out of the fog, so they could see the eclipse. They were weaving all over the highway like crazy people, trying to find a road that would take them farther east, into the promised sunshine.

Apparently no one had told them about the likelihood that the morning eclipse would be obscured by fog. No one had told all the other people lined up on the sidewalks, backs to the ocean, looking expectantly at the sky.

To be fair, the sun had come out earlier. But as the temperature dropped, the early morning fog had returned.

Not that Tia cared—or rather, not that she cared the way everyone did. She kept glancing at the clock, hoping she could find her sister Joyce before totality.

Joyce was off her meds and in the middle of a breakdown. Tia could only hope that Joyce wasn't seeing this—the confused driving, the strange people with their eclipse glasses stepping out of the fog—because Joyce really would think that the people were androids or maybe aliens disguised as humans, trying to take over the world.

And then the eclipse...Joyce might see that as something supernatural as well.

Totality would happen in forty-five minutes.

Tia was trying hard not to panic. She had been so nasty to her brother for losing Joyce a week ago. Then Joyce had showed up on Tia's doorstep and Tia thought everything would be all right. She begged for a few days off work to get Joyce level. Then Tia got Joyce to the local hospital, reinstated her meds—

And Joyce slipped away, before dawn, and Tia hadn't noticed.

She had known that Joyce's disease made her both paranoid and cunning; somehow Tia had thought she could deal with it on her own—at least until her brother arrived.

And they had decided he wouldn't arrive to take Joyce back to the resident care facility (*Mental hospital*, Tia thought. *It was a mental hospital. Just call it what it was*) until Eclipse Day passed.

Eclipse Day. A nightmare in and of itself.

The entire state of Oregon had gone into a panic. The total eclipse, which would cross the United States in less than ninety minutes, hit landfall in Seavy Village first. Every official and expert on eclipses had predicted that the tiny coastal towns would get overrun with tourists, but so far, it had been a bust.

Hardly anyone was here. Most of the tourists had all gone to the high deserts of Central Oregon, where sunshine was guaranteed.

Totality would occur at about 10:15, and Tia couldn't be driving then. Those warnings she *had* heard. They said that people would stop in the middle of the road and look up and you wouldn't be able to see them in the dark and there would be bad accidents.

Although if the total eclipse mimicked night, then she had no idea why she wouldn't see anything. Her car's lights would go on, and she would drive as if darkness fell.

But she was going to heed the warnings, just because the last thing she needed was to get into a car accident.

The last thing she needed was to lose track of her sister too.

Although she had. And it hadn't even been hard.

Joyce had slipped off the limited cellphone watch that Tia had given her for Christmas. Joyce had shut the watch off completely the first time she had gone missing, but she had been in a different stage of her disease at that point.

The cunning stage. She had thought that their brother Howard was going to hurt her, so she shut off the watch. He couldn't track her easily, and he hadn't called the cell phone company to see if he could get help.

Tia had been about to do that when Joyce had knocked on her door, with a tale of harrowing escapes and possible murder.

All of that could have been true or none of it. Joyce was slipping into the hallucination/paranoia part of her disease. Apparently she hadn't been medicating for at least a week.

The hospital emergency room had given her a few shots, and Joyce had slept. But they hadn't administered the regular medication, giving Tia the pills instead.

Tia gave them to Joyce, but Joyce hadn't taken them. After Joyce had disappeared that morning, Tia had found a Kleenex with slightly dissolved pills in the middle of the whiteness.

Joyce had pretended to swallow, then spit them out when Tia left her alone.

Tia had trusted too much, and now Joyce was missing. On a day that could send her over the edge completely.

Tia was driving south. She was just relying on instinct now, instinct and past experience. Joyce loved the bay, and the bay was walking distance from Tia's house.

No one near Tia's house had seen Joyce. Tia had let the police know as well as the volunteer fire department. But they had initiated emergency protocols (expecting hundreds of thousands of tourists, when there were actually fewer than a normal summer weekend), and informed her—because of those protocols—that they couldn't do an all-out search.

So she was on her own.

And worried.

And scared.

And wishing she knew what to do.

Bryce Walker stepped onto the deck of his oceanfront hotel suite. The deck faced west, since most people who came to the Oregon Coast wanted to see the ocean. Ironic that today, everyone wanted to look east.

The ocean was invisible today. He could hear it shush-shushing but could not see it. It was enshrouded in fog.

He knew there were people below him. He could hear them when the partial eclipse began. They all gasped audibly—something he had heard a dozen times before.

It didn't matter how many times people saw videos of an eclipse, viewing one for the first time—even a partial—was awe-inspiring.

Not that he felt like being inspired.

If asked, he would say he was here by accident, although that really wasn't true. He was drawn to an eclipse, even when he really didn't want to see it.

And as a result, he was staying in the most expensive hotel on this part of the Oregon Coast. He had told himself that it would be a treat to stay here once he turned in the final draft of his book. He wrote nonfiction about science for the masses, mostly science history dressed up as escapism.

He'd wanted to escape this last book. He'd thought a history of the cosmos would be fun—he would cover everything from Ptolemaic astronomy to Galileo—but it had turned out to be the hardest thing he had ever done.

Too broad a subject made it hard to tell an actual story. In the end, he had used the trip as a goal just to get pages done. Every day had become a drudgery, and he had promised himself that he wouldn't work once he arrived here—which was easier said than done.

The next book intrigued him. He was just beginning the in-depth research stage. This book catered to his strengths. It would combine the stories of Marie Curie, the Nobel prize, radioactivity, and x-rays. With some World War I thrown in.

He could tell an actual story with that.

Maybe that was why he was reluctant to look to the skies. He'd spent too much time examining the heavens for his previous book. And for a few books before that.

The balcony was chilly cold. The fog was a wet fog that smelled of the sea, and left water droplets on the plastic furniture covering the balcony's concrete expanse. Even the railing—also concrete— was damp beneath his touch.

He stared at the wall of seething gray before him. Occasionally, he could see the beach, with a handful of people standing stubbornly in the sand, looking east.

He was probably the only person in the path of totality in the entire United States who was stubbornly looking west, avoiding the sun as it "disappeared" behind the moon.

But he hadn't come here for the eclipse. He had seen several solar eclipses. Solar eclipses that were visible from somewhere on land occurred once every eighteen months or so, and he had gone to a variety of places including New Zealand, Turkey, and South Africa to see total solar eclipses.

On those trips, the journey had been at least as important as the few minutes of totality. Maybe even more important.

And, much as he loved his country, he didn't feel the same excitement about traveling to some remote region of North America to watch the sky turn dark. He also didn't want to sit in a football stadium or some other manmade place to watch the eclipse with a whole bunch of newbies.

He'd burned out on solar eclipses when he'd written a book on the history of the 1918 eclipse here in the States, using that total eclipse to explain the science of eclipses and how eclipses had changed the way humans saw themselves and the earth. That book had hit the stands in June and was currently sitting in the top ten of the nonfiction bestseller list.

If he were being honest with himself (and sometimes that was hard), he was here to hide from the inevitable interviews about eclipse-watching that the pundits wanted. If he had gone to the Central Oregon desert, the pundits probably would have tracked him down. He hadn't let anyone know he was coming here, and he wasn't answering numbers he didn't know on his cell phone either.

The sky was slowly growing darker. At some point, he would make his way down to the ground floor and join the handful of people praying the fog would let up. He would stare east for around two minutes, experience totality again, and then go back to his room.

Not truly exciting, but he wasn't blowing off the eclipse entirely that way either.

He had a pile of cheap eclipse glasses on the dining room table here in the suite. He had handed some out the night before, and he would hand out a few more when he went downstairs. More people lost eyesight *after* totality than before, because they missed the timing. They would be staring at the sun/moon/darkness of the totality, and then the sun would start reasserting itself, and the eye damage would be done.

He would harangue a few people, get back in touch with his geek-self, and then return to the room and start a rather intriguing-looking tome about Marie Curie and intellectual property. When he started a new project, he always read other people's biographies and histories first, just so that he knew what was out there.

He sighed, and checked his watch. More than forty minutes to totality. He wasn't sure he wanted to stand with strangers for that long in the chill.

Then a movement caught his eye.

A woman ran across the beach, tripping and stumbling as if she was in a panic. She moved in and out of the billows of fog—for a moment he could see her, and then in another moment, he couldn't. But he had a sense of her movement—west, away from the eclipse, and toward the ocean itself.

Something about her worried him. Then, as she emerged from another fog-cloud, he saw why.

She wasn't dressed for this weather. She was wearing a skirt and a sleeveless top, dressed for summer ten miles away, outside of the ocean's influence. Everywhere else in Oregon today it would be at least eighty degrees, but here, in the fog, it was barely fifty-five.

She staggered toward the waterline, and for a moment, he was afraid she would blunder into the ocean fully clothed. When she reached the wet sand, a wave retreated, and she fell to her knees. Then she put her face in her hands, her shoulders shaking as if she were sobbing.

His stomach twisted. Something was very wrong here, and he wasn't sure what it was. But her behavior was at odds with the morning, the weather—everything.

The fog closed in over her again, and he could no longer see her. For a moment, he was torn—should he remain up here and call hotel security, have them get her away from the water?

Then he realized hotel security probably had nothing to do with the beach. Plus, they probably had their hands full, even though the tourists weren't thick on the ground at the moment.

He spun, let himself back inside the room, grabbed his rain

shell, his cell phone, and a handful of eclipse glasses. As he headed out of the room, he made sure he had his key (he did), and then he ran to the stairway.

He wasn't sure exactly what made him feel so urgent, but he didn't care. He needed to act, not think. He would rather be wrong than realize later his hesitation had prevented him from saving a life.

Joyce wasn't near the bay—hardly anyone was. The fog was so thick there that Tia had barely been able to see her hand in front of her face.

But a local walking his dog claimed to have seen Joyce. The local held his eclipse glasses in his right hand as he talked to Tia, but the poor dog had the glasses tied to its little face. Good dog that it was, it didn't try to paw the glasses off.

Tia didn't even ask about that, when she normally would have. Instead, she asked the man which way Joyce had gone.

He pointed north, and said she had gone along the beach.

The problem was that the shoreline curved here. Someone running along the beach would get to a spate of hotels and tourist attractions within minutes.

Tia had to drive. The highway would take her over the largest hill in town, and then drop her on the other side, effectively adding nearly two miles to her trip.

But she couldn't drive along the beach, especially in this weather.

She would go to the Baywater Resort at the top of the hill, and see if she could see anyone on the beach. The Baywater was eleven stories tall. It would give her a panoramic view of the beach—if the fog cleared.

She had pulled back on the highway in time to see a few more cars with foreign plates try to head east. The fog was even thicker than it had been before.

She glanced at the clock—only ten minutes since the last time she checked, although it felt like hours.

Tia drove carefully to the top of the hill. It felt like she had entered a cloud. The fog was now so thick she couldn't see more than a few feet ahead of her. She knew where to turn to get into the Baywater's parking lot because she knew what the symbols painted on the road meant. She had worked at the Baywater she first moved here, and she could essentially reach it by braille.

She needed to be careful, though. The driveway to the resort itself went steeply downhill, and if the previous few blocks were any indication, the handful of stupid tourists that were on the coast would be blocking sidewalks, driveways, and entrances into parking lots.

Still, Tia didn't see anyone up here, probably because the fog was so very thick. She bumped over the edge of the driveway and circled down, unsurprised to see the parking spaces in front of the Baywater's entrance empty.

The Baywater was white brick with pinkish trim. It had been built onto the side of the cliff. Its entrance was on the ninth floor, so that arriving guests could see the view of the ocean as they entered. The dining area and some function space took the tenth floor, and a handful of penthouse suites covered the eleventh.

Because she had gone down a few feet, the fog wasn't quite as thick. But it really was getting dark.

And cold.

And Joyce had left without her coat. Without a sweater. Without anything, really, except the clothes she had worn the night before.

Tia shivered as she got out of the car. She ran down the stairs to the lobby entrance, bursting inside, and startling no one. The reception desk was empty, a sign near a gigantic metal bell saying *Ring For Service*. A sticky note had been attached: *Watching the eclipse. Let us know if you need anything!!!*

The three exclamation points meant that Louise was on duty.

Louise would have let Tia know if Joyce had come inside—if Louise had seen her, that is.

Tia ran across the lobby to the floor-to-ceiling windows.

She could just barely see the beach. The sky was whitish-gray almost to the water's edge, the ocean lost in fog and twilight darkness. The beach itself looked hazy, indistinct, something she had seen a thousand times on a foggy day, but today it seemed ominous. She couldn't even see the two-story rocks that stood like guardians on either edge of the Baywater's somewhat secluded beach.

Then the fog parted just a little, and she saw people below, looking up—those pod people with their glasses. They were facing slightly southeast so that they could see what there was of the sun between the rocks of the cliff face.

Movement caught her eye. A man was sprinting across the beach, heading directly toward the ocean. He was waving one of his hands, and holding something in the other one.

She squinted, frowned, tried to see what he was doing. A woman was walking into the water—a woman of Joyce's height, and Joyce's weight.

Tia didn't need confirmation. Joyce had often said she thought the best way to die would be to drown in this ocean. Howard and Tia would argue with her—reminding her that the ocean was ice-cold, the riptides wicked, and even then it might take twenty minutes to freeze to death or sink beneath the surface.

But Joyce had it in her head—even when she was somewhat lucid—that dying here would be noble somehow.

Tia tore around the lobby's overstuffed chairs, and ran past the elevators. They were slow. She needed to get to beach level fast. She took the concrete staircase two steps at a time, hands on the railing so she wouldn't trip, and prayed that the door to the beach level was unlocked.

She was gasping for air by the time she had gone down all nine flights. She slammed her hands against the steel bar holding the door closed, and the door banged open.

She was on the patio, near the pool, which was sending heated ripples into the foggy air. She ran past the empty lounge chairs to the beach access, ran down the five stairs, into a well of fog.

Her eyes teared up. She couldn't see anything, and she knew better than to yell. Yelling at Joyce only made her more paranoid.

"Please go away, please go away," Tia said to the fog. But it billowed around her, incredibly cold and smelling of brine.

She ran toward the water's edge, where she thought the man had gone, and hoped against hope she was heading to the right place.

The woman was already in the water when Bryce reached her. The gray water snaked around her bare feet, sometimes caressing her calves. She was staring at the nonexistent horizon and he knew, somehow, she was thinking of swimming out there—toward the nothingness.

Bryce was only a few steps behind her now. The water came up to his Nikes, and they would probably get soaked in a few minutes.

He didn't care. This woman clearly needed help.

The fog split just a little, and the tiny group of eclipse watchers behind him oohed their appreciation. The woman winced, as if the sound had hurt her, and for a moment, he thought she was going to plunge deeper into the water.

He wasn't sure how to reach her, exactly. That same helpless feeling he'd had throughout his teenage years rose again. His brother Frank had started hallucinating his last year in high school. Their parents blamed street drugs, which had probably triggered his schizophrenia early, but hadn't caused it. No one helped Frank, no one could talk him down, except Bryce, two years younger and completely inexperienced.

By the time Frank got diagnosed...

Bryce put that away. This woman was not Frank. This woman was someone else, someone in trouble. Maybe she was just depressed. (*Just* depressed. As if there should be a *just* before the word *depressed* ever.) But depressed people were usually rational, at least.

And something about this woman's posture had reminded him of Frank, something had made Bryce think she wasn't quite rational.

Even a depressed person would look at the sky right now, wouldn't they?

Still, Bryce was going to treat her the way he used to treat Frank.

"Hey," Bryce said quietly. "I have your glasses. You forgot them."

The woman stiffened, but didn't turn around. She hadn't known he was there. He had clearly startled her.

"You're going to need them," he said in that same quiet reasonable tone.

She didn't move, but he knew she had heard him. He also knew now that she wasn't "just" depressed. She was like Frank, somehow. Something was going wrong in her brain.

Bryce's heart pounded.

No one else seemed to notice the woman. No one else knew she was in trouble.

He was her last best hope.

And he didn't even know her name.

The fog parted just enough that Tia could see a man standing on the wet sand, something in his left hand. He was not that tall, but athletically thin, and he wasn't dressed for the beach. He wore a white shirt (which was partly how she could see him) sleeves rolled up, jeans, and Nikes that were starting to get soaked.

He wasn't wearing eclipse glasses. He was looking toward the ocean, and in a surprising gesture, reached his right hand out as if he were trying to appeal to someone. Then the hand fell to his side.

He had brown hair in need of a trim, a prominent nose, and a narrow jawline. From the side he looked completely unfamiliar, yet she recognized his expression.

Muted panic. A helplessness that came when there was no good way to help.

The fog billowed around him like a lover. Tia looked toward the water, and there, her back to the entire continent, stood Joyce.

She was going to drown herself. And this poor man had no idea what he was up against.

Tia did, and even she didn't know what to do about it. She could swim. She used to work as a lifeguard a hundred years ago in college. She also knew how to deal with riptides, essential to anyone here on the Oregon Coast.

But this was Joyce, who wanted to die; Joyce who had proven how strong she could be in previous episodes. Joyce, who could, with the wrong movement, kill anyone who tried to help her.

If she was in the water, that is. The key was to keep her out of it.

Tia moved closer, not quite sure how to proceed. Should she grab her sister and fling her toward the shore? Easier said that done. Joyce outweighed her by at least sixty pounds.

Tia's step forward caught the man's attention. He glanced at her. He was younger than she thought, with a long, not-quite-handsome face, and stunningly intent dark eyes.

He put a finger to his lips.

Tia nodded, then mouthed, *She's my sister*.

He nodded once, curtly, then turned back toward Joyce who, surprisingly, hadn't moved.

"Your glasses," he said in a quiet and gentle voice. "You're going to need them."

That was what he held in his other hand. Eclipse glasses. Tia shook her head. The last thing she wanted to do was bring the eclipse to Joyce's attention. It had grown even darker. Even the ocean was dark. Dark and foreboding.

"Please," he said. "You need to protect your eyes."

Joyce finally turned, her back still toward Tia.

"Glasses...?" Joyce said, in that tone she sometimes used when she wasn't sure if she had missed an important conversation. She had a way of asking a question without making it sound like too much of a question.

"For the eclipse," he said. "It's almost totality. You said you wanted to see it."

He was lying to her. Hadn't one of the therapists said never to lie? Tia couldn't remember. Her parents handled the changes in Joyce, until they died in that horrid car accident, and then Howard took point for much of it.

Tia had tried to help, but she had always been told—first by her parents and then by Howard—to live her life. *Not everyone should sacrifice their lives to Joyce's illness*, their mom used to say.

"Eclipse...?" Joyce said in that same tone. Her chin was trembling. It took Tia a moment to realize that Joyce's teeth were chattering.

"I told you earlier that a total eclipse is one of the most masterful things in the universe." The man held out his empty hand. "Watch it with me."

Joyce hovered, clearly indecisive. She had been lost in whatever delusion had sent her fleeing from Tia's house, and then ended up here. Joyce was coming to herself—just enough to be tantalizing. Tia had seen it a hundred times before.

The real Joyce would be there, and then the delusional one would return full strength.

All versions of Joyce are the real Joyce, one of the psychiatrists had said to Tia. *You have to accept that.*

The man had a half-smile on his face, a welcoming smile. Something in his expression seemed very familiar. He didn't seem threatened by Joyce at all.

Tia's gaze would've been jumping all over the place. She would have been terrified that something was going to set Joyce off, and something would have. Something still might.

The fog was clearing. Voices at the eastern edge of the beach grew louder, celebrating the fact that the sun—such as it were—was coming out.

Joyce looked toward the Baywater, clearly terrified.

"The glasses," the man said. "You're going to need them."

Joyce looked at him, and Tia braced herself for the tantrum, the *who are you/why do you think you can fool me* moment.

Joyce finally saw Tia, and her eyes narrowed. She glanced back at the man.

"How come Tia doesn't have any?" Joyce asked.

Tia started to answer, but he gave her a warning glance. Small, subtle, but very clear.

"Because I was supposed to give you both the glasses, and I was late," he said. "I'm sorry. You needed them sooner, and I didn't get here on time."

He kept his hand out for Joyce.

"Come on," he said. "It's getting cold, and it'll be cold throughout the totality. Let's get out of the water."

The sentence worked because they were both in the water. The lower part of his jeans was wet. The hem of Joyce's skirt was soaked.

Tia was still on the packed wet sand, but far enough from the waves that she hadn't gotten wet yet.

Joyce looked at his hands—both of them—one with eclipse glasses and one empty.

The pod people farther up the beach started a countdown.

Joyce looked alarmed.

"Come on," he said. "We don't want to miss it."

Joyce glanced at Tia. Tia would have smiled, but the one thing she had learned over the years was that Joyce recognized one of Tia's nervous smiles. So Tia simply nodded.

Joyce took the man's hand and let him lead her to the dry sand.

Tia would have tugged her all the way to the hotel, to the car, back home, but the man stopped, handed Joyce a pair of glasses, and reminded her to fold them.

"In a few seconds," he said, "we can look at the sun. But when I tell you, you have to put the glasses on."

"What about Tia?" Joyce asked.

Tia joined them. He handed her a pair of the cardboard glasses with some kind of weird tint over the eyeholes as well.

She took them, and folded them. He nodded and smiled. His smile was reassuring. No wonder Joyce listened to him.

"...two..." the pod people said. "...one..."

It got dark, nighttime dark. Lights came on near the hotel's pool.

"Let's look," the man said. "But you have to promise you'll listen to me. When I tell you to put on the glasses, you will."

"I promise," Joyce said, sounding less confused.

He kept his hand threaded in hers, then told her to look up.

The pod people were gasping and shouting with enjoyment.

Tia turned and looked up too, glasses in hand. The fog had receded just enough that she could see the moon in front of the sun, the corona, the red light around the sun. It looked like the photographs but not like the photographs.

Saying you'd seen a total eclipse because you'd seen the pictures was like saying you'd eaten a meal filled with garlic and spices and ingredients you'd never had before just from looking at a picture of it.

The air was crystal cold, the light was both bright and dark at the same time, and there was a tangy scent that might've been the ocean, might've been her, might've been Joyce. The atmosphere felt electric and strange and powerful.

"Okay," the man said in that same soft voice, "put on your glasses now."

Joyce did as she was told. Tia didn't. She looked at her sister, not at the sky. The man had his glasses on, and so did Joyce, and they were staring upwards like everyone else.

Joyce remained still. She seemed entranced. After about a

minute, the man removed his glasses and glanced, almost without moving, at Tia.

He nodded toward the hotel.

Tia nodded as well.

She understood him, strangely enough. They were going to try to get Joyce inside. After that, it would be anyone's guess.

But he didn't move. He stayed perfectly still as Joyce held his hand and looked at the sky, her eyes protected by the glasses.

"It's magic," she said after a moment. "It's real magic."

"It is," he said, and there was a warmth in his voice that hadn't been there before. "I had almost forgotten."

They stood for another five or so minutes, her sister enraptured, the man almost immobile, Tia waiting breathlessly.

So much could still go wrong. Tia didn't want to lose this moment, though. This strange sense of possibility, as if she could—just maybe—get her sister home and safe.

Thanks to the kind and good-looking stranger holding her sister's hand.

Then a shudder ran through Joyce.

"It's so cold," she said.

"It is," he said. "We're going to go inside now, and warm up."

He didn't make any other suggestions. He didn't lead Joyce anywhere. He waited.

Tia wouldn't have done any of those things.

Joyce brought her head down. "Can I take off the glasses?"

"Only if you promise not to look at the sun anymore," he said.

"Okay." She tugged the glasses off her face, then smiled at him.

Then her smile ever so slowly faded.

Tia's heart started to pound. She recognized the look. It was the look Joyce got when she was about to melt down.

"I don't know you," she said.

"That's right," he said in that calm voice. "We just met because of the eclipse. I'm Bryce."

Joyce's eyes narrowed. He had given her just enough information that she couldn't figure out what she knew and what she

213

didn't. Had he meant that they met before the eclipse and she had forgotten it? Or had he been referring to what happened on the beach?

It was a brilliant maneuver, one Tia had never thought of.

Joyce frowned at the hotel. Surely she recognized that.

"I'm cold," she said, clearly deciding not to deal with the details. "Do they have hot chocolate?"

"I'm sure they do," Bryce said. "Let's go inside and find out."

The walk up the beach took forever. Bryce didn't know the woman whose hand he held, and while she was similar to his brother, she wasn't his brother. She was heavyset, her face round and puffy from medications she probably had stopped taking.

Her emotions shifted like the dry sand beneath his feet. Whenever Bryce felt like he was on solid ground, she changed it up again.

Her sister—Tia, apparently—unsettled him as well. She had a runner's build, thin and wiry. Her hair was dark, and her eyes matched. She had a nervous energy, but Bryce couldn't tell if that was because she was worried about her sister or because she was always one of those jittery nervous people.

She was beautiful, though. He was trying not to notice that.

The heavyset sister wouldn't let go of his hand. Her grip was tight, almost painful, particularly as they approached the clump of tourists still gazing at the sun.

"I'm c-c-cold," the sister said again, her teeth chattering.

"We can go back to the room," he said with a glance at Tia, hoping she approved. It was going to be important to get the sister warm and dry, so that she calmed down. "We can order room service."

"Our room...?" the sister asked, and he could hear that edge, the one that meant some bad emotional reaction was on the way.

"My room." He wasn't going to lie to her.

"With Tia," the sister said, emphasis on her sister's name, as if Tia could protect her.

"Tia will join us," he said, not allowing any misunderstanding. He didn't want the sister to think the room was his and Tia's. Heaven knew what kind of mess that would create.

"Okay," the sister said. "Do we order on the way up?"

She hadn't forgotten the hot chocolate. He hadn't either. He hoped the hotel had some.

"Once we get to the room," he said.

He glanced at Tia. She was following a half-step behind, her mouth in a determined line. He recognized her expression. Disaster averted, for the moment, but disaster could return any second.

He would normally have suggested Tia get a coat or something for her sister, but he didn't think Tia should leave them. They needed to play this moment by moment.

The tourists were making the sister nervous. She kept glancing at them. So he moved ever so slightly to block her view as they reached the concrete stairs up to the pool level.

The stairs were too narrow to go side by side, so he went up one step, still holding her hand, and helped her up as if he were an old-fashioned courtly gentleman. The sister smiled at him—the first real smile since she had been watching the eclipse—and let him help her.

Tia followed not to close to her sister, but not too far away either. The fog had returned, bringing even more chill with it. Steam rose off the water of the pool, and for a brief moment, he worried that the sister would jump in. But she avoided it, heading toward the door beside him.

He was about to grab the door to let them into the Baywater, when Tia walked around them. She held the door open, so that he could continue holding the sister's hand.

She was shivering. She had gotten a bad chill. They were going to have to warm her up somehow, and he doubted hot chocolate would do it.

Tia had already made it to the elevators. She clutched her eclipse glasses in her hand and watched worriedly as he led her sister toward her. Tia didn't smile, and he wasn't sure why, but he had to trust it.

At least the sister was nowhere near the water now. At least she was safe—for the moment.

But she had clearly gotten away from her family. It was hard to keep track of full adults with mental illness. People always blamed the families when something went wrong, but they didn't know how very difficult it was.

He knew. And that still didn't make Frank's death any easier.

Bryce's heart twisted. He wouldn't think about that, not right now. He'd managed this far. He and Tia would continue to manage, until they got the sister stabilized.

The elevator binged. The doors slid open revealing a normal-sized carriage. He wondered how the sister would view it, if she would think it too close, too narrow or too wide.

Tia went inside, and to his relief, the sister followed. She turned around, just like a healthy person would, and waited for the doors to close. Somehow she kept her cold fingers wrapped in his.

He didn't dare give Tia any kind of communicative look. There were too many mirrors all over the elevator, and the sister would see any little look. The smallest thing could set someone like the sister off.

The doors closed, and the elevator lurched upwards. He gripped the remaining eclipse glasses with his pinkie, ring finger, and middle finger, and used his index finger and thumb to pull his key card out of his back pocket.

Tia watched, but didn't reach for anything. He recognized the wariness of someone who had lived with this for years and years. He also appreciated her caution.

At least the sister wasn't like Frank. At least small spaces didn't enhance her delusions.

The elevator stopped, then bounced once, and the doors eased open. The sister stepped out first. Bryce heard Tia suck in a breath: he recognized the watchfulness. Was the sister going to run, again? And how to stop her?

He followed, his hand no longer entwined with the sister's. She was standing barefoot on the carpet, her skirt dripping, her entire body shaking. He stepped past her and unlocked the room, listening to make certain that nothing happened behind him.

The women were quiet. He pushed open the door, then turned. The sister stood and shivered. He extended his hand, and she stepped inside, gingerly. She looked at the windows. The fog was receding as the sun was returning.

The beautiful day that had shown such promise before the eclipse began had returned.

Besides, it was hard not to look. This entire suite was set up around the views of the ocean. Views on three sides, with the furniture positioned so that the waves were visible.

Not that he had looked much. His books covered every available space. The sister didn't seem to notice. She walked to the windows, dripping and shaking.

Tia came inside, and mouthed *thank you* as she did so. He grabbed some books off one of the couches and set them on a side table.

Then he said to the sister, hoping against hope he wouldn't set her off, "I'm going to order hot chocolate, coffee and pastries. Would you like anything else?"

She shook her head, still staring out, arms wrapped around herself.

"You look really cold," he said in his most gentle voice. "Why don't you take a shower while we wait?"

Her entire body went rigid, just like she had on the beach. His breath caught. He hoped he hadn't done anything wrong.

Tia remained in front of the door, so that the sister couldn't just run through it. But Tia probably didn't know that there were sliders to her sister's left. She could run onto the balcony and then jump to the concrete below.

"I don't have clothes," the sister said.

"There's a big fluffy robe in the closet here," Tia said quietly. "You can wear it while we dry your skirt downstairs. You can keep your shirt."

The sister turned, eyes flashing. Her gaze fell on Bryce.

"I don't remember you," she said.

"I'm Bryce," he said. "We met because of the eclipse..."

"I *know* that," she said. "I don't remember you from before."

"Because we only just met," he said.

"Then why should I trust you?" the sister asked.

He didn't have an answer for that. He had learned with Frank not to underestimate questions like this. Because they sometimes came from a sharp intellectual place, and sometimes they came from the delusions. But they were important.

"You should trust him," Tia said quietly, "because I do."

It took all of his strength not to look at her in surprise. She had no real reason to trust him. But she seemed to.

The sister frowned at him, and then at Tia

He almost told the sister to remember the magic, but that could boomerang too. He decided to remain silent.

"I want eggs," the sister said. "Scrambled. And hot chocolate. And toast."

Then she looked around.

"Where's the bathroom?" she asked.

"Here," he said, and felt a stab of fear. Too much like the past. "Let me just make sure there are clean towels."

He stepped into the bathroom first, his heart pounding. There were clean towels—the hotel was overly generous with them—but he still had to move quickly.

He grabbed his razor, his hair clipper, and the scissors he had carried since the days when he had a beard. He grabbed the two glasses from the counter, and anything else that could be used to smash the mirror. He wrapped everything in the towel he had used that morning, wishing he could wrap up the mirror too.

Then he stepped out.

The sister was near the bathroom door, holding the fluffy robe that had been in the closet since he arrived.

She handed him the eclipse glasses.

"Thank you," she said, and walked into the bathroom as if there was nothing wrong.

She closed the door. It didn't have a lock, thank heavens, but he didn't like the snick as it shut.

He glanced at Tia. She swallowed visibly, so nervous that he could feel it.

The shower started up.

He walked to the table and set down the towel. It opened to reveal all the things he had removed from the bathroom.

Tia's face paled.

"You've been through this before," she said so softly he almost didn't hear her.

He nodded. "My brother."

"Is he...?" She tried again. "Did he...?"

There was no delicate way to ask these things. Nor was there a delicate way to answer.

"My brother was an untreated schizophrenic," Bryce said softly. "My parents got him help too late. He killed himself when I was seventeen."

"Seventeen," Tia said. "Oh, my. I'm sorry. This would have brought it all back."

He looked at the door. This incident did bring everything, but not in the way that she thought. It made him realize how alone he'd been ever since. How protected he had kept himself.

How closed off.

"I'll take this stuff to the bedroom, then I'll call room service." He sounded curt, but he didn't know how to sound any other way when it came to his brother. It was over and done with, and years of therapy had gotten him through.

Years of therapy, and spending time alone. Writing. Losing himself in the cosmos and science and history and the past.

Tia remained near the door, and he didn't blame her. Because it would be so easy for her sister to burst out of the bathroom, and then run to the hallway.

He stepped into the bedroom, put the towel and the items wrapped in it on the upper shelf of the closet, and closed the door. Then he picked up the hotel phone, ordered breakfast (they had hot chocolate!) and asked to be connected to the gift shop. They had had sweatshirts about the Great American Eclipse and some generic (if overpriced) sweat pants.

He ordered three sweatshirts, one pair of sweat pants, and three baseball caps with the hotel's logo, and asked them to be delivered to his room.

Then he returned to the front room.

Tia still hovered near the door. She had latched the chain, but she seemed nervous.

He didn't blame her.

The shower still hummed.

"Food's on the way," he said. "And I got clothes."

"I'll pay for it," she said. "I just have to go to the car—"

"Not right now," he said. *Not ever*, he thought. "Let's just get her calmed down. Does she have meds?"

"At my house," Tia said. "I don't think I should leave her though."

"Does she live with you?" he asked.

"No," she said. "Joyce lives in a facility in the Valley. She got out, went to my brother's, and then ran away again. Somehow she made it here."

The Valley—the Willamette Valley—was more than an hour away on a good day. Someone had given the sister—Joyce—a ride.

"What are you going to do?" Bryce asked.

"My brother is coming for her, with someone from the facility. But not till the eclipse traffic has cleared up. Probably tonight."

Tia rubbed her hands together.

He couldn't help himself. He took them in his.

Electricity flowed through him. She looked at him, startled. Had she felt it too?

"You're really kind," she said, not pulling away. "You didn't have to help her."

"I did, though," he said.

She studied his face, hers filled with compassion.

"You were there, when your brother died, weren't you?"

He didn't quite know how to answer that. He had been in the next room. Not quite the same thing. "I didn't...expect it," he said

Because no one had explained how the disease went. Because no one had told the family how insidious it was, how the person who had the disease often knew that nothing was right anymore, and wanted it all to end.

"She was sobbing," he said quietly. "Before she headed into the surf, she was..."

"She thinks it's a good way to die," Tia said.

He closed his eyes for a brief second, then shook his head. "They know that at her facility, right?"

"They do," Tia said.

"And you'll get after them for not policing her?" he asked.

Tia shrugged. "They can only do so much. It's the best place in the state."

Her words hung between them. The shower continued its hum, and then someone knocked on the door.

Tia got out of the way. He opened the door. A man in a black uniform handed him a pile of clothing. Bryce had told them to charge it to the room, but he still gave the man a tip, before closing the door again.

"Thank you," Tia said. "I have no idea what I would have done if you hadn't stepped in."

Bryce took the clothes into the living room, pulled the clothes out of the plastic bags, and stuffed the bags under the sink.

"You were just a few seconds behind me," he said.

"But she wouldn't have listened to me," Tia said. "She would have fought me—"

"Maybe," he said. "I think she was having second thoughts."

Or she wouldn't have turned around, wouldn't have stopped.

He had pounded on his brother's bathroom door for seemingly hours, and Frank hadn't opened up. Nothing had changed his mind. Nothing would have.

"She's using up all your hot water," Tia said.

"Not mine." He smiled. "The hotel's."

"Thank heavens it's the middle of the morning." Tia smiled at him—a real smile. She was stunningly beautiful.

He hadn't expected that.

"What do you do when you're not rescuing women on the beach?" she asked.

"I write books," he said, surprising himself. He usually never told anyone that.

"And you're writing something here?" she asked.

"Researching," he said.

"Eclipses?"

He shook his head. "I've done that already," he said. "I wasn't sure why I was here. I thought they had lost their luster for me."

Tia frowned a little. "That was nothing like I imagined."

"It never is," he said.

Then the second knock. Breakfast.

He opened the door, wheeled in the tray himself, and took it into the main room, after writing a tip on the bill.

And then the shower shut off.

Tia's heart pounded. This was one of those moments. The door could open, Joyce could bolt, and then they'd be running all over again.

Or she could step out and be normal.

Tia could hear her rustling around inside the bathroom, and she didn't hear anything loud or scary.

Still, she closed and locked the main door, turning the deadbolt, setting the chain, and wishing she could put a chair underneath the doorknob.

The bathroom door opened in a waft of steam. Joyce stepped out, hair wet, eyes bright. As if her meds had kicked in, even though she hadn't taken any.

"I smell hot chocolate," she said.

"Over there." Tia swept her hand toward the kitchen area.

Joyce padded in, barefoot, and Bryce handed her an already full mug. She clutched it, and hugged it to her.

He was a good man. A nice man. Tia hadn't met anyone like him before. Especially someone who would understand her family situation.

Men usually fled when they found out her sister was mentally ill. Sometimes, though, Tia refused to get close because she didn't want to discuss Joyce yet again.

"Shirts," Joyce said, wandering toward the couch.

"For all three of us," he said. "But the sweatpants are for you, so you don't have to wait for your skirt to dry."

Joyce grinned at him, surprising Tia. Then Joyce set the mug down, grabbed a sweatshirt and pants, and went back into the bathroom.

Bryce turned and ran his hands over the silverware. His brother had really traumatized him.

"How long are you here for?" Tia asked.

Bryce shrugged. "As long as I want to be."

"Then let me show you around," she said. "After, you know..."

He nodded, smiled. "You don't owe me anything."

"Oh, I do," she said. "But that's not why I'm offering."

His gaze met hers. It was warm and it pulled her forward. She liked him. And he seemed to like her.

"This is a pretty special place, isn't it?" he asked.

"The resort?" she asked.

"The coast," he said.

She nodded as the bathroom door opened again. Joyce, in a Great American Eclipse sweatshirt and matching pants, looked almost normal.

"Magic," she said, running her hand along the image of the moon over the sun.

"Yes," Bryce said, his gaze still on Tia's. "Magic."

Tia decided his eyes were the best thing about his face. She liked that intensity.

She said, "Sometimes the world just has to remind you how magical it can be."

"Yeah," Joyce said, walking past her, seeming like her old self. "And then there's hot chocolate."

Bryce laughed, and Tia smiled, feeling some of the tension leave.

Her sister probably wasn't past her difficult morning. They still had struggles ahead. The day would be up and down.

But Tia could take advantage of the up. And she had a bit of help, at least for a little while.

"There's sunshine," Joyce said. "I didn't think I'd ever see it again."

"That's the best thing about totality," Bryce said. "It makes you see everything new again."

He had probably deliberately misunderstood her. Not that it mattered. Because Tia agreed.

She hadn't realized how much she had shut herself off, how much her life had focused around the difficulties, and not the good things.

Little things. Like sunshine and hot chocolate.

And someone who understood.

Bryce patted the chair beside him, and Tia sat down, as if she belonged there. As if she had always belonged there. At his side, having a quiet breakfast.

On an unusual day, at the beautiful Oregon Coast.

THAT SUMMER ON BLUE HERON ISLAND

DAYLE A. DERMATIS

As I mentioned in the introduction, Dayle A. Dermatis's story "That Summer on Blue Heron Island" provided the inspiration for this entire volume. Once I read the story, I had to have it for Fiction River. *The story didn't fit in any of the upcoming volumes, so Dayle let me hold the story until I could create a volume around the story itself.*

Dayle shares a love of the modern gothic with me. It was only a matter of time before one of us wrote a modern gothic. Dayle got to it first, and set the story in a made-up version of the lakeshore area she grew up in on Lake Champlain, her cousin's property on Saranac Lake, and "a healthy dollop of idyllic fantasy."

Dayle is good at fantasy. Her novels What Beck'ning Ghost *and* Waking the Witch *are spooky modern gothics,* Ghosted *and* Shaded *are urban fantasy, and she has sold a lot of fantasy (as well as other genre fiction) to* Fiction River. *In fact, she's appeared in our pages sixteen times, including "Girl with a Mission" in* Hard Choices, *"The Florentine Exchange" in* Special Edition: Spies, *and "Follow You" in* Stolen.

Dayle has also edited two volumes of Fiction River. Doorways To Enchantment *will appear in July, and* Fiction River: Secrets *will appear in the next year or so.*

Settle in, and go on a summer vacation filled with thunder, lightning, romance, and yes, darkness. See why I decided summer needed a bit of sizzle. Enjoy "That Summer on Blue Heron Island."

I woke to arrhythmic jolting, every shake sending a flare of agony through my head, nauseating me. Rain sheeted against my face. I tried to raise my hand to block it, but my body didn't want to respond.

A flash of lightning, followed almost immediately by a long, slow grumble of thunder that seemed to go on forever, illuminated the face above me. Will Madigan, my summer crush.

Wet black hair plastered his skull. His face was pale, his lips parted as he sucked in air. He was carrying me through the dark woods, his feet thudding on the rocky, uneven path as he jogged.

I tried to ask him to stop, to put me down—my head hurt so bad—but all that came out was a low moan.

His voice was rough with emotion. "Don't you die on me, Lizzy Sloane," he said. "Don't you dare die on me."

It's Elizabeth. *Nobody calls me Lizzy anymore*, I thought grumpily, and then everything went black again.

For as long as I can remember—which means about seventeen years, since I'm twenty now—my family has been spending summers on Blue Heron Island in Saranac Lake, New York. I think it was my great-great-grandfather who bought the island (probably bilking some Indian tribe in the process; I'm given to believe previous generations of my family didn't amass all our wealth by the most ethical of means).

My arm of the family had been the first to arrive this summer, as usual, on the heels of the cook and housekeeper (the gardener/handyman had opened up the buildings and done the grounds work, and would come back every few days as needed).

The next day, Uncle Jeremy (who was my father's half-brother) and his wife, Delilah, showed up. They have five kids: Cortland, Braeburn (Brae), Paula, McIntosh (Mac), and Fortune, all named after apples because the family had made their money with orchards. When craft brewing started to take off, they created a line of hard ciders, which was doing amazingly well. So well, in fact, that Jeremy and Delilah must have celebrated a *lot*, because Fortune was a late-in-life baby for Delilah. At eighteen months, Fortune was more than twenty years younger than her oldest bother, Cortland, and the first four kids were clumped together in age.

Cortland and his pregnant wife were here, as well as Mac, but

Brae and Paula had skipped this summer. Brae was backpacking through Europe, and Paula... Well, I don't know.

Paula and Mac were a year apart, and she and I were the same age. She'd been my closest friend and confidante in the extended family for years, but in the last year or so, she'd basically ghosted me. Stopped answering my texts. Ignoring my calls. In fact, I hadn't seen her in a about a year; Delilah and Jeremy hadn't come to the island last summer, and I'd had several migraines during this past Christmas holiday, which meant I'd missed some of the family get-togethers.

It hurt, but I'd mostly shoved it aside. I'd ask Aunt Delilah when I had the chance, but I wasn't going to let Paula, or her absence, ruin my summer on the island.

That still meant there would be a bazillion people coming and going. My two aunts on my mother's side had eight kids between them, and Dad's other four siblings had...this was where I had to start counting on my fingers, because I have a *lot* of cousins. Some of them might be my oldest cousins' children. If I sat down and charted it out, I'd know how everyone was related, but who wants to spend their summer vacation doing that?

Not everybody stayed all summer. Some came only for long weekends, or for a couple weeks in the middle. My older sister had just started her first year as a law clerk, so she was going to be scarce; my younger sister and brother were still in high school, so they were here but grumpy at the lack of cell service and Internet. You wanted to make a call, you went to the main lodge or the guesthouse and used one of the phones there.

Anyway, this year, Mac had brought his friend Will.

I was sunbathing on the beach when they arrived, lying on a towel on the sun-warmed rock, a cooler of ice and Diet Coke next to me. Extra-coverage sunglasses kept the worst of the glare away from my eyes; really bright lights could trigger my migraines, but this was my favorite place in the world, and I'd learned to adapt. I didn't have my headphones on; instead, I listened to the breeze whisper through the pines and the occasional, ethereal call of a loon echoing off the water.

Perfection.

I heard the pontoon boat well before it came around the jut of land into the cove. I stood and tugged on my khaki shorts, and met them at the dock.

They'd sent ahead the bulk of their luggage, so I helped offload duffels and laptop bags and Fortune's diaper bag, hugging each family member in turn and answering the same questions every few people (when had we arrived, who else was here, how was I doing, didn't I look good?). We were loud enough that a couple of crows startled out of the trees, cawing their annoyance at the interruption of their serenity.

Mac caught me up in one of his big bear hugs. He looked as though he'd been here all summer already, with his hair a sun-bleached blond and eyebrows to match, and smelling of sunscreen. He let me go, thumped me on the back, and said "Elizabeth, this is my friend Will. Will, this is my cousin Elizabeth."

I turned with a friendly smile, and then my tongue glued itself to the top of my mouth.

Thank you, Mac, for bringing the most gorgeous friend you could find.

Thick black hair waved to his shoulders, brushed back from a high forehead and strong brow. Dark eyelashes framed intense, denim-blue eyes. Something about him looked vaguely familiar, but if I'd known someone this gorgeous in the past, I'd remember, right? Maybe he reminded me of some actor.

He grinned, a motion that lit up his face, and I found myself obsessed with his mouth. I wanted to kiss it.

I also wanted to say something witty and profound, and stop looking like an idiot.

"Hi," I said.

Damn. Not quite the pithy response I was going for.

"Nice to meet you," he said.

"Crap, my sunglasses are still in the boat," Delilah said. "Can someone grab Fortune?"

"I've got her, Mrs. Sloane," Will said, reaching out and pulling the redheaded toddler into his arms. Fortune had been fussing, but she quieted down, stuck three fingers in her mouth, and stared around, wide-eyed.

"Warning: there are going to be a lot of Mrs. Sloanes here," I said. "You might want to start calling her Aunt Delilah."

His eyebrows went up. "As long as Mac doesn't mind me joining the family."

"You're here," I said. "You don't get invited to Blue Heron Island without passing a few tests you didn't know you were taking."

I leaned my face close into Fortune's. "But you, my wittle adorable gooshy-cheeked chipmunk, you belong right here." I booped my nose against hers, and she laughed.

Will hefted Fortune more firmly in his arms and headed up the path, behind most of the rest of the group. I slung the diaper bag over my shoulder, grabbed a soft-sided cooler, and followed.

He had a great butt in a pair of tight, faded jeans. I could follow him anywhere. It was all I could do not to fan myself. My freshman year boyfriend had been nothing to write home about in the end, and I'd been too busy with school to date seriously for the past two years. The summer was definitely looking up—and it had been pretty darn good to start with. Blue Heron was my happy place.

We came out of the trees and hiked up the broad steps cut into one side of the long, sloping lawn, formed by turf and old railroad ties. We piled the luggage on the flagstone patio, and Delilah took back Fortune, and the family went in to say hi to my parents and siblings.

Will stayed behind. At first this delighted me, but then I couldn't read the expression on his face as he surveyed his surroundings.

I saw the enormous but yet somehow cozy log lodge, the vast

lawn that held the ghosts of a thousand games of tag, the shushing pines that surrounded us.

I was starting to worry that he, however, was scanning for a cell tower or TV dish.

"So, what is there to do around here?" he asked finally.

"It's not so much what to *do*, but how to *be*," I said, failing to keep the irritation out of my voice. It was the problem of bringing in someone new: they sometimes didn't *get* Blue Heron.

I'd had such high hopes for Will, but he was failing my test, dang it.

"It's a place to come and relax. Aunt Shannon does needle-point, Uncle Buster annoys the cook because he loves to bake and keeps getting in the way, and my dad works on his never-ending novel. Everybody reads—there are tons of books if you don't have a Kindle. We've got board games and volleyball and badminton and croquet and kayaking and swimming and fishing. If you're really hankering for a party, there's the big Fourth of July bash that everyone comes to. Massive picnic, G&Ts out the wazoo, and yes, fireworks." I ran out of breath, sucked in some of the clean, pure mountain air.

He held up his hands. "Woah, sorry. Didn't mean to offend. Mac had warned me that it could be kind of slow, but honestly, all that sounds great. This last semester kicked my ass; it'll be nice to just kick back for awhile." He stuck one hand out. "Truce?"

Maybe I had been a little too prickly. Yeah, I had the tiniest bit of a headache coming on. "Truce."

Oh. *Oh*. His hand was warm, his fingers long and strong, curling around mine in a firm grip that went on just a little too long for my sanity. When he let go, I almost whimpered from the loss.

"How about you give me the grand tour?" he suggested.

Hell yeah. I glanced at him. He was wearing grey T-shirt with *Cornell* in red letters, the aforementioned jeans, and brown Dock-ers. "You might want to put on socks," I said. "Potential poison ivy."

He gave me a long, slow look, down and then up again. I felt myself flush.

"You might want to put on *clothes*," he said.

"Well, yeah," I retorted. "Duh."

Smooth, Elizabeth, real smooth.

I also needed to grab my towel and cooler from the beach, and knock back some pain meds before the headache became a full-blown migraine.

When I was on Blue Heron I had the least number of migraines than anywhere else. My doctor figures it's because I'm so relaxed here. But they still happen every so often, and if I catch them early enough, I'm good. This one was probably a holdover from the stress of college.

I was back in my element while I showed Will around, because I could give this tour like nobody's business. Still, I'd get caught up in showing him something, turn to look at him, remember how gorgeous he was, and feel my stomach do a flip. Kind of like how it felt when I was younger and would roll down the lawn, feeling deliciously out of control.

First I showed him the rest of the lodge, the oldest standing building on the island, which was built in the 1880s and briefly served as a tuberculosis sanatorium when that was all the rage. A mix of rustic and elegant, it's like an enormous log cabin, with a two-story open living room, ten bedrooms that all have their own sinks, and enough sleeping porches, parlors, and private nooks that even when we're here in full force, it doesn't seem full. Bookshelves and artwork vie for wall space along with a couple of sad trout trophies and one moldering deer head with a faded July 4th plastic tiara dangling from one antler. His name, as I told Will now, was Fred.

"Poor dead Fred," Will said with a chuckle.

"How did you know?" I asked. "We actually call him Fred the Dead Head. I think my grandfather is responsible for that."

"Great minds think alike, I guess," Will said.

Must be.

There was one older building, at the opposite end of the island, a great stone house on a cliff overlooking the lake, which had been destroyed by fire well before I was born. Half of it is gutted; the other half a dangerous warren of rooms with fallen beams and charred wood floors. The combination of the mostly missing roof and empty windows means the wind makes some unique and spectacularly creepy moans and wails. It's a rite of passage for the younger kids to dare each other to go inside. I don't think any of us get past what would have been the foyer before running back out screaming little high-pitched kid screams.

(On a quiet day, you could hear the shrieks of the latest crop of kids all the way to the lodge, and we'd all chuckle and shiver in memory.)

There's also a guesthouse and a bunkhouse, both built in the thirties, and the gaming cabin, which is basically one big room used as a children's play space when it's raining. It has a stage at one end with a closet of clothes for dress-up, hopscotch marked out on the floor, and shelves and shelves of games.

"That's new," Will murmured.

"What?" How would Will know something was new? He hadn't said he'd been here before.

He pointed to the TV and Wii and Xbox. "The gaming consoles are clearly from a more modern era."

"Well, yeah. Brendan and Constance's kids threw a hissy fit. They don't even come here much, but they insisted."

Even the other younger kids—we called them the littles— would rather be outside on a nice day. The island was paradise. Hard-packed dirt paths meandered up and down between the trees, leading to open meadows, a pond, the cove with the outthrust of rock that was the best place for fishing.

We got back in time for supper on the patio. Aunt Shannon and Uncle Buster had arrived with their five kids, all young, and we chowed into honey-glazed ham and fresh biscuits and homemade coleslaw and corn on the cob, plus Uncle Buster had made chocolate cupcakes with white frosting, our initials written on them in purple and gold.

When we were finished, Aunt Delilah had her arms full of dishes when Fortune started to fuss.

"I'll take her," I said. I cleaned her chubby cheeks and hands with a wipe, then lifted her out of her highchair into my arms. "Hello there, you squishy noodle," I crooned as I followed Aunt Delilah and Uncle Jeremy into the house.

"Hey, so how's Paula doing?" I asked.

The plates Aunt Delilah had been carrying clattered into the sink.

"Oh goodness, she's fine," she said.

"I just haven't heard from her in ages." I shifted Fortune to my other hip. "She hasn't been answering my texts."

"She's fine," Aunt Delilah repeated. "So busy with school." Her voice seemed a little high, a little shrill, but as Paula and I and the others often joked, Aunt Delilah was so jittery, she made coffee nervous. She usually calmed down by the end of the summer. Blue Heron Island worked its magic on everyone.

"She got a great internship," Uncle Jeremy said, taking over at the sink. He turned on the water to rinse the dishes, raising his voice as he added, "Really great. We won't see her all summer."

I still didn't get why Paula had ditched me like last year's fashions, but I wasn't about to say that to her parents. Aunt Delilah held her arms out, and I transferred Fortune into her arms just as I heard Mac and Will's voices as they carried in more dishes. Distracted, I ran my hands through my hair and hoped I didn't have toddler drool on me.

Afterwards, Mac, Cortland, Will, and I stretched out on the lawn along with my sister, Cathy, and my brother, Ed, and watched the stars and the fireflies come out to dance. We sipped beers and caught up on life since the Christmas holidays, bitched about school, that sort of thing. I was constantly aware of Will on the blanket next to mine. When he laughed at my jokes, I felt a happy glow.

"Midnight swimming or Cards Against Humanity marathon?" Cortland asked finally.

We voted for swimming.

"Coming, Lizzy?" Will asked.

"It's Elizabeth," I said. "Nobody's called me Lizzy since I was a kid."

I'd been introduced as Elizabeth. Why would he call me Lizzy? Behind his back, as he turned toward the lodge, I frowned.

Then he elbowed Mac, laughing about something, and I figured Mac might have slipped and referred to me as Lizzy at some point. (He wasn't the only one who occasionally did—my dad still called me that, but my dad was the only person allowed to.)

We tossed on our suits, ran down to the lake. The water was cold, but we were stubborn. We raced out to the raft, tried to convince Will there was a lake monster (while I distracted Will with the story, Mac ducked underwater and grabbed his legs and pulled him under), and swam until our skin was wrinkled and goosebumped.

The adults were sitting around the fire pit, drinking whisky, but they headed to bed when we returned, leaving us to our beer and marshmallows over the fire. We huddled around its warmth, hunched in our Adirondack chairs, damp towels slung across our shoulders.

When the fire burned down (and we poured the remains of our beer on top of the embers, just in case), we finally called it a night.

Will paused outside my bedroom door. "Good night, *Elizabeth*," he said. My heart stuttered as he leaned close. I could smell the wood smoke in his hair. He brushed his lips against my cheek, and then he was gone.

I lay awake for a long time, thinking about that kiss.

The upstairs bedrooms had tall casement windows, and a high, fat moon glowed through, spilling on the wide, whitewashed plank floors. I'd always loved clear nights like this; as a kid, I felt like I could swim right up the moonbeams.

I shared the room with Cathy, who slept peacefully in her own twin bed, a lump of body beneath a pile of quilts. She'd always been a quick sleeper once she burrowed down, no matter how warm it was. I was the hot sleeper, preferring the window open and no more than a light blanket, and I was the tosser and turner.

Especially tonight.

I kept hearing Will's laugh, and seeing the way the moonlight played off his bare chest when he pulled himself, dripping, onto the raft.

I hadn't expected a summer fling, and I chewed on that for a bit. I wasn't used to strangers on the island, except when a girl-friend or boyfriend was brought into the fold—and almost always, if someone brought a person they were dating, marriage followed. You didn't bring someone to the island unless you were serious about them.

Oh, occasionally one of us would have a friend visit, but that was usually for a long weekend, not the whole summer.

I wasn't upset with Mac bringing Will, not by a long shot. It would just take some getting used to.

I wouldn't have the relaxing, familiar summer I'd expected...but familiar was overrated. Will was more like an enhancement to the island. He brought excitement. The buzz of adrenaline, the flutter in my stomach—that was his fault.

My hand rose, touched my cheek where he'd bussed the kiss, barely touching my skin.

I flipped my feather pillow to the cool side, punched it a few times for good measure.

And continued to lie awake, thinking about kisses and Will.

We all spent the next day by the lake, unsurprisingly. It was a glorious early summer day, the sun beating down but not too warm, the sky blue except for a few wispy cirrus clouds to keep things interesting. When the littles weren't splashing and shrieking, you could hear the breeze communing with the tops of the pines, and the raucous screams of blue jays countered by the trilling of warblers.

Most of us alternated between swimming and lazing on the shore. The adults favored lawn chairs; the rest of us sprawled on towels. Kayaks went out and back; inner tubes were deployed for some closer-to-shore desultory paddling. Tiny Fortune, slathered with sunscreen and bundled in a life vest so puffy she looked like an orange with pudgy arms and legs, had a toddler-sized inflatable donut. I took her out into the water, barely waist deep for me, and she gleefully squealed and kicked her feet and slapped the water with her hands.

Lunch was hot dogs over a fire with whole-wheat buns and all the trimmings, plus coleslaw and potato salad and watermelon and brownies. You didn't worry about calories here. There was like a magical island calorie-banishing fairy, I swear.

Everything was the same as it always was—close to perfect, really—and yet different. That was Will's fault, although he didn't know it. Or maybe it was my fault, my own reaction to him.

The island was familiar, but he wasn't, and I was constantly aware of his presence, even when I relaxed into the habitual flow of family and summer vacation. Will was an outlier, but not in a bad way. He just made me...more mindful, alert. Maybe even a little self-conscious, although I didn't change the way I did things.

No, I did. Generally we all do our own thing except at meals, when we were expected to gather. Small group activities were spur of the moment. If Mac didn't ensure Will was included in some plan, I tried to step in.

I told myself I was being polite, gracious.

Funny how we choose to see things how we want to see them sometimes. I knew I lied to myself, but I didn't care.

I was attracted to Will, and I wanted him to like me, and I wanted to get to know him better.

"So, where are you from, exactly?" I asked. I was lying on my towel on my stomach, head cradled in my arms, my face half-swathed in my sunglasses. He and Mac had just stretched out again after a race to the raft and back.

He beat a gentle tattoo on his wet stomach with both hands. He smelled brackish from the lake water.

"Moved to Albany when I was a kid, but I've spent some summers and winter vacations in the Adirondacks," he said. "That's why I'm studying law, actually—I want to be an environmental lawyer, protect all of this. That, and my dad's a lawyer, so he kind of nudged me in that direction."

"And your mom? What does she do?"

"She's an entrepreneur," he said finally.

"An entrepreneur of what?" I asked.

He rolled onto his side and looked at me. I couldn't read the expression in his gaze. "Why does it matter what my mother does?" he asked. "Checking to see if my family fits in the same tax bracket as yours?"

I flushed. I'm not normally a blusher, but I could feel the heat on my chest, my cheeks, even in the warm sunshine.

"Of course not," I said. "I'm just making conversation—trying to get to know you. You already know all about my family, thanks to Mac."

He snorted. "Guys don't talk about shit like that, Elizabeth. We're too busy arguing over who got more points throwing things at the trash basket or discussing the merits of some girl's ass."

Now I heard the humor in his voice. "Have you discussed the merits of my ass?" I asked, pulling my sunglasses down my nose so I could look at him with an arched eyebrow.

"Don't be ridiculous." He lay back down. "You're his *cousin*, for crying out loud."

Now I snorted, and reached over to get a Diet Pepsi out of the cooler. I was pretty sure Will checked out my ass when I did, and I hid a smile. Boys were so predictable.

Although it was interesting that he'd gotten prickly when I asked about his family.

I shoved the thought away.

―――――――

As the afternoon sun's rays lengthened and the air grew a little chillier, small clumps of people detached and drifted up to the house, to shower and dress for dinner, and switch from iced tea and soda to pre-dinner cocktails.

We tended to group by ages, the younger sets happy to have the freedom from boring parents, the older folks enjoying adult conversation instead of herding children.

There were two non-adult groups, essentially. Once a kid was old enough to be wandering around on their own and not be constantly monitored by a mom or nanny or older sibling, they joined the younger group, which we affectionately called the littles. At some point, usually in high school, they transitioned to the older group. If there were enough kids in the middle range— middle school-ish—sometimes they had a group of their own.

Thus Cathy and Ed, my younger siblings, generally were hanging out with Mac and Will and me. Cortland did as well for some of the time, but he wanted to spend quality time with Vanessa, his wife—and because she was five months pregnant, she understandably wasn't up for every midnight swim or high octane volleyball game.

Cortland was transitioning out of our group, I realized as I stood on the lawn, watching him with a drink in his hand, chatting with my parents, one arm around Vanessa. He wasn't the first to go, but the first I was fairly close to. I felt my stomach clench as I wondered how soon after college I'd be expected to ease into the adult dynamic. I wasn't looking forward to it.

For one thing, I'd have to drink G&Ts. I shuddered. Gin tasted like the tears of despairing pine trees.

Not this summer, though. This summer was still about fun and sun and possibilities.

The sun cast long rays over the lawn, the lower part of the slope already in shadow from the tree line of tall pines at the bottom. In anticipation of dinner, the littles were ramping up their appetites by flinging themselves down the slope, rolling and shrieking with laughter, and then staggering dizzily back up the lawn to do it all over again.

"What...are they doing?" Will asked.

"You've never rolled down a hill before?" I was aghast. It was practically a requirement of summer.

An odd look flashed in his eyes, furrowed his brow, but then it was gone, and maybe I'd imagined it. "Guess I've never lived anywhere hilly."

"Aunt E, Aunt E!" Brett shouted. It sounded like "Auntie," something I encouraged.

"Coming!" I shouted back, and dropped to the ground. I stretched my arms over my head, glanced downslope to ensure I was properly parallel to the tree line and no one was in my path, and gave a wiggle to get me going.

Blueskygreengrassblueskygreengrass flashed faster before my eyes as I picked up speed. A giggle of pure delight bubbled out of my throat. It wasn't exactly like flying—hang gliding was more like that—but there was something gloriously wonderful about being almost out of control, spinning helplessly.

The ground leveled out just before the trees, just before a spot where the grass gave way to a few flattish rocks that had heaved their way out of the soil. Normally you slowed down by then, but one of the first things even the littlest kids learned was how to gauge when you were close and not roll onto the rocks. Muscle memory, not conscious thought, reminded me to fling out my arms and spread my legs and come to a gentle halt on my back.

I was laughing between gasps of air. The world still spun, and the high tendrils of cirrus clouds, white against the perfect blue, blurred and danced. The grass was cool, tickling my bare arms and legs, the scent of earth surrounding me. I spat out strands of hair that had caught in my mouth during my flight, tasting bittersweet conditioner.

Bliss.

A body bumped mine, gently, and I turned my head to see Will, on his side, facing me. He was laughing, and he blinked hard a few times, dark lashes obscuring his sparkling blue eyes.

"How many are there of you again?" he asked.

"Sloanes? No idea—no math allowed on the island."

"No, Elizabeths. There seem to be at least two of you."

"That's part of the joy of rolling down the hill," I said.

"I can see that," he said. "Unexpected bonus."

His face was very close to mine, and my own spinning sensation was fading, so I could see every detail of his face. I was mostly distracted by the ring of darker blue around his denim eyes, and the warmth of the proximity of his body, even though we were barely touching.

I wondered if he wanted to kiss me, and then I decided, why wait? I pulled myself up onto one elbow to face him.

The next thing I heard was peals of laughter, followed by small bodies swallowing up the sight of Will as children piled atop both of us.

"Oof!" I said as I fell back and a tiny knee hit my stomach.

Between little limbs, I saw Will rise to hands and knees, children clinging to him like lamprey. He made a mock growl and pawed the ground. One of the kids screamed "Horsie!" and others took up the refrain.

The dinner bell rang out from the deck.

"First person to the top of the hill gets double dessert tonight!" I shouted.

The press of bodies vanished in an instant and the shrieking started up again.

"C'mon," I said to Will. "If we don't follow them, they'll come back."

I thought he was going to grab my hand—I wanted him to—but then he said, "Race you," and I said, "Oh, you're *on*," and off we went. On the way, he scooped up the straggler, Alice, and swung her from her arms ahead of him as she squealed with delight.

I would've beat him anyway, I swear.

And we, along with Mac and Cathy and Ed, snuck into the kitchen later that night and got our own double desserts of cherry pie and vanilla bean ice cream, which we ate on the deck while playing Uno and watching for shooting stars.

As it turned out, Will could keep up with me pretty well.

A few days later, after breakfast, I decided to go for a run. Running was another thing that helped keep my migraines at bay, and running outside was best, and trail running on Blue Heron Island was best of all.

Will saw me lacing up my sneakers and asked if he could join me.

"I could use some stretching out," he said. "Mac's threatening a badminton challenge later, and when he threatens, I know it's going to be vicious."

"It's like Calvinball," I said. "The rules change mid-play. You may need to lie down afterwards."

"I've heard you're a hell of a runner," he said. "I may need to lie down after *this*."

I'd raced him up the slope of the lawn; he had speed, but stamina remained to be seen. Still, this morning I wasn't running for time or distance, just to stretch out myself and enjoy the island.

The groundskeeper kept the various paths through the forest reasonably clear while still maintaining the natural landscape. Plants and branches were trimmed, especially large rocks removed, but otherwise, there was packed dirt with roots and small rocks embedded in it, and a few places where the path swerved around a tree.

I knew these trails better than I knew the streets of New York or around Dartmouth. Like I did with the lakeshore, I recognized the subtle changes each year: a downed tree (cut back only so far that it didn't block the path), a fairy ring of mushrooms, a new blue heron nest high up in a tree.

I started slow, letting my own muscles loosen and my legs reacclimate to running on a non-flat surface. Running on the street or a track or a treadmill just wasn't the same. As my joints warmed up and remembered how to accommodate the surface changes, I picked up the pace a little, felt my heartbeat speed up a little, both from the exercise and from joy.

Insects buzzed, breaking off abruptly as we passed and then picking up again behind us. The air smelled of warm dirt and leaves. Sunlight dappled the path as it dripped between branches and leaves as my feet thudded against the ground. If I'd been alone, I'd've spread my arms and laughed at the pure pleasure of it.

But Will was with me, and although that changed things, it didn't really cramp my style. I had a moment or two of self-consciousness about getting sweaty and flushed, but remembered he would, too, and if he didn't like me sweaty and flushed after a run, we didn't stand a chance.

In fact, there was something to be said for having someone to share things with, like spotting a heron nest or pointing out the path that lead to the pond, or giving him the heads-up about a small streambed we were coming up on and would have to leap over.

Sometimes I was sorry the groundskeeper didn't leave the fallen trees; an occasional obstacle would have been a fun challenge.

Will responded with a few choice words, like "Gorgeous" about the scenery (yes, it was) or "Are there turtles?" about the pond (also yes) and "Got it" about the stream, which he cleared with ease.

Our strides fell into sync, and that was nice, too. We didn't have to talk, and hearing his measured step and breath match pace with mine was comfortable, easy. I found I could extend an arm to indicate which path we should take—they crisscrossed the island, and I had a rough plan in my head of how far I wanted to go this morning—and he would understand, turning with me.

In fact, at the final juncture, he made the arc before I even pointed.

This was where I usually picked up speed and sprinted back, and I briefly stumbled before I did so automatically, surprised he'd known which way to go. Will stepped up his pace, too, and kept level with me. We weren't racing, really, but we were subtly challenging each other, and my lungs were burning by the time we burst out of the forest onto the edge of the lawn.

We slowed, using the wide swath of grass as a cool-down lap, both of us gasping a little and laughing at the same time.

"How'd you know which path to take at that last intersection?" I asked when talking was possible again.

"Didn't you show me that first day?" he asked. "Or maybe it was when Mac and I did some hiking around."

Made sense. It wasn't as if I'd been with him and Mac all the time. "I'm going to put my suit on and cool off in the lake. Join me?"

He did, and we met on the patio soon thereafter and walked down to the lake. My leg muscles felt a little weak, but in a good way, a satisfying "I used these muscles" way, and I was looking forward to a final stretch in the water. I could almost feel it, cool and soft against my skin as I lengthened my body into a crawl.

Will said Mac was just waking up. Slug. At least I didn't feel guilty for taking Will away from Mac, the friend who'd brought him to the island.

Maybe my legs were weak because I was getting to spend more time alone with Will.

That was, until we got to the dock and found Uncle Jeremy and Aunt Delilah sitting at the edge of the lake with their feet in the water. They had little Fortune in her puffy orange vest and slathered with sunscreen. Aunt Delilah was spinning her in slow circles in the water, and Fortune was giggling madly.

My aunt and uncle didn't look like they were having nearly as much fun. They were facing away from us, toward the lake, when Will and I approached. Their heads were close together as if they were having an intimate conversation, but the tenseness in their backs and shoulders suggested the topic wasn't a happy intimacy.

"Hey!" I called out in greeting, feeling as if we should announce our presence as early as possible.

They jumped apart, almost guiltily. "Good morning, Elizabeth, Will," Delilah said. She had a wide mouth and a smile that normally lit up her face, but her expression looked a little pinched right now, with a tightness around her eyes.

It looked more than just being tired—and at her age, dealing with a baby must be exhausting. Were she and Uncle Jeremy having problems? I'd read about couples having another baby to patch up their failing relationship, and how it rarely worked out.

But she and Jeremy chatted with us as if nothing was wrong, and I dismissed my concerns. It wasn't my business, and there was nothing I could do either way. Really, I was probably overthinking everything right now, between Will occupying my brain and the fact that I was supposed to be spending the summer deciding whether to change majors or not (regarding the latter, so far avoidance had been working well for me).

After I stretched my muscles with a swim, it was almost time for lunch, and this time, Will did grab my hand as we jogged up the path to the lawn. He smelled like healthy male sweat and lake water. I couldn't keep the goofy grin off my face as I showered and dressed, but at least I managed to tone it down before we all gathered on the patio for roast beef and horseradish on rye with pasta salad and fruit salad, and blondie bars for dessert.

It was going to be a great summer.

The cook and housekeeper were given a day off every week. Sometimes the cook left us a cold meal of veggie pasta salad and grilled
chicken or something like that; sometimes my father grilled steaks
outside, with potatoes in foil and a tossed salad; and sometimes a
few of us were volunteered to pull something together.

This week it was our turn—meaning those of us in high school
or college—and it meant we'd had to plan ahead so the cook could
ensure we had the necessary ingredients. I usually volunteered to
do the dishes instead, but because Will would be in the kitchen, by
God, so would I.

In fact, Will had taken over. He'd been the one to plan the
menu: lasagna (both meat and vegetarian, and one with béchamel
instead of red sauce), Caesar salad, garlic bread, and brownies.

Despite its size, the kitchen always felt homey to me.
Gleaming white subway tile with dark grout covered the lower half
of the walls, and the floor was still the original hexagonal white
tiles with a dark green border. Under the windows set into the long
wall was an enormous, deep stainless steel sink and drain board. In
the center of the room was a massive island, the butcher block
sanded and resealed at the end of each year to minimize the nicks
from a summer's worth of sharp knives, and above that was a huge
wrought-iron pot rack, from which also hung dried herbs and
fragrant garlic. There was a walk-in fridge/freezer, an eight-burner
gas stove plus a griddle, lots of cabinets, and a pantry.

Right now the lower part of the windows were steamy thanks
to the two huge metal pots of red sauce and one of béchamel
bubbling on the stove. I kept dipping hunks of fresh sourdough
bread into the red sauce. It was so good that it took everything I
had to not repeatedly burn my mouth because I didn't have the
patience to wait for the sauce to cool. Sweet tomatoes, basil and
oregano, and a ton of the aforementioned garlic—I knew, because
I'd minced about a million cloves of it.

I'd been on dish duty enough times to know where things were
stored, but Will moved around the kitchen as if he owned it. He'd
disappear into the pantry and emerge with armfuls of ingredients

and bowls, pull the right spoons from drawers, and I half-expected him to start juggling knives like a chef at a Japanese restaurant.

Cathy and Ed had claimed my old dishwashing job and fled, so it was Mac, Will, Cortland, Vanessa, and I. Vanessa sat at the island, mixing brownie batter, and Mac and Cortland were browning the beef and onions. Me, I held a big bowl for Will to ease the noodles into after he'd pulled them from the boiling water with tongs. Behind me on this end of the island were several large pans, waiting to be layered with tasty ingredients.

He didn't have to look up any recipes; he had them in his head. "These are easy ones," he said. "The only difference is that I'm not used to cooking for quite this many people. Had to do a bit of math on the amounts of ingredients, but Ms. LeFebvre helped with that."

"Ms. LeFebvre?"

He glanced at me, and his mouth tightened for a moment, as if in disapproval. "Your cook?"

"Oh! Chef Ef. When Cathy was little, she had trouble pronouncing her name, so Chef Ef suggested the nickname. It's been so long, I'd forgotten her real name."

His expression smoothed out. "That's cute," he said. "So she's been with you a long time?"

I wondered about his reaction, but let it go as I thought back. "I was eleven or twelve when she came, I think. One cook left, and then we had one for only one summer, and then Chef Ef since then."

He pursed his lips as if he was about to say something, but then he shook his head once and focused on stirring the noodles gently with a slotted spoon. Then he said, "You remember them all. That's nice."

I shrugged, shaking the bowl a little to get the noodles to settle. "The regulars, yeah. If someone's here only for a season, that's one thing. But when someone's been around for a while..." I snorted. "Sometimes I get to know them better than I know some of my second cousins thrice removed."

"What's my middle name?" Mac joked.

"Granny Smith," I said, because of the whole apple-naming thing in his branch of the family.

"Mr. Competitive," Will said.

"Annoying As Fuck," Cortland said. To Vanessa, he added, "He's my younger brother. They're *all* annoying as fuck."

"Younger sisters, too," she said. "They're always stealing your clothes."

"Solidarity," I said.

"Your older sister would have something to say here," Vanessa said, and I rolled my eyes, laughing.

"My younger brother has never stolen my clothes," Will said.

"That's because he has good taste," Mac said.

Will lobbed a faded red oven mitt at Mac's head.

I didn't have an issue with what Will was wearing: a plain grey T-shirt that fit him nicely, black cotton shorts, deck shoes, and one of Chef Ef's white aprons. I'd been trying not to spend too much time contemplating the dusting of hair on his forearms, or the dexterity of his fingers as he sprinkled herbs into the sauce, or the way his black hair rumpled when he ran his hand through it.

"Seriously, either you're really good at faking this, or you know what you're doing," I said as he eased more noodles into my bowl.

"I never fake anything, and I do know what I'm doing." He flashed a grin that made my knees go weak. "I've been learning from my mom since I was big enough to climb up on a stool and stir things. My brothers and sister, too."

"She sounds like a smart lady," I said.

"She is," Will said, and I heard affection in his voice, but he didn't elaborate.

I started to ask where his mom learned to cook, but Mac said, "Meat's done. What now?"

"Drain the fat and then dump the beef in one of the red sauces," Will said. "We'll let it simmer all together for about ten minutes while the rest of the noodles cook. Can someone slice the zucchini for the veggie lasagna, please? Li—Elizabeth, could you grab the ricotta and shredded mozzarella from the fridge? Oh, the parmesan, too."

When I brought him the cheeses, he huffed through his nose. "Damn, someone put the ricotta on the shelf closest to the freezer."

"Good lord, how do you know that?" I asked.

He ran a spoon through it. "See how it's got some icy chunks in it and it's watery at the top? It's too cold on that shelf—things start to freeze."

I had no idea. He must've been spending more time in here with Chef Ef than I realized. Although when he had time, I couldn't imagine. Didn't he sleep?

Then Mac couldn't find the colander to drain the beef, and we started an assembly line to make the lasagnas, so it wasn't until everyone else, tired and sweaty, had fled the kitchen that Will said, "Elizabeth Sloane, you make an excellent sous-chef. You're welcome to assist in my kitchen anytime."

I put my hands together and sketched a bow. "Will Madigan, I look forward to learning more at the feet of the master."

It was only partially true. I still didn't enjoy cooking. But maybe I could get some private lessons from him.

The next weeks went by like all summer weeks should: slow and lazy, with the biggest decisions being whether to get out the badminton racquets or just boot the volleyball back and forth, or whether to re-read Harry Potter or try the new Nora Roberts.

Mac and Will, being friends, spent most of their time together, but as often as not it was the three of us, since Cortland obviously wanted to spend time with his wife. I saw a lot of Will, but didn't get to spend a lot of time alone with him, which was frustrating. I definitely had a crush on him, and when he looked at me, it was as if I was the only person in the room, or on the lawn, or wherever, so I was pretty sure he felt the same.

I liked his sense of humor, especially when we played Cards Against Humanity, possibly the rudest game in existence. I liked how he was always courteous to my family—by the end of the first week he'd broken down and was calling people "aunt" and "uncle," but his tone was just as respectful. I liked how he'd play patiently with the younger kids, and throw the ball for someone's golden retriever when even more family descended on us one weekend.

I just didn't like how few chances we had to be alone together, especially after the fresh wave of family descended. The lodge had enough space that it didn't feel crowded, but it wasn't quite big enough to necessarily have a room to yourself if you weren't in the bathroom, and although there were a fair number of bathrooms, hogging them because you needed private time was frowned upon.

To make matters worse, because of the fresh influx of bodies, the single menfolk were banished to the bunkhouse.

But we found our ways.

We shared our first kiss out on the lake. We'd taken kayaks out, just Will and I, after dinner. It had been an impossibly clear blue day, but a cool one, and everyone else was around the campfire or in the lodge, drinks in hand, games out. The sun was setting behind the trees, and the water was still as a mirror, only our paddles and kayaks disturbing the surface.

It was the first time I'd experienced silence all weekend, and it was blissful. I'd felt the beginnings of a migraine coming on, so I'd taken my meds and explained things to the crowd and then fled to the lake. My stomach flipped as if I'd rolled down the slope of the lawn when Will said he'd join me. I think he was a little over-whelmed by the sheer volume of Sloanes, and I didn't blame him. We were a force to be reckoned with, and even I got peopled out by the end of the busiest weekends on the island.

I wanted to believe, though, that Will had joined me because he wanted to spend time alone with me.

We paddled in companionable silence, even dipping our oars gently as if not wanting to shatter the stillness. We were out far enough that I could just make out the house on the next island over, another private residence. I think the owner was a congresswoman.

I paused, letting my kayak drift as I tracked the course of a blue heron overhead. When I looked back down, Will had slid his kayak next to mine. He was watching me. My heart skipped, came back beating faster. He leaned, and I leaned, and we met in the middle.

His lips were soft and cool, but they warmed quickly. He tasted of mint from the ice cream we'd had for dessert. It was perfect, unhurried and exploring as we learned how we fit together. Everything in my world narrowed to the bubble that contained just us, the moment that slowed time to just this kiss. I felt as though I'd been waiting for it all my life.

However, you can't fully concentrate on kissing when you're balancing a kayak, so it didn't last long. But it was oh, so sweet.

I smiled. He smiled back. We turned our kayaks and headed back to the dock, while a loon called mournfully behind us.

Even with the additional people that weekend, we managed to find a few more moments of private time. Due to some renovation before my time, one of the screened sleeping porches was only accessible through a closet. All that was out there was a bulky, white wicker sofa with flowered cushions. The sofa itself was too big to be maneuvered through the closet door, although the cushions obviously got stored during the winter; otherwise they would have gotten mildewed.

I'd nearly forgotten the room existed until I lay awake one night, scheming places to sneak off to with Will.

Will had me by the hand, and we both giggled as we pushed through the extra raincoats in the closet and stumbled through to the porch, our own secret Narnia.

He tasted like the Adirondack Brewery IPA we had cases of on the island—or maybe that was me, because I'd been drinking it, too. The grounds had been recently mowed, and the smell of fresh grass, a little damp from an earlier light rain, permeated the porch. I'd never thought of it as a sexy smell until now...and I had a feeling I always would from now on.

Will kissed as though he had all the time in the world, languid and deliberate, taking his time, exploring. And I met him, kiss for kiss, tongue for tongue, putting all the longing I had into the way our mouths touched and moved. He cupped my face in his warm, strong hands and I pressed against him, working my hands around to his back, splaying my fingers against the muscles that flexed there.

In some ways, we did have all the time in the world; the summer still stretched before us, weeks without responsibility or care. That afternoon, we probably could have necked for hours—I know I could have—but the dinner bell rang the ten-minute warning, and our absence at supper would be noted and frowned upon. We reluctantly drew apart, although we leaned in for another quick kiss, then another, and even as we stood up, we kept doing it, and giggling.

My giggle caught in my throat when I heard voices in the outer room, a parlor of bookcases crammed with books old and new, and overstuffed chairs and reading lamps. I glanced at Will, which was a mistake, because he was stifling his laughter, too, but I could see it in his blue eyes, and it almost set me off again.

We hadn't been doing anything wrong, and I wasn't ashamed, but it was the tone of the voices that gave me pause. Low and urgent, stressed. It was a conversation we shouldn't be listening to, I knew that in my bones.

But we were trapped—the only way out was through the closet into the parlor. The closet door was closed, but it was louvered, so it didn't really block sound.

A moment later I recognized the voices: Uncle Jeremy and Aunt Delilah.

"I agree that it's not a good idea for her to come here," Jeremy said. "Not until she stops fighting us. Maybe we shouldn't have come—maybe we should go home—"

"The separation may be a good thing, though," Delilah said, although she didn't sound convinced of her own words. "The more space, the more time...she'll have to come around and realize we're right eventually."

They had to be talking about Paula. I wondered if she'd screwed up the internship, or college entirely.

"I'm just worried that she'll—" Jeremy began.

"Don't even say it," Delilah said firmly. "Look, we'll give her a call the next time we're off-island, see how she's doing. She knows, deep down, that we love her, no matter what."

"I hope so." It was Jeremy's turn to sound dubious.

"I have to get Fortune so we can get to dinner," Delilah said. "It'll be fine. She'll be fine. We'll be fine."

I heard a quick kiss, and then two pairs of footsteps on the wooden floor, fading away.

That was weird. What was Uncle Jeremy worried Paula would do? Should I ask them about it, privately? Maybe I could reach out...?

"I'm going to pretend I didn't hear any of that," Will said, still pitching his voice low. "Not that I have a clue what they were talking about."

"Good plan," I said. "With a family as big as ours, it's best to keep out of people's business unless they ask for help. It gets messy otherwise." I wasn't ready to share my concerns with him. He didn't know Paula, and as well as he was fitting in, he was still new here, not one of the family.

Although the summer was still young....

We pushed through the raincoats and into the parlor, made sure the coast was clear, then headed down the hallway. I ducked in the bathroom before going to the dining room, allowing Will to get to supper before me. My cheeks were flushed and my eyes were bright, and I wondered if anyone would be able to tell my lips were a little swollen.

I ran a finger over them. Everybody had secrets. This was our little secret, Will's and mine. For as long as it needed to be.

Finding time—and space—continued to be the challenge. Strangely enough, it was the littles who sparked the idea for me. They wanted to camp outside one night, and Will and I ended up chaperoning them, all of us in a big tent on the lawn. We made s'mores over the fire, wrangled them all into sleeping bags, and after they'd all finally fallen asleep, Will and I held hands and kissed and whispered about everything and nothing.

We certainly weren't going to do more than that with the littles sprawled all around us. And I liked talking to him almost as much as I liked kissing him, although that was starting to get a little frustrating.

The next day, I pulled him aside while a bunch of us were walking outside to whack a volleyball around, and said, "Meet me at midnight at the start of the running trail."

He leaned close, his voice low. "An assignation?"

I tried not to giggle. "Something like that."

Just before midnight, I snuck out a window in my bedroom. Along that side of the lodge, for fire safety, ran a narrow balcony with stairs at both ends. It had been added well after the lodge was built, so it was accessed through the large casement windows rather than doors. Leaving that way was quieter than trying to sneak down the hall past half the bedrooms, even if I did know from years of experience which boards creaked underfoot. This way, I was unlikely to run into someone making a bathroom run or sneaking down to the kitchen for a snack.

Cathy, of course, didn't twitch from beneath her pile of blankets.

I'd already set things up, out in the meadow past the pond. Sleeping bags spread out, shallow clay pots nicked from the potting shed and filled with dirt, with votive candles set in them. (I thought it best not to set the island on fire.) I'd considered small speakers to hook my phone into, but in the end I decided I didn't want music. The island had music of its own.

Will was a few minutes late, muttering something about Mac's weird sleep patterns. But then, there at the edge of the forest, he gathered me up and kissed me so well, I felt it down to the tips of my toes.

The skies had cleared, and a full moon spread its pale glow over us. I took Will's hand and led him through the woods, down the paths we'd run every few days so far this summer, past the pond, still and pearly in the moonlight, where the frogs sang.

I paused to light the votives with the long lighter I'd brought. Then we kissed again, for a long time, just standing there. He cradled my face in his hands and I threaded my fingers through his hair, and I savored the taste of him, toothpaste-minty and familiar.

When we finally eased apart, I said, "There's only one problem: no condoms. We'll have to wait for that until we can get off-island."

Like magic, Will had one between his fingers. "I keep one in my shaving kit," he said. "Only one, though, unless I can rifle through Mac's and see what he's got stashed."

A relieved laugh bubbled out of me. "One will do for now," I said. I suspected we'd wish we had more, but one was better than none, right?

And it was, plus we found other ways to be creative, until hours later when we crept back into the house before dawn, and shared one last, lingering kiss before we went to our separate rooms, carrying our shared secret with us.

Over the next few weeks, things progressed.

By unspoken agreement, we were discreet. My parents may or may not have assumed I was sexually active, but even if they did, I doubted they wanted it flashed in their faces. Plus Mac had brought Will to the island, and it wouldn't be fair to steal all of Will's time, no matter how much I wanted to bunk down with Will in the guesthouse and pretend everyone else didn't exist for a while.

Will made love like he kissed, passionate but solicitous; it wasn't about him, or even me—it was about *us*. Well, not every time was drawn out...sometimes we could steal away for only a short time before someone might notice we were gone, or stumble onto us. And those times were even more thrilling, more of a secret to share.

We scrounged up a few more condoms, and found other ways to explore each other when we needed to.

I enjoyed being with him the rest of the time, too, whether we were debating books or whacking croquet balls or swimming with the rest of the crowd.

The only thing we really didn't talk much about was the future. A little about college, sure, but we skirted and danced around anything beyond our courses next semester, him at Cornell, me at Dartmouth. He would be going to law school, somewhere. I might end up going to grad school, somewhere. So many unknowns, unspoken.

I think it was partly fear, but more that summer was a bubble we didn't want to pop. Blue Heron Island had its own magic, and the idea of life outside of it was too much to contemplate.

I knew, though, that if this was just a summer crush, I was going to get my heart broken, shattered like the stillness of the lake when a blue heron plunged from the sky for its supper.

According to the weather reports, we'd be getting a storm the next day, and the weather would be bad for a few days. A group decision was made to take the pontoon boats and head to the mainland, both for stocking up on supplies and for having an evening out in town. People wanted to make phone calls while they had cell service, and there were movies some people wanted to see, and eat at a fantastic restaurant, Great Peaks, that specialized in local fish and game.

Will and I thought we might be able to use it as an opportunity to have some quality time together (he'd put in a condom request with Mac, who knew what we were up to the moment we started, and who rolled his eyes but said nothing), but the gods were not favoring us. I was feeling the beginnings of a migraine coming on, my first one in ages—which, ironically, I'd been planning to claim as an excuse to stay behind.

Then Delilah said, "Well, crap. Since you were staying, I was hoping I could talk you into watching Fortune, but if you don't feel well..."

"That's okay, Aunt Delilah," Will said. "I can help keep an eye on her."

Will was great with the younger kids, even fussy Fortune. He said it was because of taking care of his younger siblings.

The cook had left supper for us and Fortune—she and the housekeeper had the day off as well, and had gone to the mainland earlier, also to pick up supplies, because she'd been complaining we'd been eating extra the last couple days.

"That would be wonderful," Delilah said, looking relieved. "You know Fortune goes down early, and once she's asleep, she'll be out for the night."

I stretched out on one of the tan leather couches in the living room, a Black Watch plaid wool blanket pulled halfway up, while Will ran around on the lawn with Fortune after supper, catching fireflies and wearing her out. I wished I could've been out there with them, but I knew better. Still, I was sorry to miss the time with, well, both of them.

We both trooped upstairs to put her in her crib, and even though she struggled to keep her dark eyes open, she was so wiped out that she was asleep in minutes.

"Nighty-night, Snugglecheeks McGooshyToes," I murmured,

touching my fingers to my lips and then to her downy reddish-brown hair.

We put our half of the baby monitor on the coffee table in the living room and tried to watch a DVD on Will's laptop, but the picture was a little too much for me to concentrate on. The medication was keeping my migraine down at a dull roar, but I was still going to have to ride it out.

The change in barometric pressure wasn't helping. It was also making me antsy, making something feel...off.

"Wind's starting to pick up," I said, listening to it shaking the pines. "Storm's coming in sooner than we thought. I hope the rest of them make it back safely tonight."

I was dozing on Will's lap while he read when a loud bang startled both of us.

The sound had come through the baby monitor.

It was probably just a loose shutter in the wind. We went upstairs, hoping Fortune hadn't woken up.

But Fortune was *gone*.

I stared at the empty crib, my hand over my mouth as if that would stop the panicked sounds rising in my throat.

The window was indeed open, the shutter banging.

The groundskeeper had mowed today, ahead of the storm, and there were flecks of grass tracked between the window and the crib, and out to the narrow balcony.

"Someone's got Fortune," I whispered, because if I spoke too loud, I thought I might start screaming. Someone had that sweet squooshy baby, and God only knew why, or what they were going to do to her. "Someone else is on the island."

I said the words almost before I thought them, and speaking them aloud sent a horrified chill through me.

Someone else was on the island.

"The boat dock," Will said. "We can catch them before they leave."

We ran downstairs so fast I almost stumbled over my own feet. Will went straight for the utility closet off the kitchen, grabbing two of the industrial flashlights from the row of chargers on the closet wall. He tossed one to me and then we were out the door and off the patio, running down the railroad-tie steps at the edge of the lawn to the path that led to the boathouse and dock.

Something bothered me about the flashlights, but I couldn't quite grab hold of the thought, the way my head was pounding.

It wasn't fully dark yet, although the lowering grey clouds made it seem night was coming early. I mostly kept my eyes on the uneven ground so I didn't twist an ankle. My head throbbed with each step, but I ignored it. I hoped Will was keeping an eye on the trees.

No boats at the dock or in the cove, no motor board noises on the water, and we hadn't caught up with anyone. There hadn't been enough time for someone to get here ahead of us with Fortune and gotten so far out onto the lake that we wouldn't see them. We checked the boathouse, just in case. Empty except for the kayaks.

"They're still on the island," I breathed.

"How did they get here?" Will asked.

"They could have docked at the fishing rock," I said. "We never do because it's on the other side of the island."

The clouds had reluctantly released a few drops of rain, but the storm hadn't broken yet. It would soon. It needed to.

"They've gone somewhere under cover if they have any sense, rather than head out now," I said as we hurried up the path.

"Not the lodge," he said.

"Not the lodge," I agreed. "Guesthouse, bunkhouse, or the play cabin."

"I'll go to the fishing dock, and you check the guesthouse and bunkhouse," Will suggested. "We'll meet at the play cabin."

"Are you *crazy*?" I shouted, all my panic manifesting in my voice. "Have you never *seen* a horror movie? I'm sticking to you like white on rice."

Plus I didn't know how many people there were. Plus they could have guns.

Plus I knew the island better than he did....

And that's when it came all together for me. All the pieces. In one lightning flash.

He'd known exactly where the emergency flashlights were.

Just like he'd known where other things were, and how to navigate around the island, and that the gaming consoles in the play cabin were new. Just like calling me Lizzie.

He'd been on Blue Heron Island before.

He'd had an explanation for everything, or I'd explained things away myself. What he said had always made sense: Mac had shown him, or Chef Ef had said something, or it was a logical guess.

Shit, had he been gaslighting me all along?

We made it back up to the lawn. My mind raced, split between how to find Fortune and what was going on with Will. The skin on my forearms prickled a split second before a flash of light and loud *crack* split the air.

All the lights in the lodge went out.

I shrieked, then swore. The surprise galvanized me, though, and I took off running to the ragged line of pines on the other side of the lawn, heading for the guesthouse, Will at my heels.

Maybe I was being paranoid. Maybe Mac or Cortland or anyone else had shown him where the emergency supplies were, or he'd had a reason to go into the utility closet for something else earlier in the summer.

Maybe I was just freaking out about everything because I had a good goddamn right to freak out about the fact that someone had broken into the house and taken Fortune—someone who knew which room to go to.

But I didn't have time for freaking out. I had to calm my pounding heart and pounding head, take some deep breaths, prepare myself for whatever had to happen next.

Will might be in league with the kidnapper, for all I knew.

After all, if the window hadn't banged through the monitor, we wouldn't have known Fortune was gone for hours.

The thought chilled me. I didn't dare look at him, in case my thoughts were obvious in my eyes.

But I'd figure it out when I had to. Finding Fortune was the important thing, before someone could hurt her.

She wasn't just my cousin. She'd somehow stolen my heart in the few times I'd met her. She was my squooshy-cheeked snuggle-bug, and the person who had invaded our sanctuary and taken her was going to be in deep, deep trouble.

Even if that included Will.

I hoped it didn't. But I couldn't be sure. I couldn't ask him, because that would be letting him know I knew.

We ran across the island to the fishing rock. It was a slower pace than the ones we'd done together before, because of the gloom. Some of the trails weren't on my normal running route, so I didn't know all the tree roots and rocks. Flashlight beams weren't enough.

It was fully dark by the time we got to the rock. Our flashlight beams danced on a battered aluminum rowboat tied to the rusty, fat eyebolt sunk into the rock and banging against the jutting stone as the waves churned up.

A boat I didn't recognize—and I knew all the boats of the family and staff and even owners of neighboring islands.

"They're still here," I said.

"Then we need to check everywhere else."

Fortune wasn't in the guesthouse or the bunkhouse. I yanked open the door to the play cabin, but it, too, was empty.

I paused, hands on my knees, catching my breath after all the running. More fat raindrops plonked down on us now that we were back out in the open, but they were still intermittent; the storm hadn't broken yet, and the electric tension was rising again. The air practically whined with it.

Will rested his hand on my back, a comforting, energy-giving gesture. My body responded even as my mind questioned. I didn't want to have been wrong about him. I wanted to believe he was on my side; I wanted that solid shoulder to lean on.

Could I trust him?

Right now, I felt like I had no choice.

"Where else?" Will asked.

"The only place we haven't checked is the old house," I said.

I didn't think the place was haunted, not like I did when I was young. But it was still creepy, and dangerous. Was there even enough roof left to shield someone from a storm?

Maybe we should have stayed at the fishing rock in case the kidnapper came back. Maybe we should go back and check. Maybe we *should* split up. My own indecision brought frustrated tears to my eyes.

I had to pick something.

"Old house, and then we'll circle back to the lodge. We can see if the phone still works."

Back through the tall pines. In the darkness, with only our bobbing flashlight beams to guide our way, the trees seemed to crowd closer.

If the person who took Fortune was at the old house, it meant they knew the island, and well—not just the lodge and the regularly used areas. That thought creeped me out even more.

Then, out of the gloom and spotting rain, the crumbling house loomed. Three stories, up on a cliff, the dark grey stones black in the night. Empty windows like blindly staring eyes. I thought I saw a light inside, and my heart thudded.

The light gave me hope—and fear.

Will held up a hand. "I'll go first," he said, his voice pitched low.

"We'll go in together," I said. I didn't need him to protect me. I didn't know if I could trust him.

The front door was gone, the open space wide enough for two.

The floor was gone, too, so we had to step a foot down off the threshold onto dirt and rocks. A few hardy weeds even poked through here and there. I tried to walk as silently as I could, but my feet still crunched on the pebble-strewn ground.

The front area was a wide, open room, the walls of the foyer gone. On the far side of the room, the remains of an archway led into a room beyond. We checked the back room in case someone was hiding behind the half walls, but it was empty, too. The roof and upper floors were mostly gone. The worst of the fire had been out here; it had probably started in the big fireplace, unattended, sparks leaping out to set alight a rug, and the stone walls had since crumbled.

The wind moaned through the ruins, and even though I knew what it was, I shivered.

About half the staircase remained, twisting up into darkness and a hall that still mostly had a roof. Even as kids, we never tried to climb it—we were young and stupid, but not *that* stupid. But would a kidnapper be desperate enough to be stupid, and assume nobody would check up there?

Will grabbed my arm and pointed to an adjoining room. I was pretty sure the kitchen had been back there. He aimed his flashlight down so the beam wouldn't be obvious, but also to allow me to see there was a glow coming from that area.

A moment later, I heard Fortune make a babbling toddler sound, followed by someone shushing her. As if that ever stopped a toddler from making noise. Relief flooded my body. Fortune was alive, and probably not hurt, or else she'd be crying or silent.

We crept forward. I was barely breathing.

Then I heard...singing?

Unsure of what I would see, or what would come at me, I poked my head around the doorway and pulled my flashlight beam up.

The person sitting in an open windowsill and holding Fortune on their lap said, "Stop it—she doesn't like the light in her eyes."

I stepped all the way in, dumbfounded. "Paula?"

Will was at my side. "Paula?"

If he was part of this, he was doing a damn good job of sounding like he didn't know anything.

"My cousin—Mac's sister," I explained. To Paula, I said, "What are you doing here? I thought you had an internship somewhere."

"That's what they wanted you to think," Paula said. "My parents. They lied because they don't want anyone to know."

I had moved my flashlight beam to the left, next to her head, leaving her face half in shadow. Concern gnawed at my belly. She didn't look right, and I didn't think that was just a trick of the light. Her shoulder-length auburn hair looked tangled and messy —but then again, mine probably did too, between the wind and rain.

Still, something was wrong. Off.

Seeing darling Fortune in her arms chilled me to the bone. She'd snuck into the lodge, taken Fortune from her crib.

"Lied about what?" I asked.

She lifted her chin to indicate Will. "Who's he?"

"This is Will, Mac's friend from college. He's spending the summer here."

She picked up her flashlight where it had been sitting on the stone sill next to her and pointed it at him. She narrowed her eyes.

"Do I know you from somewhere?" she asked.

"No, I don't think so," Will said. There was a strange note in his voice, though, slightly strangled, and I looked at him.

In the glow of her flashlight, he seemed pale.

It didn't seem like they were in this together—I didn't know about him, but I didn't think she was that good an actress. Then again, something about Paula seemed to be bothering him more than just the fact that she'd apparently snuck through a window in the lodge, taken Fortune, and hidden out here.

Fortune didn't seem to be entirely distressed. She had three fingers stuffed in her mouth and was staring around as if analyzing the situation.

I panicked on her behalf. There was about half of a roof left in here—the floor above had only half-collapsed—but it still wasn't somewhere we should be lingering. Not to mention the question of why Paula was here, and why she'd taken her sister out of the lodge, which was downright creepy.

Paula wasn't well. Fortune wasn't safe.

"Why don't we go back to the lodge before the rain really starts coming down," I said gently, trying to be soothing despite the fear churning in my belly. "Will can carry Fortune if she's getting too heavy for you."

"No." Paula hugged Fortune closer, and now Fortune whimpered, her eyes even wider. She held out her arms to Will, a trusting gesture that made my heart twist, and wiggled in Paula's arms.

"Why don't you want to go to the lodge?" Will asked. He too pitched his voice so he sounded reasonable. Something was clearly upsetting Paula, and he was doing what he could not to upset her further.

"Because my parents will be there, and they'll take Fortune away again," she said. "I just want to be with my baby."

Ohhh.

It all made sense now.

"Fortune's your baby," I said. "Of course she is. Look at that hair." I smiled, hoping it looked sincere and gentle.

Why had my aunt and uncle passed off Fortune as Aunt Delilah's late-in-life baby? Why hadn't they wanted to the rest of us to know Paula had gotten pregnant? Had she even been on an internship this summer?

If not...?

If not, where had Paula been?

The question bordered on terrifying.

Now, I guessed, was not the time to ask.

"She's beautiful, isn't she?" Paula said, almost dreamily.

Distantly, I thought I heard voices. Maybe even someone calling my name. Or it could have been the wind moaning through the house. I wanted to look at Will—I could sense him close to my right shoulder, just behind me—but I didn't dare turn away.

My mouth was dry. Paula clearly wasn't okay. The rest of the family turning up might completely freak her out, and there was no telling what she'd do. Oh, my cousin, my dear old friend, what had happened to you?

I wrenched my painful brain back to the last words Paula had said. "Oh, she's so beautiful," I said, pouring the truth into my words, "but you don't want her to catch a cold, do you? Or scrape herself on a rusty nail? It's not safe in here."

Paula glanced down at Fortune as if assessing the toddler's condition. I figured that was a good sign, so I took a step closer.

Once I had Fortune in my arms, we could figure the rest of it out.

A flash and another boom of thunder, and then the storm broke. Rain sheeted down, pelting the island.

Paula flinched so hard she knocked her flashlight off the sill. I heard it rattle and bounce off a series of rocks down to the lake—the house was built right on the edge of the cliff—far enough that I couldn't have heard the splash even without the sound of the downpour.

At the same time, Fortune reached out again, squirming and kicking her fat little toddler legs, which I knew were stronger than you'd expect, especially when she wanted *down*.

The movement threw Paula off balance. Backwards.

I didn't have time to think. I leapt forward and grabbed for Fortune, getting my hands on her upper arms as Paula fell backward. Paula held on, her arm tight around Fortune's waist.

Fortune shrieked her displeasure.

Will was at my side again.

The sudden weight of Paula's descent yanked me, and my head slammed, hard, into the stone side of the window opening.

I lost my grip on Fortune.

I heard Paula scream as she fell.

No...

Then I heard Fortune crying and knew Will had her, just before my world went black.

———

I woke to arrhythmic jolting, every shake sending a flare of agony through my head, nauseating me. Rain sheeted against my face. I tried to raise my hand to block it, but my body didn't want to respond.

A flash of lightning, followed almost immediately by a long, slow grumble of thunder like waves on the shoreline, illuminated the face above me. Will.

Wet black hair plastered his skull. His face was pale, his lips parted as he sucked in air. He was carrying me through the dark woods, his feet thudding on the rocky, uneven path as he jogged.

I tried to ask him to stop, to put me down—my head hurt so bad—but all that came out was a low moan.

In the distance, a long, low rumble of thunder, like waves on the shoreline.

I tried again to shield my face, and this time my hand flopped against my forehead. I grabbed onto my own sodden hair so my hand wouldn't flop down again. The tug against my scalp was nothing compared to the pulsing squeeze in my skull.

"Don't you die on me, Lizzy Sloane." Will's voice was rough, coming through his harsh breath. "Don't you dare die on me."

It's Elizabeth. *Nobody calls me Lizzy anymore*, I thought grumpily, and then everything went black again, just for a blissful moment before the jolting brought me back.

I licked my lips. How could they be dry in the rain? "Fortune?" I managed, the word broken into two distinct syllables as he jogged down the path, but also broken by my heart, because I was so afraid for her. I remembered talking to Paula, and then a blur of motion...

"She's safe. Uncle Jeremy has her."

Relief washed over me like the rain. But I needed to know more. I fought through the pain in my head. "Paula?"

"Your dad...he's looking for her."

Okay. Okay. Nothing I could do there. My heart ached, even as my thoughts were muddled from the agony of the migraine. I wished Will would stop jolting around, just give me a moment to rest. The pain was making me nauseated, and I didn't want to throw up on Will—I didn't think our relationship was strong enough to handle that.

Did we even have a relationship? Was he even someone I could trust? I swallowed hard against the need to puke.

"Will..."

I wasn't sure if I breathed his name aloud, but then he answered.

"I know. I know, Lizzy. You've got to trust me. I just need to get you home and safe.

Who are *you?* I tried to ask, but my brain wouldn't send the words to my mouth.

If he'd been a part of this, he wouldn't be trying to save me.

I clung to that thought as everything went black again.

———

I was emergency lifted off the island. The chopper was impossibly loud, from the *whopwhopwhop* of the blades to the ambient roar to the medical personnel shouting over it all, making my head hurt even more. Rain sheeted blackly across the windows, and I missed Will.

There was the doctor in the hospital, tall and bald and wearing gold wire-rimmed glasses. If he told me his name, it's gone now. But I distinctly remember him explaining to me that I had a nasty concussion and that it would take a few days before I felt better, because—and this part is crystal clear—my brain had sloshed around in my skull.

The very concept made my stomach churn.

I later learned I was in the hospital only overnight. The next memory I had was waking up in my own bed on the island, and feeling a wave of relief. I was home, and everything was going to be okay even if my head felt like a tiny man was digging at my skull with a rusty spoon.

The window was open, the filmy white curtain fluttering in the warm breeze. I breathed in the scents of pine and grass. Across the room, Cathy's bed was neatly made; she'd been booted to the guesthouse while I recovered. In fact, nobody was supposed to visit me, to let me rest, and I was going out of my mind with boredom.

At some point during my recovery, I woke to voices outside my door, which was half-open, as if someone had just left. One was my mother, and I had a vague sense that she had been with me moments before.

Then Will slipped in through the open window. He wore blue shorts and his grey Cornell T-shirt, and he clutched a handful of white Queen Anne's lace.

Delight at seeing him suffused me like sunlight, overpowering even my knee-jerk reaction that I hadn't showered in several days and what did my hair look like? It didn't matter, because he kissed my forehead, crouched by the bed, and said quietly, "I can't stay long; you're not supposed to have visitors. But I missed you."

I groped around until I found his hand. "I missed you, too. Are you okay? Nobody will tell me anything. How's Fortune? Paula...?"

He smiled. "Me? Not a hair out of place. Fortune doesn't remember a thing. Paula...she's pretty banged up, broken bones and stuff, but she'll recover. Delilah and Jeremy have left, of course, and so have Cortland and Vanessa, but Mac and I stayed."

He cocked his head, and I heard footsteps outside. "Gotta go," he whispered. He brushed another kiss on my head and disappeared out the window.

I let out a long breath. I hadn't realized how tense I'd been, not knowing.

And how tense I still was, because in my happiness at seeing Will, I'd almost forgotten all the many unanswered questions I had about him.

A few days later, we prepared for the biggest weekend of the summer: Fourth of July.

It was overcast; not the best conditions for fireworks, but we Sloanes make do. We're stubborn like that.

I was on an Adirondack chair on the patio, the Black Watch plaid wool blanket over my lap, wearing a sweatshirt because the evening was cool, thrilled to be sprung from my bedroom prison.

My mother was still keeping an eye on me because of the concussion, but I was *not* going to miss the fireworks.

Almost everyone else was inside because of the temperature; they'd emerge when it was time for the show. Cortland and Mac had come of age two years ago to be in charge of the fireworks, and they'd taken my brother and sister as their apprentices.

Will was with me. It was the first time we'd been alone together since that night, except for his very brief visit to my room. Mom hadn't allowed me visitors for any length of time, and she'd noticed that bouquet of Queen Anne's lace.

I already knew the basics of what had happened after I hit my head. The rest of the family had made it back to the island just before the storm broke—fairly shortly after we'd left to look for Fortune, really. They'd fanned out and checked everywhere, and my father and Uncle Jeremy had arrived at the old house ruins just after Paula fell. Jeremy took Fortune and my father went to look for Paula, because Will had insisted on carrying me back to the lodge.

The whole sordid story had come out after that. Delilah and Jeremy had decided to claim Fortune as theirs because they wanted Paula to finish university and have a normal life. Paula had agreed with all of that until Fortune had been born, when she suffered from some pretty serious post-partum depression and possibly a minor psychotic break. But the lies were already in motion— Delilah had worn padding and we'd all believed she was pregnant— so they insisted on maintaining the subterfuge.

A lot of people in the family were angry about not being told, but they'd get over it the next time our family had to close ranks against some outside threat. Another Sloane trait.

Will might be that threat.

Thus far, though, he hadn't been booted off Blue Heron Island, probably because I hadn't told anyone my suspicions about him.

Now, however, he was going to tell me what was going on. I'd made it clear he had no choice. I kept my hands beneath the blanket, unwilling to touch him before I knew how betrayed I should feel.

"You don't remember me, do you?" he asked now.

I shook my head—carefully, because too much motion made the world spin. "Remember you from where?"

"My mother was the cook you mentioned who was here only one summer," he said. "I was twelve. I...wasn't very nice then. I had a chip on my shoulder because my father had left us and my mom could barely make ends meet. Plus I had glasses and an overbite and a mouthful of braces, and my mom had shaved my head before we got here because I'd had lice. It was awful. *I* was awful."

I squinted, trying to imagine an awful, homely boy beneath those gorgeous features and kind mien. I put a hand to my mouth. "Billy? Billy...something. Not Madigan."

He shook his head. "My mom remarried the next year, and my stepdad adopted me, so I took his name. But yes, Billy."

"You *were* awful," I said. I'd been bookish and shy, comfortable mostly only around my own family. My cousins had tried to include the cook's son, but he refused. He called us snobs, and pinched me once, hard, on the upper arm when I came into the kitchen hoping for an extra slice of Uncle Buster's cherry pie.

"It was just that one summer," I said. "Nine years ago. That's probably why I didn't recognize you."

"Well, I hope I look at least a little different now," he said, with such horror in his voice that I had to laugh.

"Yes, yes you do."

"My mom met a wonderful man that fall—my stepdad. He's a lawyer, so my mom was able to go back to school and become a chef. She owns Great Peaks, among other restaurants, and she created a line of organic frozen meals that really took off."

"So, why didn't you tell any of us this?"

272

He set his hand on the arm of my chair, palm up. I considered it. After a moment, I took it, and he wrapped his warm fingers around mine.

"Lots of reasons. I was embarrassed to have been the son of the help, for one. I hate to say it, but your family can be kind of snobby sometimes."

"Don't apologize," I said. "It's true. I've had a lot of lectures about dating beneath me."

"Exactly," he said. "Thanks to my stepdad, I pulled myself together and started studying hard, and I got a scholarship to Cornell. I met Mac by accident—we were already friends before I clued in to who he was. He's...more laid back than a lot of your family."

"Also true," I agreed.

"When I realized, I didn't want to tell him, because I didn't want him to think I'd befriended him on purpose. And then when he invited me here for the summer..."

Will ducked his head, his long lashes shadowing his eyes. This was hard for him, and it made my heart hurt.

Finally he looked back up, looked me straight in the eye with those gorgeous blue eyes of his, and said, "Believe it or not, I had a crush on you all those years ago. I agreed to come because I wanted to find out what kind of woman you'd become, and see if maybe there could be something, still. I figured I'd have to win your heart by showing you who I am now."

"You *liked* me? You pinched me so hard, I had a bruise for two weeks!"

"I think that was when it happened," he said. "You didn't cry. You stared at me with tears welling up in your big, beautiful brown eyes...and then you hauled off and punched me in the arm. *I* had a bruise, too. You were—you are—one of the strongest people I've ever met. When Fortune went missing, I knew you weren't going to fall apart. You just took charge."

"I was terrified," I said.

"But you didn't let that stop you," he said.

I felt tears welling again. I blinked them away. "Dammit, Will Madigan. I think I'm in love with you."

He cocked his head toward the house. "Is that going to be a problem?" he asked, and I knew he meant my family. Because he was going to have to come clean, and although my parents are generous and kind to the help, socializing with them was another matter entirely.

But Will was making something of his life, the same way my great-great-grandfather had (only hopefully with more ethics). And my father did know his father's name, and his mother was a very successful businesswoman now and sort of a famous chef to boot.

"You saved Fortune's life," I said. "If they ever, *ever* question my being with you, I'm going to remind them of that. So on behalf of all the Sloanes and Sloane-adjacents, welcome to the family."

His grin as always, charmed me down to my toes.

"I love you too, Elizabeth Sloane."

"You are allowed to call me Lizzy," I said, and then I kissed him, as a loon's cry echoed over the lake and across Blue Heron Island.

ABOUT THE EDITOR

Called "The Reigning Queen of Paranormal Romance" by *Best Reviews,* bestselling author Kristine Grayson has made a name for herself publishing light, slightly off-skew romance novels about Greek Gods, fairy tale characters, and the modern world.

She writes historical mysteries as Kris Nelscott, and she also writes in a variety of genre, from literary to science fiction to romance, under her real name—Kristine Kathryn Rusch. She has won dozens of awards for her writing

As Kristine Grayson, she also edits the romance volumes of *Fiction River: An Original Anthology Magazine.*

For more information about her work, go to www.kristinegrayson.com and sign up for her newsletter.

FICTION RIVER YEAR SIX

Feel the Love
Edited by Mark Leslie

Special Edition: Spies
Edited by Kristine Kathryn Rusch

Special Edition: Summer Sizzles
Edited by Kristine Grayson

Superstitious
Edited by Mark Leslie

A subscription to *Fiction River* saves you money and ensures that you receive the very best short fiction from some of today's best authors. Subscriptions are available in electronic and trade paper formats and begin with the very next volume. Don't wait! Subscribe today at www.FictionRiver.com.

Missed a previously published volume? No problem. Buy individual volumes anytime from your favorite bookseller.

Unnatural Worlds
Edited by Dean Wesley Smith & Kristine Kathryn Rusch

How to Save the World
Edited by John Helfers

Time Streams
Edited by Dean Wesley Smith

Christmas Ghosts
Edited by Kristine Grayson

Hex in the City
Edited by Kerrie L. Hughes

Moonscapes
Edited by Dean Wesley Smith

Special Edition: Crime
Edited by Kristine Kathryn Rusch

Fantasy Adrift
Edited by Kristine Kathryn Rusch

Universe Between
Edited by Dean Wesley Smith

Fantastic Detectives
Edited by Kristine Kathryn Rusch

Past Crime
Edited by Kristine Kathryn Rusch

Pulse Pounders
Edited by Kevin J. Anderson

Risk Takers
Edited by Dean Wesley Smith

Alchemy & Steam
Edited by Kerrie L. Hughes

Valor
Edited by Lee Allred

Justice
Edited by Kristine Kathryn Rusch

Wishes
Edited by Rebecca Moesta

Pulse Pounders: Countdown
Edited by Kevin J. Anderson

Hard Choices
Edited by Dean Wesley Smith

FICTION RIVER PRESENTS

Fiction River's line of reprint anthologies.

Fiction River has published more than 400 amazing stories by more than 100 talented authors since its inception, from *New York Times* bestsellers to debut authors. So, WMG Publishing decided to start bringing back some of the earlier stories in new compilations.

VOLUMES:
Debut Authors
The Unexpected
Darker Realms
Racing the Clock
Legacies
Readers' Choice
Writers Without Borders
Among the Stars
Space Travelers

To learn more or to pick up your copy today, go to
FictionRiver.com

PULPHOUSE FICTION MAGAZINE

Pulphouse Fiction Magazine is returning twenty years after its last issue. The first issue comes out in January 2018, and the magazine will be quarterly, with about 70,000 words of short fiction every issue. This reincarnation will mix some of the stories from the old *Pulphouse* days with brand-new fiction. The magazine will have an attitude, as did the first run. No genre limitations, but high-quality writing and strangeness.

For more information or to subscribe, go to www.pulphousemagazine.com.